CW01497750

STEVE FRECH lives in Los Angeles. In addition to writing, he produces and hosts the *Random Awesomeness* podcast, an improv-comedy quiz show that has been performed at Upright Citizens Brigade, The Improv, iO West, and Nerdist.

Also by Steve Frech

Dark Hollows
Nightingale House
Deadly Games
The Good Husband

The Detective Somerset Series
Secrets to the Grave
Want You Dead

No Turning Back

STEVE FRECH

ONE PLACE. MANY STORIES

HQ
An imprint of HarperCollins*Publishers* Ltd
1 London Bridge Street
London SE1 9GF

www.harpercollins.co.uk

HarperCollins*Publishers*
Macken House, 39/40 Mayor Street Upper,
Dublin 1 D01 C9W8
This edition 2025

1

First published in Great Britain by HQ,
an imprint of HarperCollins*Publishers* Ltd 2025

ISBN: 9780008739652

Printed and bound in the UK using 100% Renewable
Electricity by CPI Group (UK) Ltd

MIX
Paper | Supporting
responsible forestry
FSC™ C007454

This book contains FSC™ certified paper and other controlled sources
to ensure responsible forest management.

For more information visit: www.harpercollins.co.uk/green

For all the friends who make Los Angeles 'home'.

Chapter 1

'Keith? We're here.'

For the first time since picking him up outside the club on Sunset Boulevard, the incredibly intoxicated, early thirty-something guy splayed across the back seat of my car opens his eyes. It's only 9 p.m., so Keith has either had the best night of his life or one of his worst. He spots his apartment building outside, breathes a heavy sigh and begins struggling with the seatbelt.

After a few moments, Keith stops, stares down at his lap . . . and lets out a short, staccato burp, followed by a painful groan.

Please don't puke in my car. Please don't puke in my car. Please don't puke in my car! I mentally plead but say nothing because I don't want to interrupt his efforts to get out as he resumes the battle with the seatbelt. I'm also afraid of what's going to come out of Keith's mouth if he tries to speak. The air in here is already a noxious cocktail of booze, sweat, and cologne. There's no way I'm going to be able to hide the stench of vomit from Julia.

Keith finally wins the war with the buckle on the seatbelt. Once he's free, he reaches for the door handle but stops to let out another frothy burp.

Come on, Keith. You got this. Just get onto the curb and you can let it fly.

The moment passes and he's able to get his fingers under the handle and push the door open. A merciful gust of cool night air gently circulates through the cabin.

Keith pulls himself out of the car with all the grace and agility of a rag doll. He steps onto the curb and reaches back to shut the door but misses. He staggers backwards off the curb and unintentionally closes the door with his butt. He stays there, leaning back against the car.

I wait a few seconds but he doesn't move.

Finally, I hit the switch on my left to roll down the passenger window.

'Keith? You okay?' I ask.

He starts upright with a snort.

Did he just pass out while leaning against the car?

He mumbles something, pushes himself upright, and begins pinballing his way toward the entrance of the apartment building.

'Have a good night,' I call after him.

I need to stay in his head.

Relying heavily on the handrails, Keith climbs the five or so steps to the glass door. He reaches into his pocket, pulls out his keys, promptly drops them, and then almost face-plants on the concrete stoop as he bends down to pick them up. Hooking a finger into the key ring, he stands, and slaps the keys against a sensor mounted next to the door. A faint buzzing reaches my ear before Keith opens the door and staggers inside.

That's my cue to start staring at my phone.

Please, Keith. Please remember that I'm out here.

In his present state, I'd be surprised if Keith remembers anything.

When I picked him up, he didn't even recognize the light with the logo of the rideshare app sitting on my dashboard. I have to put it there because it's the law, but also so that people know I'm their ride. Keith was so out of it, I had to roll down the window and call his name. I'm glad Keith played it safe and called for a

2

ride, but I also really need him to tip me. He's in his early thirties. He's partying in Hollywood on a Thursday night. He lives in a very nice apartment building in a very nice part of Los Angeles. So, I'm pretty sure he's got the money and I need the tip. Even if it's just a couple bucks.

Ding-ding-ding.

My phone chimes with an incoming text from Julia. Because I've got it in my settings, the text is read out over the car's speakers in that automated female voice.

'*Are you still at the office?*'

Dammit.

I take the phone out of its cradle on the dashboard, disconnect it from the speakers, and begin typing.

Yeah. Sorry. We're scrambling to finish this project. I'll let you know as soon as I'm on my way home

I hit send.

Pinky swear? she replies.

I smile as I type *pinky swear* and hit send.

A few moments later she replies with, *Make that money, babe!*, followed by a string of emojis consisting of money bag, money bag, baby, baby, and finally a kissy-face.

Despite my situation, which Julia has no idea of, I can't help but smile. She's the love of my life and her little texts always have that effect on me.

I reply with my own series of kissy-faces and hit send.

I return the phone to the cradle, reconnect it to the speakers, and look back at the entrance to the apartment building.

Come on, Keith. Help me out. Please.

I hate lying to Julia. It's the worst thing I've ever done, but I don't have a choice . . . well, at least I made a choice about two months ago that I can't take back, but I had to lie because any day now, we're expecting a baby girl, Sophia (we're already calling her 'Little Sophie'), and we had to get married because of the insurance – I mean, we were going to get married anyway, but

3

we had to get married when we did so that she could get on my insurance from work, but two months ago I was let go, and now the insurance is gone and Julia doesn't know. I couldn't tell her because I was worried what the stress might do this close to the birth, but I racked up thousands of dollars of debt buying health insurance to get us through the delivery in case—

The rideshare app chimes with an alert, causing my heart to leap in my chest.

Thank you, Keith!

Maybe he's so drunk that he tipped me a hundred bucks or more. Those kinds of tips are legendary in the rideshare app driving world. There are stories of lucky bastards who gave a CEO or lottery winner a ride home and ended up with a tip of a thousand dollars. Are those stories real? I don't know, but for a fraction of a second, I let myself hope.

The screen on my phone cycles through and my heart plummets as quickly as it rose.

No. Keith didn't leave me a tip that will buy me some more time. The alert is the app letting me know that I've got another rider to pick up somewhere in the Hollywood Hills.

A crushing wave of depression sweeps over me and I stare motionless out the windshield at the quiet street.

Did I really let myself get worked up over the possibility of a few extra dollars from a drunk thirty-something, Sunset Boulevard partygoer? Am I really that desperate?

Well, let's see.

My life is rapidly coming apart. I'm lying to my wife, with whom I'm expecting a baby girl in the next week or so, we're drowning in debt, but she doesn't know that, and this rideshare driving thing is the equivalent of bailing out a sinking ship with a teaspoon.

So, yes. I truly am that desperate.

The phone chimes once more, instructing me to hit the accept button, which will lock me in to picking up this new ride.

Okay. I got this. Eyes closed. Inhale. Hold it in. Exhale. Eyes open.

I've been trying yoga as a way to deal with the stress. Not at a studio or anything. I don't have the money for that but you can find anything on YouTube.

The phone chimes again with a last warning to accept the ride or it will be given to another driver.

I check the gas gauge. That's another thing you'll learn when you're counting the pennies. I need to use every drop of gas before filling up, because if I don't, it's just money sitting in my tank. As long as this guy isn't going across town, I should be good, but he is definitely my last ride of the night.

I double-check that the rideshare logo light on the dashboard is still on and then lean over to hit accept on my phone.

I put the car in drive and pull away from the curb, on my way to pick up my last ride of the evening.

Some guy named Damon.

Chapter 2

The Hollywood Hills are nothing like what you've imagined.

From the tabloids, TV shows, and movies, you'd think that the roads are lined with massive mansions, offering breathtaking views of the city, and that every resident is a famous movie star, hip-hop artist, model, executive, or tech startup founder. While there are some of those up here, most of the mansions are in the gated communities closer to Bel Air and Beverly Hills.

The roads that wind their way through the Hollywood Hills are narrow two-lane ribbons with rusty guardrails as the only thing keeping you from plunging into the darkened basin just off the shoulder of the road. Sometimes, you don't even have the luxury of a rusty guardrail. Only a drop into oblivion.

From time to time, you will come across a mansion or two, but for the most part, the streets are dotted with small multi-unit apartment buildings and smaller homes that are far too close to the road for comfort. There is no rhyme or reason to their architectural styles. They were built anywhere from the 1930s to yesterday and while they're modest in size, their zip code ensures that their prices are not.

Go ahead.

Check out the prices on any real estate site. It'll blow your mind, but the biggest shocker to anyone experiencing the Hollywood Hills for the first time isn't the price of the homes.

The biggest shock is how dark and silent these streets are.

Like a lot of young and naive transplants from other parts of the country, Julia and I expected Los Angeles to be filled with, as the famous theme song proclaims, 'swimming pools and movie stars.' We spent the first few days exploring the different parts of the city only to discover that Hollywood is gross and depressing, most of the Beverly Hills/Rodeo Drive area is a tourist trap, and no one swims at the beach. It was a crash course in reality, but it was that first nighttime drive through the Hollywood Hills that finally put an end to all our previous notions of what Los Angeles would be.

We were expecting mansions, parties, and hundred-thousand-dollar cars. Instead, we found ourselves carefully navigating the twisting, dangerous roads. When we did have a chance to stare at palatial homes, it was in confusion. There weren't nearly as many as we thought there would be. On some stretches of road, there was nothing but shrubs, scraggly trees, and unsettling darkness. The lights of the city burned all around below us in the distance, but the Hollywood Hills were almost pitch-black, save for the pools of light cast by scattered houses or the occasional streetlamp that illuminated a treacherous turn.

This is the first time I've been up here since that night with Julia almost two years ago and not much has changed.

As I navigate to the address where I'm supposed to be picking up Damon, I do my best to keep my eyes forward and not stare into the dark oblivion just out the window to my right. The fall could be only a few feet, broken up by trees or shrubs, or it could be a hundred, so I take the turns cautiously in my old, reliable, gray Honda Civic. I had a newer car, but I traded down before we left Pennsylvania to get us some extra cash. I shouldn't say 'old'. It's just 'older' but it has everything I need.

I check the screen again to make sure this is the right way

because I'm not seeing anything in the distance. The internet reception up here is shit, which causes the app to periodically recalculate, but it's saying that I'm on the right route.

I really hope this rider, this Damon, is going to be worth it. I'm trying to stay positive but the agonizing pace of the narrow roads and the lack of visual stimulation has me thinking, and recently, that's when a voice that sounds suspiciously like my father starts whispering in my ear.

You really think that this ride is going to change anything? it asks.

I try to ignore it.

You're deluding yourself.

I bite my lip.

I've been hearing a lot more of this voice recently, especially as the birth of Little Sophie draws closer and closer. It's a voice that haunts me while I lie next to Julia and try to sleep. It's a voice that interrupts every glimmer of hope. It's a reminder of how young we are, how naive I've been, and just how deep a hole I've put us in. It's been invading every quiet moment with each second we get closer to Little Sophie's arrival.

When will you give this up? it asks, insistently. *When will you stop lying and just let it all fall apart? Because that's what's coming. You're only delaying the inevitable, and when Julia finds out—*

I jab my finger at my phone, banishing the map to a corner of the screen and pull up a music streaming app. I don't care what it plays. I just need something, anything, to make this voice shut up, but with the crappy internet, the app just hangs on the load screen. You'd think for one of the most expensive expanses of real estate in the country, it would have better coverage.

The voice laughs.

I switch on the radio and hit scan, but it's all static.

I bring the map back up.

Through the occasional recalculating, the directions say that I've got less than a mile to go, but the more I look around, the more I start to feel that this can't be right. There's nothing out here. There's the opening to a driveway every now and again, but other than that, it's shrubs, trees, and dirt.

Maybe the crappy internet has me heading to the wrong spot and the real address is one of those huge mansions on the other, much more densely populated, side of the hill. Even if these directions are correct, there's no possibility that I'm on my way to pick up some high roller who is going to be my fairy godmother tonight.

And you were counting on that, weren't you? the voice asks over the static coming through the radio.

Fuming, I shut off the radio in frustration.

I know that voice is me. It's my growing insecurities. It's my imagination taunting me. I used to be so self-assured, but the events of the past year have shattered my confidence. For the first time in my life, I'm questioning if I'll be enough and when those doubts start coming on, the only thing that quiets that voice is sitting with Julia, talking about Little Sophie, and feeling her kick inside Julia's belly.

That's where I want to be right now. I want to be sitting on the couch of our studio apartment in Van Nuys. We haven't been able to afford any streaming services, so all we've had is YouTube and our recent obsession has been watching clips of police chases. Maybe because it's a novelty. There weren't many police chases back in Pennsylvania, but there seems to be three or four a week here in Los Angeles. We always marvel at the thought process of running from the cops, especially when the helicopters show up.

Why would any sane person keep running?

Thinking about sitting with Julia makes me want this night to be over. If I arrive at this place and this Damon guy, whoever he is, isn't waiting for me, I'm canceling the ride and heading back to the apartment. Maybe Julia and I can watch a movie or just talk about what it will be like when Little Sophie gets here.

But what about that extra three-dollar tip Julia and Little Sophie are counting on? the voice asks and begins laughing.

I grit my teeth and check the phone.

The pickup is only five minutes away. Thanks to the turns and switchbacks as I descend the hillside, my top speed barely reaches twenty-five.

Finally, the road straightens out. I'm halfway down into the basin of the canyon and it's especially dark.

The destination appears as a blue dot on the screen of my phone, but I don't see anything in my headlights.

'Where the fuck are you?' I whisper.

Now, now. Language, the voice says. *You have to keep up that cheerful smiling facade for your rider so they won't know what a fuckup you are.* The voice starts laughing, again.

That's it.

I don't want to do this anymore tonight. I don't want to take 'Damon' to wherever he wants to go. I don't want another Keith who might vomit in my car. I don't want to make small talk. I usually don't talk to my riders anyway because I hate doing this. I don't want to pretend that this isn't utterly hopeless, humiliating, and soul-crushing. I don't care what it does to my all-important customer rating on the app. I reach out to cancel the ride, but just before my finger hits the button, a shape appears at the edge of my headlights.

There's a man standing next to a mailbox at the end of a driveway that leads to a house, illuminated by a solitary light over the garage. The man has cropped black hair and stubble to match. He looks to be in his mid-forties, fit, and wearing a black hoodie with a backpack slung over one shoulder. Maybe he is some sort of tech bro. He waves as I approach but is forced to stop and shield his eyes against the glare of the headlights.

I pull up, stop beside him, and hit the switch to roll down the passenger window.

'Damon?' I ask.

The question is unnecessary because he matches the picture on the profile of the person I'm picking up, but the app company requires that I ask for them by name so that the rider knows I'm legit.

'That's me,' he cheerily replies while opening the back door. 'You Lucas?'

'Yep.'

'Who else would you be, right?' he asks with a smile consisting of perfectly white teeth.

'Right,' I reply.

I look past him as he tosses the backpack onto the back seat. The driveway dips and then rises in the distance. At the end of the driveway is a one-story mid-century home. There's a fence around the side and I can make out the blue glow of a pool. Anywhere else, the house would probably run somewhere between two hundred thousand and half a million dollars, but in this neighborhood, it's a few million, easy. There are two cars sitting in the driveway. One is a nondescript Toyota. The other is a gleaming sports car. I can't pin down the make and model, but it gives me hope that maybe Damon does have money.

In any case, even if he isn't a multimillionaire who's going to turn this pumpkin of a human being into a crystal coach, at least he seems like a cool guy.

I hit the button on my phone's screen to acknowledge that I've picked him up. The app thinks for a second as it calculates the route to his destination. Just like taxi drivers, the app won't show us drivers where our rides are going until we pick them up, for fear of discrimination.

Damon settles into the back seat as the app takes a moment longer due to the poor internet reception.

Finally, my phone plays three ascending chimes and displays the route.

As with every other step in this process, I have to accept the route by hitting a button but I stop.

This says that he's only going a little more than a mile down the road. It's a five-minute drive, at most.

I get that it's a walk you wouldn't want to make on this road, especially at night, and if you were drunk, you definitely would want to play it safe, but Damon seems perfectly sober. If one of those cars in the driveway is his, why not just drive?

But more importantly, why am I questioning this?

It's a little odd, sure, but who cares? He seems chill. Maybe he'll leave a nice tip and I can—

'Everything okay?' Damon asks.

'Yeah,' I reply and point at the screen. 'Is this correct?'

He leans forward between the seats. His face, illuminated by the faint glow of the dashboard and my phone, appears ghostly in the rearview mirror as he checks the image on my phone.

'Yep. That's it.'

'All right,' I say with a shrug. 'Here we go.' I tap the accept button, and pull onto the road.

There are a few moments of silence, then there's the sound of Damon unzipping the backpack.

'How's your night going?' Damon asks as he rummages through its contents.

'It's all right,' I answer back. 'How about yours?'

'Good, man. Good, but listen,' he says as he finds what he's looking for. 'Can I ask a huge favor?'

'Uh, sure.'

He leans forward. He's holding a phone in his hand.

'Oh.' I nod down. 'There's a charging port in the back of the center console and some cables in the seat pocket in front of you if you need—'

Damon chuckles. 'Nah. It's got plenty of juice, but functionally, this thing is on its last leg. The speakers don't work. If I need to make a call, the only way I can do it on this phone is through Bluetooth.' He motions to the dashboard. 'Is it cool if I connect to yours? I promise I'll make it worth your while.'

'Of course,' I reply. I would have let him do it anyway, but he added those magic words: *I'll make it worth your while*. I reach over and turn off my phone's Bluetooth.

'*Disconnected*,' the automated female voice announces.

'Thank you, sir,' Damon says, sitting back and tapping away on his phone.

Moments later, the automated female voice fills the car once again. '*Connected*.'

There's a dial tone.

I keep my eyes on the road, fully prepared to become invisible as Damon makes his call. I've done this routine a few times. There have been couples screaming at each other in my back seat, seemingly unaware of my presence. I've had people on their phone, tearfully pleading with their significant other while I pretended not to listen or even exist, but a passenger using my car's Bluetooth is a new one.

The dial tone is cut short as Damon presses the buttons.

There's one higher-toned beep followed by two lower ones.

I blink.

I've never had to dial that number, but I've watched enough television to recognize it.

There's the purr of ringing on the other end.

I inadvertently take my foot off the gas and begin to turn. 'Is everything all r—?' I get just far enough to glance backwards at him before snapping back around to face the windshield. 'Jesus!'

'Keep driving,' Damon says. 'And do not make a sound.'

His cheery tone is gone.

This is a joke. It has to be.

'*Drive*,' he hisses.

My heart is pounding. My head is spinning. My brain latches desperately onto the one instruction it's been given, and my foot finds the gas. I swallow down the sudden swell of bile in my throat and center the car in the lane.

'Nine-one-one. What is the nature of your emergency?' a voice asks through the car's speakers.

'Send the police to three-oh-six-six Runyon Canyon Road,'

Damon says with cold deliberation. 'There, they'll find the bodies of three people I just killed.'

'Sir, are you saying that you—?'

Damon ends the call, tucks the phone into the backpack, and watches me in the rearview mirror.

This isn't happening. This isn't happening. This isn't happening.

'Lucas?'

'Y-yes?'

'You're slowing down, again.'

I look down at my feet. Even though I can't see it, my foot has come off the gas. I find it and accelerate.

'L-listen,' I sputter. 'I don't know what you—'

'Just keep driving.'

'Okay . . . okay . . . okay . . .' I repeat.

I steady myself and the car. I'm still breathing heavily. My eyes begin flicking between the road and the rearview mirror. In the faint glow emanating from the dashboard, I can see the barrel of the gun that Damon is pointing at the back of my head.

'Wh-what do you want?' I ask.

Damon leans forward so that his face is once again illuminated by the ghostly glow of the dashboard.

'I need you to listen to me, Lucas. I need you to stay calm. I need you to focus. I need you to do everything I say, because tonight . . .' Damon lightly presses the barrel of the gun against the back of my skull. 'You and I are going to make history.'

Chapter 3

They put them in the freezer. That's what made the candy bars so good at the local swimming pool in Millersburg, Pennsylvania, but not all the candy bars. Just the peanut butter cups and the Whatchamacallits.

The other candy bars were solid all the way through. If you got one, you had to wait for it to thaw before you could eat it without cracking a tooth but adult swim only lasted fifteen minutes. Waiting for it to thaw meant you missed out on valuable pool time. If you set it aside to enjoy an hour later during the next adult swim, the summer Pennsylvania sun would turn it into a melted, sticky mess.

But not a Whatchamacallit. Since a Whatchamacallit wasn't solid all the way through, you could eat it right out of the freezer and not miss out on any pool time.

This was all my ten-year-old brain could think about as I counted the heads in the line in front of me at the concession stand while a Top Forty radio station played over the speakers around the pool.

I held the folded dollar bills between my thumb and middle finger slightly away from my body to keep them from getting wet. Well, *wetter*, anyway. There had been no time to dry off. Mom had parked our stuff in the shade, which was on the opposite side of the pool grounds from the concession stand. Once the whistle for the start of adult swim had sounded, I pulled myself out of the pool and ran to our plot of grass to get a few dollars from her. She was talking with Mrs. Detmers as they laid on their towels, so it took a second to get her attention. I kept glancing back, watching the line at the concession quickly grow. The old analog clock hanging over the menu was counting down the seconds to the end of adult swim.

Finally, Mom opened the large duffel bag she always brought to the pool and searched through the goggles, bottles of sunblock, and towels and fished out two one-dollar bills from the bottom and handed them to me.

I quickly turned on my heel and took off.

'You're welcome,' Mom called after me.

'Thank you!' I replied over my shoulder. I was sincere but I also had somewhere to be.

I 'walked' as quickly as possible past the diving boards in that stride that every kid learns around the pool; the speed just below where lifeguards will tell you to slow down. The concrete was hot under my feet, but it was cooled by the water running down my body.

Because Mom had set up our stuff at the opposite end of the pool grounds, there was already a sizable wait at the concessions stand by the time I got in line. I began to worry that I wouldn't be able to get my candy bar before adult swim ended. I started counting the number of people in line until it was my turn to order, but the blond girl in front of me moved, blocking my view. I shifted slightly, trying not to lose count, when she moved again. I shifted again and almost instantly, so did she. Frustrated, I stopped and studied the back of her head. She was a little shorter and her wet hair clung to the back of her neck as she fidgeted back and forth, shuffling her weight from one foot to the other and back again.

I figured she was just as anxious as I was about running out of time when she suddenly turned around. She had blue eyes and a smattering of freckles on her worried face.

'I have to pee,' she announced to me.

'. . . okay,' I replied. What else was I gonna say?

'I don't want to lose my place in line,' she added.

I cast my eyes to the bathrooms, which were right next to the concession stand.

'. . . okay,' I replied because, again, what else was I gonna say?

'If I go to the bathroom, will you hold my place?'

'What?'

'Will you let me back in line?' she asked urgently, dipping slightly as she pressed her knees together.

For a second, I considered the advantage of having one less person in line in front of me.

'Please?!' she pleaded.

I was a little embarrassed and I felt bad for her. Who hasn't been there, frantically tensing every muscle in the hopes of making it to the bathroom?

'Yeah. Okay,' I replied.

She lifted her hand toward me and extended her little finger.

'Pinky swear?' she asked, as if this was a matter of life and death.

I was so stunned that I could only stare at her finger.

'Pinky swear!' she insisted.

People nearby started casting sideways glances at us.

'Okay, okay. Fine,' I said.

I hooked her pinky with mine. She gave it a squeeze and one solemn up-and-down motion before letting go and hurriedly shuffling off to the bathroom, leaving me standing there, avoiding eye contact with anyone who had watched what had transpired.

'Move up,' someone said behind me.

I stepped forward to fill the gap left by the girl.

We trudged forward, little by little. All the while, the minute hand on the clock over the menu crept toward twelve.

There were five minutes left and I had nearly forgotten about the girl when she came out of the bathroom, her face the definition of relief.

She slowed a little as she saw that I was almost at the counter. I think she was worried that I might not honor our sacred pinky swear. She looked almost scared. I guess the urgency of getting to the bathroom had given her confidence before, but now it was gone.

She looked at me with those big blue eyes and any thoughts I had of trying to go back on our pinky swear vanished.

I motioned for her to hurry up and get in front of me. She quickly stepped over and took her place back in line.

'Hey,' someone protested behind us.

'She was here,' I said, loud enough for them to hear but not turning around to look at them. 'She just had to go to the bathroom.'

There were grumblings but no more outright protests.

The last person in front of the girl got their ice cream bar and walked away. The girl stepped up.

'Skittles, please,' she said, placing a damp five-dollar bill on the counter. She paused and then turned to me. 'What are you getting?'

'A Whatchamacallit.'

She turned back to the teenager behind the counter. 'And one Whatchamacallit.'

I started to protest but the teenager plopped a packet of Skittles on the counter and then opened the freezer chest at their feet. They pulled out a Whatchamacallit and added it to the Skittles on the counter.

'Four dollars,' the teenager said, taking the wet fiver. They rang it up and gave a her a single. 'Dollar is your change.'

The girl took the candy and the dollar. 'Thank you.'

She turned and handed me the Whatchamacallit.

'Here.'

18

I took it and we both stepped away from the counter.

'You didn't have to do that,' I told her.

She shrugged and began wrestling with the Skittles wrapper. 'I know, but you let me back in line.'

She succeeded in opening the packet and dropped a few Skittles into the palm of her hand.

'Thanks,' I said, tearing open the Whatchamacallit.

She popped the Skittles into her mouth.

'I'm Julia,' she said, crunching into the candy shells.

'I'm Lucas,' I replied through a mouthful of cold chocolate, caramel, and crisped rice.

We awkwardly looked at one another as we enjoyed our candy.

The moment was broken when the lifeguards emerged from their little office and began making their way to the chairs positioned around the pool.

'Time to swim,' Julia announced, shoving another handful of Skittles in her mouth as she turned to leave. 'Bye, Lucas!'

'Bye, Julia!' I called out while also cramming the rest of the candy bar into my mouth.

Neither one of us knew how much our lives had just changed, but at the time, we had places to be.

Chapter 4

Damon lets his words about making history hang there before turning back and working with something inside the backpack. I take a quick glance in the rearview mirror. There's a manila envelope in his hand, which he promptly returns to the backpack. There's a metallic *clink* as he shifts the contents of the backpack.

My mind races, desperately trying to make sense of what's happening.

'What did you mean by that? What did you mean when you said "we're going to make history"?'

'You'll see,' Damon replies.

I check the directions on my phone, resting in its cradle on the dashboard. There's only a few minutes until we reach the destination and I'm terrified of what happens when we get there.

Every over-the-top true crime documentary that I've seen or podcast that I've listened to has emphasized that if you're ever caught in this exact situation, you should never go to a second location. That's where they kill you. This guy could shoot me in the head, take my keys, roll my body down the canyon, and drive off in my car. It would take the cops days, weeks, or even months to find my body, if they ever found it at all.

I have to figure out something, some way to escape, before we get to that blue dot on my phone. Keeping my head as still as possible, my eyes flit around the interior of the car.

Above my head, there's the emergency services button next to the cabin light. I can try to hit it, but what good would that do? If I go to press it, Damon might shoot me, and even if I was successful in calling them, what could they do before Damon kills me? There's the dial button on the steering wheel. My thumb is only centimeters away but unlike the overhead button, I'd have to stipulate who to call, and then, it's the same problem as before; Damon would just shoot me and take the car.

I glance out the window to my right, where the ground drops away into black nothing. I could yank the wheel and intentionally plunge the car into the canyon. Damon might be injured in the crash and if I somehow made it out unscathed, I could run. Or we might both die. Or, I could die while he lived, and then I would have done his work for him. Or we could both live and he could just shoot me afterwards and then—

'That's good, Lucas.'

My eyes return to the rearview mirror to find him watching me.

'What's good?' I ask.

'You're looking around. You're trying to find a way out of this.'

'And why is that good?'

'It means you want to live. It means you want to survive and eventually, you'll understand that the only way that happens is if you do what I say.'

His words do nothing to calm my fear and panic as that blue dot on my phone gets closer.

'L-look, man,' I stutter. 'I – I don't have a lot of money but there are some credit cards in my wallet. You can take those—'

'Stop it.' Damon says with a disappointed sigh. 'This isn't a robbery.'

'Then . . . what is this?'

He takes a moment before answering, 'This is something more.'

His tone, the gravity with which he says it, the fact that it

21

sounds like the three people he killed back at the house is just the beginning, makes me nauseous.

The dot on my phone is getting closer.

'What are you going to do to me?' I ask him in the mirror.

He shrugs. 'Depends on what you do for me.'

'Like what?'

'I already told you; I need you to do whatever I tell you to do.' The gun appears between the seats, pointed at my head. 'Can you do that, Lucas?'

I lightly nod.

'Good, because we're going to need to trust one another.' He nods to the windshield. 'And we're coming up to our first test.'

A mailbox appears at the edge of the headlights, coinciding with the arrival of the blue dot on my phone's screen.

'Stop here.'

I slow the car, pull onto the shoulder, and stop next to the mailbox at the opening of a driveway.

'Put it in park.'

I do.

I cast my eyes down the driveway. About thirty yards away, I can just make out the shape of a house. Every window is dark.

'Who lives here?' I ask.

'I have no idea,' Damon answers and leans forward. 'Now, very slowly, I want you to hand me your phone. Do not turn around.'

I reach forward and lift the phone from the plastic cradle. I'm so distracted by searching for any signs of life from the house, that I begin to twist my torso as I go to hand him my phone.

Damon presses the gun against my temple. 'Nope.'

I nearly drop the phone as I snap forward. 'Sorry! I'm sorry— . . . sorry.'

'Let's try that again,' Damon says calmly as he backs the gun off my head an inch or two.

I take a breath and slowly offer the phone over my shoulder, keeping myself facing forward to watch him in the rearview

22

mirror.

Damon's eyes never leave mine as he takes the phone from my hand.

'Good. Now, put your hands back on the wheel and keep them there.'

My hands return to ten and two and I wrap my fingers around the steering wheel.

He keeps the gun trained on me with one hand and looks down as he begins tapping away on my phone with the other.

'I'm letting the app know that you've dropped me off . . . and now, I'm terminating the app. That was your last ride of the evening. Go ahead and put the light on your dashboard away.'

With shaking hands, I pull the light with the rideshare logo from the dashboard, switch it off, and put it in the glovebox.

Damon continues typing on my phone in the back seat. The light from the screen illuminates his face as he looks down. 'Give me the PIN for your phone.'

'Why?'

No sooner do I say the words than Damon's face tightens in anger and the gun makes contact with my head, again.

'Okay, okay, okay. Oh-five-two-four.'

His eyes narrow. 'Is that a date? May the twenty-fourth?'

It's Little Sophie's due date. One week from tomorrow. I changed my PIN the moment we got the news six months ago but I'm not telling him that. He can't know about Julia and Sophie, so I shake my head. 'It's just a number.'

He regards me with that quizzical stare and then returns to the phone. 'I'm changing the PIN so that I'll be the only one with access to your phone. I'll also be holding onto it.' He sets my phone on the back seat and holds out his hand. 'Next, I'm going to need your driver's license. As before, do it slowly and do not turn around.'

I release the steering wheel with my right hand and slowly dig into my pocket. I lift my hips off the seat, extract my wallet, and

23

offer it over my shoulder.

'I didn't ask for your wallet,' Damon says. 'Only your driver's license.'

'The driver's license is in my wallet, so you can—'

'I told you, Lucas; this is our first little test. This isn't a robbery. I need you to take your driver's license out of your wallet and hand it to me. Now that I've called the police to come to the house back where you picked me up, we need to get going. You can use both hands. Just take it nice and slow.' He smiles and adds, 'You don't want to make me nervous.'

Was that a joke? Was he trying to break the tension? All he's done is make it worse.

I slowly let go of the steering wheel with my left hand, open my wallet, extract my driver's license, and hand it over my shoulder.

'Thank you,' Damon says, taking it. 'Hands back on the wheel, please.'

My hands return to the wheel as Damon reaches up and hits the button, turning on the cabin light to study my driver's license.

It's the first time I have a good look at him up close. His eyes are dark, matching his black hair and stubble.

As he studies my driver's license, I strain my eyes to the right to look again at the darkened house at the end of the driveway.

Please. Please, someone be home. Look outside and notice the car sitting at the end of your driveway. Aren't you wondering what we're doing there? Turn on a light and come out onto the porch. Ask us what we're up to and please, please have a gun.

But the house stays dark and silent.

A million questions are swirling around in my head. Why is this guy doing this? What could he possibly want? But looking at the house raises a different question.

'Who were they?' I nervously ask.

'Who were who?' Damon replies, wrapping up his inspection of my driver's license.

'The people back at the house . . . the people you killed.'

24

'No one you know,' he responds nonchalantly.

'Why did you kill them?'

'We'll get to that.' He reaches up and turns off the cabin light. 'You can have this back.'

My driver's license appears over my shoulder.

'Put it back in your wallet.'

I glance down at my driver's license and back at him in confusion. 'What was the point of looking at my dr—?'

'You don't know the people I killed back at that house, but now I know you . . . Lucas Walker . . . who lives at one-one-three-two Houghton Way, Apartment C.'

My stomach is suddenly filled with ice.

The dread on my face has to be obvious because he's grinning at me with those perfect teeth.

'It's not personal, Lucas. It's just one more way to ensure that you're going to do exactly what I say.' His 'reassuring' smile slowly fades as he continues to speak. 'Because if you don't, if you screw up my plans, plans that I have been working on for years, if by some miracle you're able to get away from me tonight, I will find you. I will hunt you down. If you try to hide, I will go through everyone you care about. I will make them suffer. I will make them hate the fact that they ever knew you until I find you . . . Do you understand, Lucas?'

His smile is completely gone, replaced by grim determination.

This has gotten so much worse. He knows where we live.

It's not just me in this car, anymore. It's Julia. It's Little Sophie.

I have to do everything I can to keep him away from them.

'Lucas?'

'Yeah,' I say, weakly nodding.

He shakes his head. 'No, Lucas. I need you to *tell me* that you understand.'

'. . . I understand.'

He stares me down, making sure that I truly do understand that this is not an idle threat.

25

As we stare at one another in the rearview mirror, we both see it.

High up on the hill, back the way we came, flashing red and blue lights appear.

The cops are arriving at the house where I picked him up.

Damon takes a deep breath.

His body language is clear; we've passed a point of no return.

'Okay, Lucas. Here we go.' He steadies the gun against the back of my head. 'Drive.'

Chapter 5

'One . . . two . . . three . . . four, five, six-seven-eight-nine!' I shouted in triumph.

'That was eight,' Julia said, hands on her hips.

'It was nine!' I protested, pointing back to the surface of the river where the ripples from my perfectly skipped rock were fading. 'That last part was two skips.'

Julia shrugged. 'Okay. I guess I didn't know that about you.'

'Know what?'

'That you're blind or you can't count.'

'Yur blyn or yu cang count,' I mockingly replied, as she bent down and carefully selected a flat stone from the riverbank.

Julia and I started hanging out at the pool after our encounter at the concession stand. We'd see who could hold their breath the longest. We'd join in games of Sharks & Minnows, and play Gutterball during adult swim. Julia wasn't athletic, but she was playfully scrappy and loved trying new things.

But our meeting at the concession stand was two years ago.

Since then, we had been hanging out more and more outside of the pool, just the two of us.

In the summer, we'd ride our bikes to each other's house or to the woods on the outskirts of town to explore or just hang out.

One June afternoon, we had ridden out to the Ned Smith Nature Center and walked one of the paths to the Wiconsico Creek. There, we engaged in one of our favorite activities; skipping rocks.

I had been playing Little League baseball for a few years and fancied myself an expert. Julia, who had none of the 'extensive training' that I'd had, threw rocks for distance rather than skips. I tried to coach her, which she usually turned into a joke, but she had fun trying to learn.

'It was eight,' she repeated as she settled upon her perfect skipper from the sand, stood upright, and set her feet. She paused and then dramatically popped a finger into her mouth, pulled it out, and held it up, as if testing the direction of the wind.

'Oh, just throw it,' I groaned with a smile.

'Hush,' she said. 'Let me do this my way.'

I took a step back to give her some space.

She brought her hands together like a pitcher working out of the stretch and stared down the river with intensity. She was perfectly still until a lock of her curly blond hair fell into one of her eyes, forcing her to blow it aside while trying to stay deadly serious. Finally, she awkwardly kicked her leg toward the water and flung the stone.

Instead of a flat spin, the rock tumbled end over end, striking the surface of the river and immediately sinking.

She turned to me and triumphantly shouted, 'Ten!'

'Ten?'

'I'm counting like how you count.'

'Oh, ha ha . . .' I replied sarcastically.

She was pleased with her joke but turned back to the river and asked in frustration, 'Why can't I get this?'

'Here,' I said. 'Let's try it again.'

I bent down and found another smooth skipper. 'Here,' I said, offering it to her. 'Show me how you hold it.'

She took the stone from my hand. 'What do you mean?' She

held the rock in her palm with her fingers wrapped around the edges for me to see. 'I hold it like this.'

'Well, that's the problem. You want to hold it like this.'

I took her hand in mine and worked her grip so that her index finger wrapped around the edge.

I was eager to show her how she might be able to skip a stone but as we stood there on the riverbank, our hands touching, something in my twelve-year-old brain shifted.

Julia and I had had physical contact plenty of times. We had dunked each other in the pool. We had 'chicken fights' where she got on my shoulders and we squared off against a pair of our friends who were similarly situated and tried to knock them off.

But something about this moment was different.

And so was every moment after.

I was suddenly nervous and excited at the same instant.

I quickly finished manipulating her grip and took a step back.

'So, think of it more like a sling, you know?' I stammered. 'And you want to throw it at the level of the water like this . . .' I pantomimed side-arming the rock a few times while avoiding eye contact.

I finally stopped and met her gaze.

She was looking at me amused, like I was harmlessly crazy.

'That's it?' she asked. 'I can throw now?'

'Yep,' I replied and motioned to the water.

Julia once again went through the motions of a pitcher from the stretch. This time, she swung her arm more to the side. Her throw was still comically awkward, but the stone flew from her hand in a flat spin. It sailed over the surface of the river and began to arc to the left before slapping the surface and bouncing upwards. It bounced again and again before achieving the holy grail of skippers and sliding across the water in a way that meant counting the skips was impossible.

Julia screamed in excitement.

She turned to me and I held up my hand. She jumped and

slapped my palm in a high-five. I was in that initial onslaught of puberty and was significantly taller than her. Her jump left her off balance and she crashed into me. She impulsively threw her arms over my shoulders to keep from falling as she laughed.

It was only a moment, but an electric shock ran through me, freezing me in place.

Julia let go and did a little celebratory dance.

'Again!' she cried and began desperately searching for another perfect skipper among the stones strewn across the riverbank.

We spent the rest of that blissful afternoon skipping rocks until our arms were sore.

Chapter 6

As Damon and I work our way west through the lonely, darkened hills, I'm getting past the denial stage of what's happening and all I can think about is Julia.

From the moment she told me that we were pregnant, it's felt as though time is speeding up. There's always been some milestone on the horizon. Telling our parents the news. The first time she felt Sophie kick. The first ultrasound. I keep trying to stop and savor the moments, but they go whizzing by and we keep hurtling toward the next one. Amid the insanity of these past few months, I've been trying to focus on the good things that are coming; like the fact that Julia and I get to do this together. We know it's crazy for us to think we can handle this. We're young and broke, but that hasn't diminished any of our enthusiasm one bit. Even though these last few months have been a nightmare with losing my job, racking up thousands of dollars in debt to buy temporary insurance, and slyly insisting that I fill out the insurance forms at our last check-in, I've never been this nervous, scared, and excited. Time's been going so damn fast and I've taken it for granted that, no matter how quickly those milestones go by, I'll still get to experience them, and here we are, days away from Little Sophie's birth, the biggest milestone of them all, and I might not be going home tonight.

No. I can't think like that. I'll make it back to Julia and Little Sophie. I just have to keep my head, and look for an opportunity to escape . . . but how can I do that? I don't even know where we're going, but I've learned a lot about the layout of Los Angeles over the past two months, enough to know what's coming up.

'We taking the four-oh-five?' I ask.

Damon regards me with a quizzical expression before replying. 'Maybe.'

'You sure you want to do that? I know it's late but even at this time of—'

'I've been planning this night for years, Lucas. I know these streets better than you do. Just follow the directions.'

Sure enough, once we reach the 405, the directions over the GPS have me take the exit to go south and we descend into the Sepulveda Pass.

Nestled between the Santa Monica Mountains, the Sepulveda Pass is a barren nine-mile stretch of Interstate that connects 'the city' with 'the valley.' There is always traffic, but due to the geography, there are no homes, no apartment buildings, no strip malls. Nothing. Only the Getty Art Museum sitting high up on the hillside.

We emerge from the underpass beneath Sunset Boulevard, which marks the exit of the Sepulveda Pass and the entrance to the West Side. All around us are cars filled with people going about their lives. Some of these people are probably heading home after a long day at work. Maybe others are on their way to the night shift. Some might be going out to catch a late movie or a drink. I wonder if anyone on this road is heading to the hospital for the birth of their child.

'Tell me about yourself, Lucas.'

I snap out of it to see Damon watching me in the rearview mirror.

'What?'

'We're going to be on this road for a while. We're about to spend a long, eventful evening together. I figured we might get to know each other a little. Tell me about yourself.'

I can't tell if he's being serious but I decide that serious or not, I'm not telling him a thing.

'If it's all the same, I'd rather not.'

He shakes his head in disappointment. 'Fine.'

We continue on, past the cluster of buildings to the east that make up Westwood.

Every now and then in the silence that follows, I glance at him in the rearview mirror. Something's happening. He's growing restless. He looks around the car and then at me, as if he's taking stock. Something's on his mind. Something's eating at him. Finally, he can't take it anymore.

'Why are you doing this?' he asks.

'Doing what?'

'This,' he says, waving his hand around the car. 'This driving thing.'

'*Me?*' I ask, incredulously. His question is so ridiculous, I momentarily forget that he has a gun. 'You're asking *me* why I'm doing *this*?'

'Yeah,' he casually replies, not seeing the irony. 'Are you in some sort of financial trouble?'

I hesitate before answering, worried that I'll give away too much, but then again, I could give away too much if I *don't* answer.

'Why would you think that?' I ask.

Damon shrugs. 'I've always wondered why people do this. I've heard the ads talking about how it's a great way to earn some money on the side. They also make it sound like it's fun, but I've got to believe that the real thing is nothing like that.'

I stare at him in the mirror.

'No,' I reply in deadpan disbelief. 'This actual experience is nothing like the ads.'

His brow knits in confusion. Then, it hits him.

'You're right. I guess the ads never mentioned anything like this,' he says with a laugh that fades into unnerving seriousness. 'So, why are you doing this?'

I'm not going to answer. I don't want to engage. I'm worried I'll slip up and mention Julia or Sophie to this murderer who knows where we live but doesn't know about them. I struggle to come up with a convincing lie, but the longer I remain silent, the sterner his expression becomes.

'Lucas? I thought we had an understanding that you were going to do what I tell you, and I'm telling you to answer my question.'

'I'm driving you to where you want to go, okay?' I snap. 'I don't want to talk to you.'

My small act of defiance throws him, if only for a moment.

'Is that something you normally tell your rides or am I just special?' he asks.

'I said I don't want to talk to you.'

His eyes narrow and he cocks his head. 'I'm only asking if you normally talk to the people you give rides to.'

'No. I don't normally talk to the people I give rides to,' I answer sharply, hoping it will end the conversation.

'Really?' he asks, a little surprised. 'No small talk? No inane chatter?'

'No. I usually have some music on.'

'Why is that? Why don't you talk to them?'

'I just – I just give them a ride, that's all.'

He thinks it over, gives me a knowing smile, and nods.

'Okay.'

'Okay, what?' I ask.

'Okay. You don't have to answer my question.'

'. . . Okay . . . Thanks,' I mutter.

'I've got all I need to know,' Damon adds, to get the last word in. He then sits back to watch the passing traffic with a contented grin.

I try to concentrate on the road. That should be it. I should keep my mouth shut until we get to where we're going . . . but

I can't. What did he figure out? If it's something that could lead to Julia, I have to know.

'Fine,' I say with a sigh. 'What was it?'

He turns his head from the window. 'Excuse me?'

'You said you got all you need to know.'

'Yes.'

'What did you find out?'

'I thought you said you didn't talk to your rides.'

'What did you need to know?' I ask nervously.

He grins, clearly happy that I took the bait. 'Well, there's only two reasons why you wouldn't talk to your rides. Reason one: you don't like them. You're just a mean, bitter person, but I don't believe that. You're, what? Twenty-three? Twenty-four? There's no way life has broken you, yet.' As Damon speaks, my brain is suddenly filled with images of my father; of him sitting on the porch, scowling at the world, of his angry expression as he stood next to the casket. 'You were also polite and personable when you picked me up,' Damon continues. 'You let me use your car's Bluetooth. That was very accommodating of you. So no, I don't think you're bitter. That means it has to be reason number two.' He pauses for dramatic effect. 'You don't talk to the people you give rides to because you hate doing this.' He pauses again, waiting for an answer I'm trying not to give, but the fact that he hit the bullseye must show in my face because his smile widens and his sense of contentment grows. 'There it is . . . So, tell me: why do you hate it, Lucas? Are you embarrassed? Maybe you're angry that you're doing this.' He waits to see if I'll respond but I don't and he continues. 'The point is that regardless of whether you're embarrassed or angry, you're still doing it, which means you *have* to do it, right? And that brings me back to my original question: Are you in some sort of financial trouble?'

This.

This is exactly why I should have stayed quiet. I didn't want to get in a conversation because he's gotten one big step closer to

Julia and Sophie. And all I said was that I didn't talk to my riders.

'I'm right, aren't I?' he asks, still happy with himself. 'Come on, Lucas. You can tell me.'

I shake my head, not in denial, but resignation. There's no point lying to him when I've made it obvious.

'So, what's the deal?' I ask as we cross Interstate Ten, still heading south. 'Are you Sherlock Holmes or something?'

To my surprise, that triumphant grin he's been sporting ebbs as he puts his focus back toward the window.

'Sort of,' he replies. 'In another life.'

'Another life? You mean like in Victorian times and now you've been reincarnated as – what? A hitman or something?'

'"Another life" as in a few days ago . . . and no, I'm not a "hitman."'

He appears to go to some dark place in his head and I'm not going to press him further.

'*Exit at Venice Boulevard and head west,*' the female voice announces over the speakers.

I maneuver into the far-right lane and, moments later, we descend the ramp to the red stoplight below.

Just outside my window, standing on the curb, is a man in ratty clothes. He's holding a cardboard sign that reads, 'Anything helps. God bless.' I stare straight ahead, not making eye contact, as I've learned to do in these situations.

'Do you have anything you can give that guy?' Damon asks.

'No,' I answer, truthfully.

'Really? Nothing? Not a dollar or some spare change?'

'No. Do you?'

'. . . No,' Damon answers with a sigh.

The light turns green and I turn right onto Venice Boulevard, which is lined with strip malls, gas stations, and apartment buildings that have bars on the windows. Once we've put a few blocks between us and the Interstate, the bars on the windows begin to disappear as the apartment buildings become nicer, as do the strip malls and gas stations, which are joined by small restaurants, pubs, and convenience stores.

'Do you have people who depend on you?' Damon asks out of the blue.

Thank God he's looking out the window to watch the buildings pass or he might have seen the panic cross my face before I answer.

'No.'

Something in my denial catches his attention, as if he doesn't believe me.

'What's your point?' I ask.

'My point is that you shouldn't be embarrassed or angry about what you're doing. If you're in some kind of financial trouble, which I suspect you are, you're doing what has to be done to get out of it. That doesn't mean that you have to like it. It also doesn't mean you'll be doing it for the rest of your life.'

'And just how long is the rest of my life?' I ask.

He thinks but shrugs it off. 'I'm just saying that you shouldn't worry. You're young, but if you're in trouble and you're willing to do whatever it takes to get by, you'll figure it out.'

My jaw hangs open. 'What are you? My dad?'

'Do you and your dad not get along?' he asks, suddenly interested.

'. . . We don't talk much,' I reply, having to remind myself that I don't want to tell him anything about me.

He studies me for a moment before moving on.

'Just saying that you shouldn't be too hard on yourself for trying to make ends meet . . . And you should call your dad.'

He goes back to staring out the window as we continue on Venice Boulevard.

'*At the next light, turn left onto Avalon,*' the woman says over the speakers.

I flip the indicator on the steering wheel.

Chapter 7

Once we're off Venice Boulevard, it's nothing but houses with perfectly manicured lawns. They're not huge, but Mar Vista is prime Los Angeles real estate. Like in the Hollywood Hills, the houses are a random assortment of architectural styles. Some of the houses that were built in the sixties remain, while others are more modern, built in a Mediterranean style or those modern designs that look like odd assortments of stacked concrete. From time to time, a house will be hidden behind a wall of hedges that lines the border of their lot, but the thing that's most striking to me isn't the varied architecture or the subtle displays of wealth. The most striking aspect is, like the Hollywood Hills, a lack of streetlights.

After a few blocks, Damon leans forward from the back seat.

'Turn off the lights and, very quietly, come to a stop right up here, just before that house behind the hedges.'

I hit the lights, slowly pull up to the curb, and put the car in park.

The house in front of us is nearly hidden by a five-foot-tall hedge. Only the windows of the second floor are visible above the wall of sculpted bushes.

'Kill the engine,' Damon says, as he begins rummaging through the backpack. Again, there's that *clink* as something hits a metal object inside.

'Whose house is this?' I ask, as the engine cuts out.

He ignores my questions and pulls a manila envelope from the bag.

'Whose house is this?' I ask again, louder.

Damon stops going through the backpack and looks at me.

'Lucas, do you want to be a part of what I'm doing?'

'What?'

'Asking questions about what I'm doing only makes you more involved. So, do you want to be a part of this? Do you want to go into that house with me and see what happens? Or do you want to stay here in the car?'

The idea of going in there and seeing what he's about to do turns my stomach.

'I'll stay in the car.'

'Good. Because you going in with me is not part of my plan. I can't have you screwing things up, so you have to stay here.' He pulls a set of zip ties from the backpack. 'Now, put your hands behind your back.'

'W-why?'

'I don't have time to explain, Lucas,' he replies, losing patience. 'We're starting to fall behind schedule.'

'Tell me why I have to put my hands behind my back. What are you going to do?'

'I'm going to zip-tie your wrists, duct-tape your mouth, and put you in the trunk.'

My heart leaps into my throat.

'What?! No! No way. You can't—'

'I'm not going to leave you here on the honor system,' he bristles. 'I'm also not going to leave you bound and gagged in the front seat for some late-night dog walker to find. I'm going to bind your wrists, cover your mouth, put you safely in the trunk, and go do what I have to do. When I come back, I'll cut the zip ties, take the tape off your mouth, and we'll be on our way. Got it?'

I've been severely claustrophobic ever since I got stuck in a toy chest during a game of hide and seek as a kid, and at this moment, there has never been a thought more terrifying than having him bind my wrists, gag me, and throw me in the trunk. Does he really expect me to trust him to come back? What if he just drives to the middle of nowhere, kills me, tosses my body on the side of the road, and then goes to the apartment to make sure there are no loose ends and finds Julia? Absolutely not.

My knuckles go white on the steering wheel.

'I'm not going in the trunk,' I quietly say.

'Lucas . . .'

I shake my head. Every muscle in my body locks up. 'No. No. I'm not letting you—'

There's a sudden rush of movement and then an explosion of pain across the base of my skull. My vision goes reddish-brown with bursting pinpoints of light. The pain and disorientation are so intense that I'm unable to speak or breathe. I'm only vaguely aware of being pulled over the center console. An arm slams down into my elbows, wrenching my hands away from the wheel. Then, my arms are pulled behind my back. My wrists are pressed together as my senses rapidly begin to return. I try to resist, but it's too late. There's the high-pitched clicking as Damon tightens the zip tie and the thin plastic band digs into the flesh of my wrists. A second later, amid my feeble attempts to fight back, there's the sound of duct tape unrolling and ripping. As more adrenaline is dumped into my body, I begin to struggle against the zip tie but a hand clutches my hair and violently pulls my head back against the headrest.

I'm about to scream but a split second before the sound escapes my lips, the air flow is shut off by a strip of duct tape being slapped over my mouth. I can't breathe. My panic grows exponentially and I begin to grunt and thrash, fighting for oxygen. I'm about to pass out before I realize that I can breathe through my nose, but it's not enough air. I wrestle against the plastic binding my wrists. I need to get this tape off. I need air.

Suddenly, my arms are thrust upwards at the wrists behind my back, throwing me forward and slamming my face into the dashboard. My arms can't go any higher, but Damon keeps applying pressure. It feels like my shoulders are about to snap. The intense pain stops my struggles and attempted cries.

All I can do is focus on the agony and fight for air through my nose.

'Listen to me, Lucas!' Damon hisses, still pushing upwards on my wrists. 'You are the one who decides how difficult this is going to be!' He pushes harder, sending shockwaves of agony through my body. I squeeze my eyes shut and release a noise somewhere between a groan and a sob against the back of the tape. 'I know this hurts but it stops when you do as I say. You're going in the trunk. You're going to stay there and not make a sound. I'm going to go inside. Then, I'll come back, let you out, and we'll be on our way. Got it?'

My shoulders are giving out. The muscles and tendons are being pulled apart. It takes everything I have to nod and whimper something like a 'yes' into the tape.

'Good . . . Now, I'm going to lower your arms. Then, I'm going to get you out of the car and put you in the trunk. I'm going inside the house and I'm taking the car keys with me. Understand?'

I nod again. I'll do anything to make this torture stop.

'Okay,' Damon says. 'Here we go . . .'

He slowly lowers my arms.

My shoulders are still on fire, but the immediate feeling that they're about to snap subsides.

Damon lets go of my arms entirely.

I sit upright, tilt my head back, and inhale rapidly through my nose. All I want is air.

The sound of Damon pulling something from the backpack and then exiting the car barely registers.

A moment later, he opens my door with one hand while using the other to aim the gun at me from his hip.

'Out,' he instructs, as he reaches in and hooks a hand under my arm to guide me to my feet. Damon quickly scans the street to make sure no one is coming before leading me to the back of the car. As he does, I notice the manila envelope he pulled from the backpack is sitting on top of the car. Once we reach the trunk, he takes the key fob and hits the button, causing the lid to open with a gentle *pop*.

'Get in,' Damon says. 'Before someone sees us.'

I stare down at the cramped space.

'Hurry up. The sooner you get in, the sooner you get out.' His tone is tense and urgent.

I glance around at the surrounding houses. There are lights on here and there, but they illuminate empty rooms or are behind closed blinds or drapes.

'Lucas,' he says through clenched teeth. 'Do not make me force you into this trunk.'

My head is still throbbing from where he struck me with the gun. My shoulders are still burning and the deep breaths I take through my nose are barely enough oxygen to keep from passing out.

I nod.

I'm getting in, but I'm not staying in this trunk. I'm not going to wait for him to come back. My mind is fighting through the pain and oxygen deprivation to rapidly form a plan.

Keeping the gun on me with one hand, Damon uses the other to help me with my balance as I lower myself into the trunk. I position myself on my side and have to tuck my knees into my chest to fit. Once I'm settled, half of my face resting on the coarse fibers of the floor mat, Damon stands over me.

'One last thing,' he says.

He reaches into the backpack and pulls out another set of zip ties. I watch in horror as he leans down and loops them around my ankles. He pulls the tab tight and, like my wrists behind my back, my ankles are now immobile.

'I had to wait until you were in the trunk,' he says off of my expression. 'Gotta make sure you're not going anywhere.' He reaches over and grabs the manila envelope from the roof of the car. 'Now, stay quiet. I'll be right back.'

He closes the lid, plunging me into darkness and, aside from my labored breathing, total silence.

I count to twenty in my head while getting as much air into my lungs as I can through my nose. The adhesive from the tape, mixed with my sweat and saliva, begins to fill my mouth with a rank, sour taste.

He's got to be at the house by now.

I'm not trusting him to free me once he's done in the house. I only have a few precious minutes. It's time to act.

I begin thrashing and kicking at my bonds, but in the cramped space of the trunk, it accomplishes nothing. I shift gears and focus all my efforts on breaking the zip tie around my wrists. I pull them against my back as hard as I can, grunting in pain as the plastic cuts into the flesh between the bones of my wrists and my hands. No matter how hard I strain, the zip tie doesn't even stretch, much less break. After a few moments of pulling, the searing pain in my wrists forces me to stop.

All my thrashing has done is burn up the oxygen in my body. I have to stop for a few moments and focus on breathing.

Okay. I can't break the zip ties. I'm not going to be able to get out of here on my own, but it's not like I can phone a fr—

Wait.

What was it that Damon said about the possibility of being spotted by a late-night dog walker? He didn't want to leave me in the front seat because someone might come walking by. I may not be in the front seat, but maybe someone passing by will notice if the car is rocking, telling them that there's someone in the trunk. They'll call the police, right?

I flip onto my back and begin rhythmically kicking as hard as I can against the side of the trunk while screaming against the tape.

I can only keep it up for a few seconds before the lack of air once again causes me to stop and come to my senses.

This isn't going to work. I can't count on someone randomly walking by in the next few minutes and seeing the car move. I also can't count on someone glancing out of the window of a nearby house and noticing, either. The street is so dark, I doubt they would see a thing.

How long has it been? Two minutes? Three? Five? How much time do I have before Damon comes back? It can't be long.

I have to get out of this trunk. If I can do that, I'll go to one of the surrounding houses and get someone's attention. I'll knock on the doors and have them call the police. I'll also send them to the apartment to protect Julia if Damon decides to go there looking for me.

But how will I do that? How can I knock on a door with my hands zip-tied behind my back and my ankles bound together?

No.

That's not the problem I have to solve right now. The first problem I have to solve is getting out of this—?

It hits me.

I've been so focused on trying to break the zip ties, getting someone to notice the car rocking, that, because I'm not really a car person at all, I've forgotten the obvious answer.

Somewhere in this trunk is an emergency latch that will open the lid. All cars have them specifically for this situation. I just have to find it.

But I can't see a thing in here.

I frantically work myself onto my side. The latch to release the lid is either on the wall of the trunk by my head or on the wall at my feet. Since I'm already oriented to this side, I hunch over, stretch my legs, and push against the side of the trunk, causing me to slide across the floor until my back is pressed up against the plastic-paneled wall. I frantically begin feeling behind me with my bound hands. I continue breathing hard against the tape as I contort and arch my back to allow my hands to search as much of the sidewall as possible while the pulse in my ears acts as a clock, counting down the unknown number of seconds I have left.

Dammit. It's not here. It has to be on the other side.

I turn myself around, scraping my cheek against the coarse floor mat as I convulse and writhe. I'm finally able to reorientate my body 180 degrees. I once again straighten my legs to slide my body across the floor of the trunk, and press my back against the opposite wall.

After a few moments of groping with my fingers, I still haven't found it. My panic begins to grow.

It has to be here.

Then, the memory hits.

I know where it is! I remember seeing it when I bought the car. I opened the trunk, saw the handle in the back corner, and pulled. Since the trunk was already open, all I heard was a click. I asked the car salesman, 'What does this do?' He gave me a pitying look and said, 'It opens the trunk.'

I turn a few degrees more and bury my face into the floor mat, which allows me to reach higher with my hands behind my back. My frantic search causes the zip ties to bite even deeper into my wrists. It feels like it has broken the skin. I don't care because as I grope in the darkness, I'm struck by a horrible thought. What if the latch is in the other corner. I didn't reach this high. What if I missed it? What if I have to turn back around and—

My finger brushes against the handle.

It's here!

I press my face harder into the floor and strain my hands backwards, giving my fingers enough purchase under the handle.

I steady myself, making sure my fingers are securely under the plastic lever, and pull.

Pop.

Fresh air pours into the trunk. I flip onto my back and can see stars overhead.

Grunting with effort, I pull myself up into a sitting position and scan the street. The houses are still dark and quiet. There's nothing to suggest that anyone is watching. I'm still on my own and time is running out.

My plan changes again.

I can't take the risk of knocking on a door or screaming for attention. If no one is home, I'll be wasting time and possibly alerting Damon.

My only hope is to hide.

If he comes out and sees that I'm gone, he may decide that he doesn't have the time to look for me. Maybe he'll drive off, since he has the car keys, and then I'll make as much noise as I need to get the attention of someone on this street.

That's the new plan: I have to hide.

I scan the street again.

There!

The only place that's close and that could provide enough cover are the bushes surrounding the porch of the neighboring house.

I swing my feet over the lip of the trunk and lurch upwards, attempting to stand. I'm able to clear the opening of the trunk and my feet land on the street, but my ankles are still bound. My momentum causes me to keep tipping forward. At the last second, I'm able to twist myself so that I hit the asphalt on my side.

I want to stop and take in the oxygen I so desperately need, but I can't. I lift my head and look toward the bushes.

Twenty yards. That's my estimate. Twenty yards over the curb, across the sidewalk and then the lawn to get under those bushes.

Suddenly, a man screams. It came from the house behind the hedges. The one that Damon went into.

I have to move. Now!

I begin writhing and lurching, eventually settling into a rhythm. I reach the curb and work my way onto the sidewalk.

My body is screaming for more air. Sweat is pouring into my eyes. The rank duct-tape-and-saliva taste is pushing me to vomit.

I work myself over the sidewalk. My cheek makes contact with the grass. I look up. The bushes are right there. I just have to keep moving, inch by inch. In another minute or so, I'll be safely hidden under the bu—

A door opens and closes behind the hedge.

I begin grunting as I continue thrashing, propelling my body as fast as I can across the grass.

There are hurried footsteps on the sidewalk behind me.

No . . . No . . . No! No! No!

Damon growls with rage.

Pain suddenly rips through my shoulders as I'm forcefully lifted from the ground by my arms and dragged back across the lawn toward the street. Damon hurls me against the side of the car. My body fights for balance. I'm about to topple over when Damon is upon me.

He pins me against the car and brings his face close to mine.

His eyes are wild with rage. His teeth are bared like a rabid animal. Only then do I notice the flecks of blood splattered across his face and the bloody blade he's holding at my throat.

'You have no idea how badly you just screwed up,' he snarls.

Chapter 8

What kind of a name is Toby, anyway?

I wasn't even paying attention to the basketball game. I barely heard the echoing thud of the ball against the hardwood floor or the squeaking of sneakers. I was too busy thinking about what a stupid name Toby was. There wasn't much to the basketball game, either. Our junior high team sucked but with Millersburg being such a small town with limited entertainment options, everyone went to the games. It was a social hangout and a place to be seen. Everyone's head would turn when someone walked through the double doors next to the bleachers. If it was a friend, they'd scan the crowd until they saw you and you'd wave them to the seat you had been saving for them. I was there with my friends Thomas and Doug, but I had been saving an extra seat.

Julia and I hadn't hung out in a month, which was a while for us. I had no doubt we were still best friends. We talked on the phone every few days. We still saw each other in the halls between classes, but we hadn't gotten together to read stories, throw stones, or just hang out like we used to.

That fall her braces had come off. My braces had come off a few months earlier and I knew how weird it felt; like you had big old horse teeth. So, we celebrated with a bubble gum blowing contest. But, after that, we hung out less and less.

I worried that something was wrong but she told me that everything was fine so even though I was sitting with Thomas and Doug at the game, I saved Julia a seat so we could hang out like old times. But then, halfway through the first quarter with the Millersburg Mustangs already down by twelve, there was movement at the double doors. Everyone's head turned.

There she was. Julia . . . attached at the hip to Toby Mauer. Toby Mauer. Our starting halfback on the football team who, like our basketball team, wasn't very good.

While most of us were still struggling with the awkward gangliness of puberty, he was tall and fit and one of his toned arms was around Julia's shoulders.

And Julia was beaming.

This surprise development sent shockwaves through the bleachers but hit me the hardest.

Julia and Toby waved to friends and scanned the bleachers for a place to sit.

Julia saw me. Her smile, now with perfectly aligned teeth, faltered just a little.

I almost automatically motioned for her to come sit next to me in the spot I had been saving, but I stopped myself, sparing us the embarrassment of Julia turning it down.

Toby and Julia found a spot up in the corner of the bleachers with a few of the other football players and some of the more popular girls.

I tried to go back to not really paying attention to the game and joking with Doug and Thomas, but I kept finding excuses to glance back to that corner of the bleachers. I would catch glimpses of Julia laughing with the girls or nuzzling close to Toby. The worst was when I saw his hand on her knee.

After that, I didn't want to look back. I forced myself to stare at the game without watching as I fumed.

Seriously, what kind of name is Toby?

I focused on his name because there wasn't a whole lot else that I could find fault with. He wasn't class president or anything but he was popular, and good looking, and talented. The Junior High Trifecta.

But where was Toby when Julia got her braces off? Where was the sparkling Toby when Julia would come over to my house and we would hang out because her parents were fighting and she was upset? Did Toby know of her love of Skittles? Did Toby know that Julia liked to write short stories about elves and dragons?

And for real; what parent names their child Toby?

The bleachers cleared out at halftime as people went to get a snack or hang out in the parking lot. Some students went around the side of the gym to smoke a cigarette. With the Millersburg Mustangs down by twenty, others simply went home.

Doug and Thomas were in the club of people who went outside to share a cigarette that Doug had swiped from his dad's pack. I didn't smoke and it was way too cold outside, so I opted to get some hot chocolate from the makeshift concession table in the lobby by the door.

I was waiting in line when I felt a tap on my shoulder. I thought Doug or Thomas may have also realized it was way too cold outside, but I turned to find Julia looking at me with an awkward, braceless smile. Her cheeks were ruddy. She had obviously just come from outside.

'Hey . . .' she said.

'. . . hey.'

'How are things?' she asked, attempting a cheery tone.

'Good . . .' I answered, matching her awkwardness. 'So . . . You and Toby are, uh . . . going together?'

That was the term at the time.

She shrugged. 'Yeah. I guess so.'

This was why we hadn't hung out in a while. I could tell that she was happy, but talking about it to me was obviously strange for her. It was strange for both of us.

'Cool,' I said, trying to play it casual.

'So . . . Are we going to do Christmas?' she asked. 'I want to read you this new one I wrote about Azamar.'

Azamar was the hero elf of a lot of her stories.

'Sure,' I answered, as if I could take it or leave it, but for the first time since she had walked into the gym with Toby, my chest didn't hurt.

Julia smiled in a way I felt sure Toby hadn't seen. She lifted her hand and extended her little finger.

'Pinky swear?'

'Pinky swear,' I said, hooking her little finger with mine.

For a second, it was like old times; just Julia and I.

'Julia?'

We turned to see Toby standing by the doors with the kids from the corner of the bleachers.

'We're going to head to Josh's house. You coming?' he asked.

'Yep,' Julia chimed. She went to join them but turned and pointed at me as she walked backwards. 'Remember: you pinky swore!'

I nodded.

She spun around and got close to Toby, who put his arm over her shoulder as they went through the doors and disappeared into the parking lot.

That's when it truly hit me.

I wasn't mad at Toby. I wasn't upset with Julia.

I had known for a while but I had never admitted it to myself. I was too young. I didn't fully understand, but now, I did.

I stood there alone in the lobby, facing one of the most thrilling, gut-wrenching, and terrifying facts a young person can wrestle with.

I was in love with my best friend.

Chapter 9

'*Continue north on Interstate four-oh-five,*' the automated female voice instructs over the car's speakers.

She's been guiding me since we left the house. Damon punched in the info on my phone and has since been too busy cleaning the blood from his face with a packet of wipes from the small first aid kit he's pulled from the backpack. The faint scent of alcohol fills the car.

I've kept my mouth shut and followed the voice's directions. Damon's only word to me since pinning me up against the car and holding a bloody knife to my throat has been 'drive.'

Is he waiting until we're further away from the house and he's cleaned himself up before making me pay a price for trying to escape? I'm staying as silent as possible. I want to become invisible up here in the front seat, but he's going to 'deal' with me sooner or later.

'Dammit!'

Damon's outburst causes me to nearly jump out of my seat.

I look at him in the rearview mirror.

Damon's hoodie is off, and he's wiping the blood from a cut on his right arm. I alternate between watching the road and watching him clean the wound. He applies a small pad, and wraps it in gauze. Then, he takes the duct tape from the backpack, tears off a long strip, and begins looping it around his arm to secure the gauze when he sees me watching him. 'Watch the road.'

My gaze goes back to the surrounding traffic but I can feel his eyes on me as we pass under the 10 Freeway, on our way back toward the Sepulveda Pass.

I could ask him why we're going back the way we came, but I'm sure as hell not going to. I'm not going to ask him why he's killing people. I don't want to know. I don't want to engage with him. The less we speak, the less of a chance that I'll slip up and mention Julia.

After he's done securing the gauze to his arm to stop the bleeding, he pulls his hoodie back on and glares at me.

'So, what was your "plan"?' he asks.

'What?'

'Once you got out of the trunk, what were you going to do?'

'I don't know,' I answer like a kid who's been caught sneaking out of bed.

He scoffs in disbelief. 'Really? You don't know? I told you to stay in the trunk and not make a sound and I come out to find you slithering around in the grass. Don't tell me you didn't have a plan.'

'I just wanted to get away.'

'And then what? Did you forget that I know where you live?'

'I don't know,' I helplessly insist. 'I was taking things one step at a time. I didn't trust you when you said you'd let me out.'

'You didn't?'

'No. I thought you might leave me in there or kill me and dump me in the middle of nowhere. I mean, why should I trust you?'

'Have I given you a reason not to trust me?'

'Other than holding a gun to my head and threatening to kill me unless I drive you around so you can kill other people?'

'I haven't lied to you about anything, Lucas. Nor will I,' he says, perfectly calm.

'And you expect me to believe that? You expect me to trust you when you tie me up and throw me in the trunk while you run off to murder someone?'

He takes a breath as we drive under Sunset Boulevard and re-enter the barren stretch of the Sepulveda Pass.

'That's what has to happen,' he finally says. 'I can't have you come into these places while I do my work.' He leans forward. 'And let's be perfectly clear: I don't *need* you to trust me but it is better if you do. It's better if we trust each other. Not *like*. You don't have to like me, but if we trust each other, it'll make my work easier and you'll have a better chance of surviving . . . Believe me when I tell you that I don't want to hurt you, Lucas, but if you get in the way of my work . . .' He trails off and is struck by a thought. 'Are you a fan of baseball, Lucas?'

'What?'

'Growing up, did you play baseball?'

'I don't— I mean, yeah. Little league.'

'Okay. We'll call your little stunt back there strike one.'

'Are you serious?'

'Very.'

I guess he feels that he made his point as he sits back to watch the traffic while using another alcohol wipe to make sure that he's cleaned all the flecks of blood from his face.

The build-up of vehicles entering the Sepulveda Pass causes us to slow down.

His mention of the apartment puts my mind back on Julia and Sophie. No matter what happens to me tonight, I have to keep him away from them. But how? How can I keep Damon from ever going to our apartment? What would make him stay away? I'm hit by a thought so perfect, I let it fly before really thinking.

'I don't live there anymore,' I blurt out.

He finishes wiping his cheek. 'What are you talking about?'

'The apartment? The one on my driver's license? I moved six months ago. I just haven't changed it because the license isn't

54

expired, but I don't live there anymore.'

He stops worrying about wiping his face and raises an eyebrow in my direction. 'You don't?'

'Nope.'

'So . . . where do you live?'

I shake my head. 'I'm not telling you.'

I hate to admit it, but these months of lying to Julia may be helping me here. I've felt miserable every time she's asked me how work was and I've made up some mundane stories, but I've gotten pretty good at it, and if it keeps him away from her, there might be a silver lining.

Damon brings his face closer. The alternating headlights and overhead streetlamps create an unsettling pattern where in one moment he's an unreadable silhouette, and the next, he's a leering ghoul. Damon aims the gun at me between the seats, out of view of the passing cars but visible to me.

'How about now?' he asks.

He's trying to intimidate me, but he's had that gun on me for the last hour. He's locked me in the trunk. He's held a knife to my throat. For a second, I'm not scared of the gun. The floodgates of fatigue, disgust, and anxiety open and I feel myself go over the edge.

'You're not going to shoot me.'

'I'm not?'

'No.'

'And why is that?'

'Because if you shoot me right now, we'll crash. And your plan for this evening, whatever it is, will get a lot harder.'

Chapter 10

When I realized I was in love with Julia, I did what my young teenage brain felt was the only logical thing to do: I buried it deep in my psyche and mistook that for getting over her and moving on.

We were fourteen. The most intense crushes, the kind that made you feel like you were destined to be together forever, came and went in a week.

Julia's relationship with Toby lasted all of a month. After that, we went back to being best friends. She never mentioned him again and I never asked. I had my friend back and I buried those feelings for her even deeper.

We started high school the following fall. Even though we'd had most of the same classmates since kindergarten, it felt different. We felt grown up.

I developed crushes on other girls. I would tell Julia about my feelings for them and she would give me advice on how to win them over. Looking back, I know those crushes were attempts to deny my feelings for her. She would tell me later that she liked me, too, but we were both terrified of what would happen to our friendship if we explored anything more. So instead, we tortured each other by seeing other people.

My first 'real' relationship started October of our freshman year; Brianna Hemsey. We were very serious, and by 'very,' I mean that we held hands in the hallway between classes. Brianna was particular about how things should be: about our friends, how she should be treated, etc. I was on cloud nine.

For a while, at least.

She agreed to go to Homecoming with me, our first high school dance, but she wasn't very impressed with the casual way I asked her over the phone. I didn't think it was supposed to be a big production, but she pointed out how her friends' boyfriends had created cute videos and posterboards, asking their dates to Homecoming. I told her I would do something mind-blowing for Midwinter dance, which would be next year. After all, we had been together for three weeks, which meant we were going to be together forever.

And Brianna *hated* Julia.

Maybe she was aware of my feelings for Julia in a way I wasn't ready to admit. I tried to explain to her that Julia and I were friends, but when Julia asked if I would save a dance for her at Homecoming, I told her I would ask Brianna if it was okay. Brianna made it clear that no, it was not.

Julia was a good sport about it. She was going to the dance with Doug, but only as friends.

I went with Brianna's friends and their boyfriends. It wasn't a bad time but even before we got to the dance, I was tired of the endless selfies and the high-pitched screams as she and her friends gushed over their dresses.

The school gymnasium was decked out in streamers and balloons. Chaperones patrolled the beverage station, making sure no one added to the punch, which was primarily Sprite and Hawaiian Punch. Brianna and I danced the slow dances. She and her friends took a million more photos, as if they were more concerned with documenting that they had been to the dance rather than enjoying it. Still, I had resolved to have a good time. I didn't want to upset Brianna.

But then Julia arrived.

I had seen her dressed up before, but this was the first time I had seen her like that. She was wearing a midnight-blue dress that made her blond hair shine and her eyes sparkle. She looked a little uncomfortable but appeared to be having a good time with Doug. They had come with Thomas and his girlfriend, Suzie.

They were joking and laughing. Doug was demonstrating some ridiculous dance move that caused them to bust a gut. I really wanted to join them. I wanted to tell—

'Lucas?'

I turned to see Brianna.

'Come on,' she said, extending her hand. 'We're going outside for a bit.'

I took her hand and we went outside. It turned out that someone had a flask of Mad Dog 20/20. Just like during the basketball games, around the side of the gym is where you went to smoke or drink. They passed around the flask and gossiped about how lame the dance was. When the flask reached me, I handed it off without taking a sip, causing Brianna to glare at me. Finally, I told her that I was going back inside. I walked away from the group but Brianna caught up with me as I rounded the corner of the building.

'What's wrong with you?' she asked.

'Nothing,' I told her. 'I'm just going back inside.'

She didn't try to stop me but I could feel her eyes burrowing into my back.

Upon returning to the gym, I walked up to Julia and tapped her on the shoulder.

She turned and lit up.

'Hey!' she cried and gave me a hug that I returned. She then looked around. 'Where's Brianna?'

'She's outside,' I replied, nodding over my shoulder. 'I just wanted to tell you that you look really nice.'

She blushed. 'Thanks. You look really nice, too,' Julia said, adjusting the boutonnière.

Brianna had pinned to my chest. We stood there for an awkward moment before a slow song began to play. Julia suddenly had a mischievous smile. 'If she's outside, do you want to sneak in a dance?'

I wanted to, very badly, but I had promised Brianna and we were still going to be together forever.

'I probably shouldn't.'

The disappointment in Julia's face caused me physical pain.

'Okay,' she said.

'I should, uh . . . I should probably find her.'

'Have fun,' Julia said, as I turned to go.

'You, too.'

Brianna broke up with me three days later.

I think about that moment a lot. I wish I would have danced with Julia. I didn't know it then, but it was the last time we had the opportunity to share a dance as innocent teenagers.

Before my life fell apart.

Chapter 11

'That's why you're not going to shoot me.'

The muscles in one corner of Damon's mouth pull his lips into an unsettling grin, as if he's enjoying our little thought experiment.

'That's an interesting theory,' he says. 'But what if I have you pull over somewhere nice and quiet and kill you there?'

'In Los Angeles? You think you can find a nice, quiet spot where you can kill me and no one will notice in this town?'

Damon's thoughtful smile grows. 'Lucas, without turning your head to look, describe the drivers of the cars to our right and left.'

'What?'

'Describe the people behind the wheel of the cars to the left and right of us.' He quickly shakes his head. 'You know what? It's dark, so I'll make this even easier for you. Don't worry about the drivers. Simply tell me the colors of the cars to the left and right of us, right now, without looking.'

I already know that I've made a mistake but I try to keep my head still and strain my eyes to the left.

'Lucas, I can see you trying to look at the cars in the mirror.'

'I don't know their colors,' I admit in frustration.

Damon nods. 'That's what I mean. No one notices anything outside their own little world. No one on this road is watching us. They have their own problems to worry about. Seriously, how often have you noticed other drivers? And I'm not talking about someone flipping you the finger for cutting them off or someone thanking you for letting them into your lane. When was the last time you looked over at another driver for no reason and genuinely wondered what was happening in their life? And even if you thought that maybe something was wrong, would you get involved?'

I don't have a response but he's right. There have been times I've been giving rides and felt that the people in my back seat didn't even notice me.

'Don't feel bad,' Damon says off of my expression and relaxing slightly. 'No one would. You don't notice them and they don't notice you. And it's not just Los Angeles, either. It's true everywhere. That's what I'm counting on, tonight. We could pull over to the side of the road or into a parking garage, I could shoot you, and no one would bat an eye.'

'. . . Then maybe I won't.'

'Won't what?'

'Pull over. If I know you're telling me to stop so you can kill me, maybe I just keep driving.'

He shrugs. 'Then I guess we're right back to where we started. I shoot you, the car crashes, and I take my chances.'

'But your plan is over.'

'Nah. It's just delayed. I would just have to add one more stop.'

'Which is?'

'One-one-three-two Houghton Way, Apartment C.'

'But I just told you that I don't live there.'

'Which was really stupid,' he says with a confused smile. 'Because why would you say that?'

My nails dig into the steering wheel.

'If you didn't live there anymore, that would have been your luckiest break of the night,' Damon continues. 'Because if you did escape me, I might never have been able to find you. There's only one reason why you would tell me you don't live there anymore and that's because you *really* don't want me to go there.'

My heart plummets into my stomach. 'I'm just letting you know that I don't live there anymore. That's all.'

'And I'm calling bullshit.'

He waits for a reply, but I stay silent and attempt to focus on the road.

'Come on, Lucas. Tell me. What's at one-one-three-two Houghton Way, Apartment C.'

'Nothing!' I angrily snap. 'I don't live there anymore!'

Damon flinches. The anger and panic in my voice caught him off-guard. The moment is fleeting but it isn't lost on me. For the first time since he aimed that gun at my head after picking him up, there wasn't an ounce of fear in me. Keeping him away from the apartment was more important.

The initial rush of rage-filled confidence ebbs but my mind is spinning out. I'm so absorbed in my thoughts that I only register at the last second that the traffic has come to a stop. I hit the brakes a little too quickly to avoid rear-ending a Prius. The seatbelt halts my forward momentum and pushes me back.

Damon, who isn't wearing his seatbelt, is pitched forward into the back of the passenger seat.

'I told you to watch the road,' he mutters and sits back with an exasperated sigh.

It's a sigh of annoyance, of exasperation, and it's not the first time I've heard it. Other riders have done the same. It's a reminder that on some level, Damon is just another rider. I already hated doing this. There was already enough uncertainty in my life, enough stress, and now, there's a murderer in my car, a murderer who knows where I live and by default, Julia. I've put her and our daughter in danger because I've been lying to her.

'Why?' I mumble under my breath.

'Excuse me?'

'Why did you need a ride? Why did you have to bring me

into this?'

'Well, Lucas, if it makes you feel any better, you were never part of my plan. I had other means of transportation, but something happened at the house where you picked me up. One of the people got outside. I chased them, but they had a gun, too. They shot at me while I hid behind the car I had arrived in. I was able to kill them and drag the body back inside, but when I went to leave, the car wouldn't start. Whatever they hit under the hood of the car while I was using it for cover must have been important. Maybe they hit the radiator or maybe they snapped a belt, I don't know, but the car was dead. I needed a ride and had to improvise.'

'What about the other car in the driveway? The sports car?'

'What about it?'

'Why didn't you take that one? It belonged to someone you killed, right? Why not take the key off of them and use that?'

'Because it was a high-end sports car with specialty license plates. When the cops arrived, it would have taken them five minutes to identify the victims, and another five minutes to figure out whose car was missing, and five minutes after that, every cop in the city would have been looking for the expensive sports car with the specialty plates. I needed something less splashy. That's why you're stuck with me.'

'But you called the cops to the house,' I protest. 'You could have taken the car and no one would have been looking for you. You could have done— . . . whatever it is you're doing and not involved anyone else.'

'I had to call the cops.'

'Why?'

'To start the clock. Everyone needs to know what these people did.'

I wait for him to explain further.

For a moment, it feels like he might tell me, but he changes gears. 'The point is, I didn't pick you, Lucas. I didn't plan for anyone else to be a part of this . . . And for what it's worth, I'm sorry.'

I scoff. 'Sure. But whatever it is you're doing is more important than me, right?'

'Yes,' he answers without hesitation. 'But that doesn't mean I'm not sorry.'

'Perfect,' I say with a helpless shake of my head. 'That is just my luck.'

Damon rolls his eyes in disgust. 'Oh, don't do that.'

'Don't do what?'

'Don't blame "luck." Don't think that the world has it out for you. The world doesn't care. The "world," or "luck," or the "universe," or "karma," or whatever the hell you want to call it? It doesn't exist. This encounter? You and me? It's pure chance. It's meaningless. There are no cosmic scales. It's just people and people are divided into two types: those who think fate determines their lives and those who get what they want – and those types of people? They don't give a shit about anyone they have to go through to get it.'

'. . . Just like you don't give a shit about me?' I ask. 'Aren't you just going through me to get what you want?'

Damon tries to think of an argument but only shrugs. 'I said I was sorry.'

'Just not sorry enough?'

He shrugs, again.

'Okay,' I reply, seizing on an idea. 'Then let me ask you something.'

'Go ahead.'

I stare at him in the rearview mirror. 'Who went through you?'

In the alternating pattern of light and darkness that crosses his face, his expression grows cold. I've triggered some dark and violent memory. The animal that pinned me up against the car and held the bloody blade to my throat is suddenly back and it's about to strike when—

Ding-ding-ding.

The screen on the console lights up with an incoming text message.

It's from Julia.

I panic and try to hit the 'ignore' button but it's too late. Damon connected my phone to the Bluetooth system of the car after we left the house to tend to his wounds.

The automated woman reads out the message through the speakers.

'*When are you leaving the office? I swear this baby is trying to kick its way out.*'

Neither of us move.

Damon's anger morphs into shock, and then smug triumph.

'Well, well, Lucas,' he says, a sinister smile playing across his face. 'I think I know what's at one-one-three-two Houghton Way, Apartment C.'

My heart goes into overdrive and my adrenaline spikes.

'No! Listen to me! Please, listen—'

'Who's Julia? Is she your girlfriend?' Damon asks.

'She's my wife,' I reply, speaking rapidly. 'She has nothing to do with this. She doesn't kn—'

'Why aren't you wearing a ring?' he asks.

'What?'

'If she's your wife, why aren't you wearing a wedding ring? And why does she think you're at the offi—?' He stops. His smile grows even wider as he puts it all together. 'Because rings are expensive and you're having financial problems. That *is* why you're doing this . . . and she doesn't know.'

'No, she doesn't, and you can't—'

'She thinks you're working at an office?'

'Yes, but I had—'

'And you're having a baby?'

My rambling and sputtering stops as my worst fear, the thing I was trying to keep away from him, comes to pass.

'. . . Yes . . .' I meekly answer.

'Boy or a girl?'

'What?'

'Are you having a boy or a girl?'

'. . . A girl . . .'

He stares at me and somewhere in those eyes, lurking behind the smug triumph and sadism, is a flash of pain.

'Have you picked a name?' he asks.

'. . . Sophia . . .' I admit, my chest tightening. '. . . Little Sophie.'

Damon nods and grows quiet, as if deciding what to do with this new information. He stares at the back of the seat in front of him and then runs his hand through his hair, almost like he's frustrated. This doesn't make any sense. A moment ago, he was beaming at this new discovery. Now, he seems pissed. Finally, he turns his attention back to me.

'Okay, Lucas. Here's the deal: for the rest of the evening, you're going to do what I say. Down to the letter because if you don't, if you mess with my plans—'

My vision blurs with tears. I know what he's about to say.

'Please, don't do this,' I beg.

'I will kill you and then I will pay a visit to your apartment.'

'No . . .'

'And I will make sure that you, Julia, and little unborn Sophie are reunited.'

'Please!'

'It's up to you, Lucas,' he says and sits back.

'This has nothing to do with them! You can't—'

'Watch the road.'

'—hurt them! They haven't done anything to you! I will do whatever you want, just pr—'

His eyes go wide. 'Lucas, watch the road!'

'—omise me that you won't—'

'LUCAS!' He suddenly lunges through the gap between the front seats to grab the wheel.

I turn to face forward as alarms start pinging and the console screen blinks red with a one-word message: *BRAKE!*

A stopped semitruck is right in front of us.

We're going to hit.

Before Damon can grab the wheel, I wrench it to the right, veering us into the adjacent lane.

Miraculously, we miss the truck by what must be less than an inch. There is the screeching of brakes all around us and a symphony of horns. Thankfully, the car in the next lane was quick enough to stomp on the brakes to avoid ramming us. The driver lays onto the horn.

All around us, people are voicing their displeasure.

I'm staring straight ahead. My breath is catching in my chest.

'Lucas?' Damon asks, calmly.

His words barely reach me over the blaring horns and my heart hammering against my ribs.

'Lucas, you have to keep going.'

I'm still trying to breathe.

'Come on, Lucas. You're blocking traffic.'

I slowly come to my senses and shift my foot from the brake to the gas. I ease into the lane and pull forward past the semitruck while Damon waves apologetically to the surrounding drivers.

I begin to accelerate.

Damon heaves a sigh and settles back into his seat. 'Okay. Let's not do that aga—'

Blip-Blip!

Flashing red and blue lights appear behind us.

Chapter 12

The reception was over.

It had been incredibly awkward and painful. It was going to be painful and awkward, anyway, but Dad had made it so much worse.

At the funeral, instead of giving a speech filled with love and remembrance of my mom's life, his speech had been filled with anger and bitterness. Some anger and bitterness would have been understandable, even expected. Mom had been taken from us so quickly. There had been no time to grieve, no time to process what was happening. A month ago, she was here. We were sitting at the kitchen table, talking about colleges. Now, she was gone. None of it was fair, but Dad could have made his speech about her. Instead, he chose to air his grievances about how unfair it was, how cruel, and to belittle the idea that there was some higher power that cared about us.

Everyone gave him a pass at the funeral, but he continued to be angry and bitter at the reception at our house afterwards, which made everything so uncomfortable. Everyone tiptoed around him. When anyone tried to express their condolences, he scoffed at them. They expressed their condolences to me, as well. I was appreciative but I was still bewildered and in shock.

Finally, Dad had enough and went upstairs to his room and shut the door, leaving everyone standing around, wondering what to do. Seeing that there was nothing else they *could* do, they began leaving. As they left, everyone took turns to tell me to contact them if there was anything I needed.

Eventually, I went out to the backyard, sat on the porch steps, and stared straight ahead, seeing nothing.

After a few minutes, the screen door opened. Julia quietly stepped out and sat next to me.

She didn't say a word. She didn't try to tell me that everything would be all right. She didn't tell me that my mother was in a better place. She didn't tell me how sorry she was. She didn't tell me that she understood what I was going through. She didn't try to touch me.

She was just there with me.

Having my best friend there, not rationalizing anything or trying to cheer me up, moved something.

The shock that had been holding back my grief collapsed.

I turned to Julia, buried my face in her shoulder and wept harder than I ever had in my life.

She held me, crying herself.

I don't know how long we sat like that. I wept to the point of exhaustion.

Julia never let go.

Chapter 13

The cars in the rearview mirror move out of the way as the flashing red and blue lights begin maneuvering directly behind us.

'*Take the next exit and pull over,*' the fuzzy, distorted, but audible voice calls from the cop car.

Damon curses.

'What do I do?' I ask.

'What do you mean, "What do I do?"' Damon spits out. 'You take the next exit and pull over. And get your blinkers on.'

I tap the button on the console. The rhythmic clicking of the hazard lights begins to keep time as I drive the fifty yards or so to the next ramp. It carries us down to Sepulveda Boulevard, which runs parallel to the Interstate through the pass. During the day, it would be choked with drivers trying to shave a few minutes off their commute by avoiding the Interstate, but at this time of night, the cars are sporadic. I pull onto the dirt and gravel shoulder and stop beneath a streetlamp. The cop car follows close behind. Its headlights and flashers practically blind me in the rearview mirror. The cop car stops a few yards behind us.

'*Turn off the engine,*' the loud, fuzzy voice calls out.

I put it in park and hit the ignition button.

For a few seconds, no one moves, then the strobing red and

blue lights go dark, but the headlights behind us stay on.

'Keep facing forward and tell me, what is he going to find?' Damon asks.

'What?'

'Right now, he's running your plates. That'll bring up your driving record. What is he going to find?'

'Nothing.'

The figure of the cop passes in front of his car's headlights. He stops at the back of my car.

'Do not lie to me right now,' Damon hisses. 'What is he going to find?'

'Nothing! I swear! I got a speeding ticket like five years ago back in Pennsylvania. That's it,' I answer honestly.

The cop finishes up whatever he's been doing at the back of the car and begins walking toward my window.

I reach for the glovebox.

'Keep your hands on the fucking wheel!' Damon spits out.

'I was getting my registra—'

'Keep your hands on the wheel until he tells you to move them.'

I return my hands to the wheel and glance at the side-view mirror. The officer is getting closer. His form is beginning to block out the glare from the cop car's headlights.

Damon speaks quickly as he begins stuffing the bloody alcohol wipes into the backpack. 'Listen to me, Lucas, because we've got about thirty seconds. You're finishing your last ride of the night. You're taking me to Sherman Oaks. Apologize for anything and everything. If he writes you a ticket, do not argue. Keep it short and sweet. If you try anything to make the cop suspicious, I will shoot the cop first, then you, then I'm taking this car, paying a visit to Julia, and then I will disappear. Do you understand?'

My eyes are on the side mirror.

'Lucas?'

The cop is almost outside my window.

'Dammit, Lucas! Answer me!'

Even though I'm focused on the approaching cop, I can feel the tension radiating from the back seat. Damon's trying to stay as still as possible and keep his voice down, even though there's no way the cop can hear him outside the window.

My refusal to answer him is not an act of defiance.

I simply can't answer him.

I can't answer him because I believe him.

I believe Damon will carry out his threat against me and Julia and our unborn daughter and now, his threat includes this cop. He's killed people. He's cut them and held that same blade to my throat. So, yes, I believe him.

But there is possible salvation right outside my window.

If I want to take this chance, how do I do it? Do I try to run? My seatbelt is still fastened and if I try and fail, not only am I dead, but so are Julia and Sophie, and possibly this cop, who may have a child of his own. Not to mention, if I try to run, the cop may think I'm attacking him and—

Tap tap tap.

The cop's knuckle gently raps against the glass, and gives the universal symbol to roll the window down.

As calmly as I can, I peel my fingers from the wheel, reach over, and hit the switch.

The window rolls down with a steady hum and the sound of passing cars on the Interstate above us rushes in.

'How we doin' tonight?' the cop asks. He's in his forties with a stocky frame and a buzz cut. His tone isn't as cheery as his words suggest, but he's not hostile. Everything about him says, 'Polite but in charge.'

'Good,' I reply.

Did he hear my voice shaking in that one-syllable response?

He clicks his pen light on and aims the beam at me and then at Damon in the back seat.

'And you, sir?' he asks Damon. 'How are you?'

Is there a fleck of blood on Damon's face that he missed? Or a bloody wipe lying on the seat? Can he see the gun that Damon is holding? I'm guessing not, because the cop makes no mention of anything out of the ordinary.

'Fine, officer,' Damon answers with perfect ease. 'And you?'

'I'm good, thanks,' the officer perfunctorily responds. He clicks off the light and puts his attention back on me. 'License and registration?'

'My, um, my license is in my wallet and the registration is in the glove compartment.'

He nods. 'Understood. You can get them out. Nice and slow, please.'

I take my wallet from my pocket, extract my license, and hand it over. Then, I reach over, open the glove box, and take out the faux-leather holder, which contains the registration and insurance information. I pull the papers from the folder and offer them to the cop, who takes them and studies them by the glow of the streetlamp overhead.

'Where are you heading this evening?' he casually asks.

'I'm taking my last fare of the night to Sherman Oaks.'

He looks up from the papers. 'Rideshare?'

'Yeah.'

He checks the front of the car and the dashboard through the windshield.

'Where's your light or decal?' he asks. 'If you're giving rides, they need to be on. That's the law.'

'Yes. I'm sorry.' I reach over and take the light from the glovebox and show it to him. 'I took the light down from my windshield, but then decided to do one last ride for the night and I forgot to put it back up.'

'Mmm-hmm . . .' the cop says and goes back to my papers. 'You know why I pulled you over?'

'I – I almost hit someone up there.'

'Yep. Everything okay?' He looks up from the papers. 'You haven't been drinking, have you?'

73

'Yes— No! I didn't mean— I mean, yes, everything is fine and no, I haven't been drinking,' I stammer. 'I just wasn't, uh, you know, I, um, I took my eyes off the, uh—'

The cop's eyes narrow slightly.

I'm blowing this.

'That may have been my fault,' Damon chimes in, coming to my rescue. He leans over toward the window so that he can make eye contact with the officer. 'Lucas and I were talking, and he told me that he and his wife are expecting their first child. A little girl. I was so happy for him that I started asking a whole bunch of questions. I'm afraid I may have been a distraction.'

Damon's tone is charming and slightly apologetic. I quickly glance in the rearview mirror. He's wearing that pristine, disarming smile that I trusted when I picked him up. Our eyes meet for a split second before he goes back to the cop.

'So, like I said, that may have been my fault,' Damon concludes.

The cop studies me. His demeanor is different.

Are my eyes still bloodshot from tearing up a moment ago when Damon threatened Julia and Sophie? Can the cop tell from my expression that something is wrong?

'That true?' he asks. 'You've got a baby on the way?'

'. . . Yes.'

Another beat.

'When are you due?'

'Next week,' I answer.

The cop relaxes ever so slightly and smiles.

'Okay,' he says with a light laugh. 'Now, I understand why you're a bit nervous. Don't take this the wrong way, but you're pretty young. So, I get it. I remember how nervous I was when that first kid was on deck.'

Damon chuckles from the back seat.

I'm the only one not joining in.

'Do you have children, officer?' Damon asks. His question is just as much for me as it is for the cop. He wants me to know that the officer has kids, to keep me in line.

'Oh, yeah. Three,' he replies, and goes back to me. 'Don't worry. After this first one, you'll be a pro.' He glances at my license, registration, and insurance card, which are still in his hand, and then gives me a reassuring smile. 'Listen, you didn't technically do anything wrong, but you did almost hit someone. I wanted to make sure you hadn't been drinking. You appear sober, so I'm gonna let you go, but promise me, from here on out, you'll keep your eyes on the road. That way, we can be sure that your daughter gets to meet her daddy, all right?'

I stare out the windshield and mechanically nod.

The cop pauses and cocks his head. 'You sure you're okay?'

'Yeah . . .' I'm able to choke out.

'Thank you, officer,' Damon adds.

'Here you go,' the cop says, offering my license, registration, and insurance card back to me. 'Get home safe, and you spoil that kid. Hear me?'

'Yes,' I say quietly. 'Thank you.'

I reach for the documents.

As I do, my hand extends out of the car and into the light cast by the streetlight overhead. I grasp the documents and attempt to pull them into the car, but the cop won't let go.

I turn my head.

He's looking down at my hand.

He sees them.

The deep, angry red and purple lines around my wrist left from the zip ties.

He lets go of the documents.

As I slowly pull them back into the car, our eyes meet.

Everything changes.

The air between us is suddenly charged with electricity. The cop's face turns to stone. That sympathy he had a moment ago, that jovial laugh he shared with Damon, is gone.

He knows. He knows that something is wrong and it's not the

impending birth of my daughter. It's something else and, whatever it is, it has to do with the man in the back seat.

The cop slowly pulls his hand back and ever so slightly begins to open his hips. His other hand moves almost imperceptibly toward the gun in his holster.

'Officer . . .' Damon says from the back seat. His easy demeanor is also gone.

The cop's hand inches closer to the gun.

'No . . .' I quietly plead. 'No, no, no . . .'

The cop turns to Damon. His hand flies to his gun.

There's a burst of movement from the back seat.

'Stop!' I scream.

It's too late.

Hell breaks loose.

Chapter 14

The gunshot is ear-splitting as the passenger window behind me is blasted outwards. The officer falls.

I lurch forward and instinctively throw my hands over my ears, which does nothing. The shot has already slammed into my eardrums, leaving a high-pitched ring.

Damon grabs something from the backpack. The car rocks as he opens the back door and exits. Gun in hand, he goes around to the cop, who is lying on his back on the side of the road, his face contorted in pain. The ringing in my ears fades and is replaced by the groans and sharp gasps escaping the officer's lips.

Damon kneels next to him in the dirt and gravel.

'You shot him!' I exclaim.

Damon inserts his fingers between the buttons of the cop's shirt and rips it open to reveal the black bulletproof vest underneath.

'He'll be all right,' Damon says.

The cop continues to writhe in pain, seemingly unaware of his surroundings.

'He'll have a hell of a bruise and maybe a broken rib or two but he'll be fine.'

It takes a second to process but Damon's right . . . and I suddenly see an opportunity. He's not going to kill the cop and he's out of the car. I begin to reach for the ignition, but Damon aims the gun in my direction.

'This cop is wearing a vest. You are not.' With his other hand, he reaches into his pocket and pulls out the key fob to my car. 'And if you try to drive off, you're not getting far.'

For a split second, I consider taking my chances, but he's right. I wouldn't make it fifty feet before the engine would shut off.

I take my hands off the wheel in defeat as Damon turns his attention back to the wounded policeman.

'Just keep breathing,' Damon tells him. He pulls a pair of zip ties he took from the bag before exiting the car and uses one to bind the cop's ankles. He then pushes the cop onto his side and pulls out a second pair of zip ties to bind his wrists behind his back. Damon quickly stands, hooks his hands under the cop's armpits, and drags him back toward the cop car. I twist in my seat to watch but am temporarily blinded by the blazing headlights of the police car. A few moments later, the lights cut out. It takes my eyes a second to adjust but I see Damon extract himself from the front seat of the cop car. The officer is lying on the ground next to the car, still writhing in pain with his wrists bound by the zip ties. Damon opens the back door of the cop car and wrestles the officer inside. He then closes the door and begins hustling back toward me. Before he reaches the car, he cocks his arm and hurls something into the darkness up ahead. As it reaches the edge of the light cast by the streetlamp, I catch a glint of metal. I can only assume that those were the keys to the police car.

Damon opens the back door and gets in.

'Go! Go, go, go!' he breathlessly instructs.

'Listen, you can just leave me here.'

'What?'

'Take the car and leave me here.'

'Lucas—'

'I don't know where you're going. There's nothing I can do to stop you. I'll only slow you down.'

I'm hoping he'll take me up on the offer and that he'll be so preoccupied with finishing whatever he's doing, I can get the police to the apartment to protect Julia and Sophie.

'Drive the damn car!'

'You just shot a cop!'

'He'll be all right. They'll find him. The only question is when. It might be an hour, it may be a few minutes, which is why we have to go. I need more time and, if I leave you here, you'll let him out and he can call for backup. I can't trust you to sit and wait, not after what happened back at the house.'

'I promise that I won't—'

'Fine!' he rages. 'I'll take the car and go straight to your apartment.'

We stare at each other in the mirror.

'And if you think for one second I'm bluffing,' he seethes through clenched teeth, 'as you pointed out – I just shot a cop . . .'

I can't hold his stare. My shoulders sag and the air leaves my chest. I start the car, pull a U-turn across the road, and make my way back to the on-ramp to go north on the 405. I cast one last glance in the rearview mirror at the police car, sitting under the glow of the streetlamp.

'He's going to be fine, Lucas,' Damon reiterates. 'And you've got other things to worry about.'

We climb the ramp to rejoin the flow of traffic, made up of hundreds of other drivers who have no idea what just happened below.

Once we've become another one of the countless, nameless cars traveling on the Interstate, I steal another glance at Damon.

His eyes dart around as he recalculates. Suddenly, he slams the palm of his hand into the back of the passenger seat, curses, and runs a hand through his hair, again. Finally, he sits back in resignation. He's still radiating frustration and anger but he's regained a modicum of control.

'You shot a cop,' I quietly say again. 'The police will never let you live now.'

'Drive the car.'

I shake my head. 'It doesn't matter that he was wearing a vest. You shot a cop. Whatever you're doing, whatever you have planned? It doesn't matter anymore. When they catch you, they are going to kill you . . . There's no way they'll let you survive tonight.'

Damon watches the passing cars. 'Fine.'

'*Fine?* How is that *fine?*'

'Because surviving was never part of my plan.'

His words stun me into silence.

Whatever Damon is doing, it ends with his death.

Will it include my death? At the end of all of this, will he let me die—?

A light appears on the dashboard.

I stare at it in shock.

'I – ummm . . .'

Chapter 15

After my mother's death, I was an emotional mess. Any romantic feelings I had for Julia were put on the back burner, but she helped me pull the pieces back together and start to move on.

My father, on the other hand, never left that place of anger and bitterness. I let him grieve. I was angry and bitter, too, but I knew Mom would never want me to stop living my life because of what happened to her. I just hoped that Dad would start living again, but by the time I went off to college, he was still angry and wanted nothing to do with the world. I tried to get him to open up, but it was no use.

Julia and I ended up going to Allegheny College. We hadn't gone there because the other was going. We decided on our own but having the other there was a huge bonus. Our friendship continued. People mistook us for a couple, which we joked about. She dated other guys. I dated other girls, but we always seemed to find ourselves hanging out together after the relationships ended. We would go to dive bars together, study together, watch movies together, or simply do nothing together. And as more time passed and I was able to move on with my life, my feelings for her resurfaced.

And I was sure she had feelings for me, too.

My junior year of college was the first time I didn't go home for Christmas. I was done trying to get my dad to start living his life, again. I had gone home my freshman and sophomore year and it had been miserable. Dad rarely spoke. I asked him if he even wanted me to come home at Christmas anymore to which he replied that I could do whatever I wanted.

That was that.

I decided to stay on campus that Christmas, but I wasn't alone. Julia's parents' marriage had fallen apart.

Like me, Julia was an only child and her presence had been the glue holding the marriage together. When she left for college, it started to crumble.

She had gone home for Thanksgiving and it had been a trainwreck. So much so that when I told her I was staying on campus for Christmas, she asked if she could hang out with me.

Despite the depressing reasons for us spending the holidays away from what was left of our families, it was one of the best Christmases ever.

My roommate, a great guy named John Kester who adored Julia, went home for Christmas, so Julia and I had the apartment to ourselves. We bought a cheap artificial Christmas tree from Walmart and decorated it. We watched every cheesy Hallmark Christmas movie we could find and provided hilarious running commentary. We cooked dinners. We ordered pizza. We drank too much wine.

And there were moments, soooo many moments, where we were on the couch, snuggled under a blanket because the walls of the apartment were little more than cardboard against the freezing Pennsylvania winter, that we almost crossed that line we had drawn for each other. The only thing keeping us from doing so was the fact we were sort of the only family we had left. If we threw that out to explore how we felt for one another and it turned out to be a mistake, the one rock-solid relationship we had in our lives would have been damaged beyond repair.

But fighting that urge took a willpower I didn't know I possessed.

*

Because we were broke college kids, we had agreed that we weren't going to get each other Christmas presents, but of course, we got each other presents.

I had bought a ceramic ornament and took it to a friend of mine who was an art student. They painted it in red and gold with our names in delicate script.

When I gave it to Julia, she choked up a little bit as she hung it on our scraggily fake tree.

After placing it on a branch, she turned to me with a smile.

'And I've got something for you.'

I shook my head. 'Please tell me you didn't get me anything.'

'It's not anything huge. Just close your eyes and hold out your hands.'

I raised a suspicious eyebrow at her.

'Do it!' she commanded.

I gave her one last glance, closed my eyes, and held out my hand.

She moved toward the kitchen.

I tried to sneak a peek and open one eye but she was waiting for me.

'Close 'em!' she said, pointing a finger at me.

I obeyed.

Her footsteps went to the kitchen and there was the sound of the refrigerator opening and closing. Her footsteps returned and stopped in front of me.

Something cold was placed in my hand.

'Okay. Open them!'

I opened my eyes to find a frozen Whatchamacallit in my hand.

'Merry Christmas!' she cried.

Allegheny College was a relatively small school to begin with but it was almost a ghost town during the holiday break.

That was fine with Julia and I. We were more than happy feeling like we were the only people on Earth for that week and a half. We called our parents on Christmas morning. I found myself a little worried about my father, since it was the first Christmas since my mother's death that he was spending alone, but if he was upset or lonely, he showed no sign of it. We said our 'Merry Christmas.' I told him that I loved him, which I did, but our conversation didn't go much further than that.

Things were harder for Julia. She called her mother and then her father, but both calls descended into Julia having to listen to one parent gripe about the other. She finally had to cut off both conversations. We spent the rest of the day playing board and card games, eating cookies, bingeing movies, and just watching the snow fall outside the window, talking about everything and nothing at all.

Even though most people went home for the holidays, a few of our friends came back early and they insisted that we come out with them for New Year's.

We didn't want to go. We were having a great time together and didn't want to burst that bubble, but it felt like we should go out. It didn't seem normal that we should be enjoying each other's company for over a week without socializing with anyone else. So we agreed to meet up.

We got bundled up against the bitter cold and walked to the crocodile statue next to Brooks Hall to meet a handful of our friends. From there, the plan was to bar-crawl through the ten or so bars that were open.

Our friends were waiting for us when we arrived. We joked and chatted. Everyone asked how our holidays had been and quickly set off for the warmth of the nearest bar.

Julia and I hung back, walking side by side on the snow-covered sidewalk as our friends led the way.

'I guess it's good that we're being social,' Julia said, unenthusiastically watching our friends have an impromptu snowball fight.

'Yeah. I guess so,' I replied, matching her enthusiasm.

We continued on for a little while in silence as our friends finished their snowball fight and now felt the need to get to the bar faster, since they had pelted each other with snow.

'I've been thinking . . .' Julia said.

'About what?'

'Well, since it's kind of a tradition, if you wanted to kiss me at midnight, that would be okay.'

There was no hesitation. No moment to think. No doubt, whatsoever.

I gently grabbed her arm, pulled her to a stop and turned her to me.

Julia cocked her head at me in amused confusion.

I put one hand on the small of her back, placed the other gently behind her head, drew her to me and kissed her.

Her initial reaction was shock. Then, she melted with me and we shared a kiss that had been building for over half of our lives.

When our lips separated, she looked at me with an uncontained smile. 'I said midnight.'

'It's midnight somewhere,' I replied.

We never made it to a bar. We immediately turned and practically ran back to my apartment, stopping only to share another kiss.

*

The next morning, we checked our phones to find a flood of text messages from our friends, nearly all of them jokingly asking where we had gone. They had turned around and we weren't there.

My favorite was one that read, *It's about damn time.*
Julia and I have been together ever since.

Chapter 16

'You're joking.'

'No, I'm not.'

Damon's jaw hangs open.

'. . . You're *joking*,' he repeats.

I motion to the dashboard in frustration. 'You were going to be my last ride. I was going to drop you off, gas up, and drive home. I wasn't planning on having to take you all over the city.'

He leans forward to see the blazing orange gas pump icon for himself just as we crest the hill to reveal the glittering lights of the San Fernando Valley below.

'How long do you think we can go before you run out?' he asks. 'How many miles?'

'I don't know. How much more of your plan do we have to go?'

He thinks and then sits back. 'Shit.'

'Are you worried that we're going to be spotted at a gas station or something?' I ask.

'No. It just puts us further behind my schedule.'

'Maybe if you hadn't taken the time to shoot a cop—'

'Shut up,' he snaps, and looks out the window while chewing his lip as the gears turn in his head.

They're turning in my head, too. I'll take every delay I can get. Every moment that he's thrown off his plan might present an opportunity to escape or at least get help if I can play it right.

'So, what's it gonna be?' I ask.

He grunts and shakes his head. 'If we need gas, we need gas.'

I flip on my blinker and begin maneuvering to the far-right lane to take the first exit out of the Sepulveda Pass, which is Ventura Boulevard into Sherman Oaks.

'What are you doing?' Damon asks.

'Going to get gas,' I answer, confused.

'Keep heading north.'

'But you just said we need ga—'

'I said to keep heading north. I'll tell you when to exit.'

I switch off the blinker.

The exit to Ventura Boulevard passes as we keep driving.

As we approach each exit, I ease up on the gas, anticipating his instruction to turn, but it doesn't come, and as we continue on, my palms begin to sweat on the wheel.

We're entering Van Nuys. Nordhoff Street is the next exit. If we exit here, we could be at the studio apartment in less than five minutes. I gave Julia grief because for the first few weeks, she kept calling it the 'Nordstrum Street' exit. From my driver's license, Damon knows the apartment is in Van Nuys, but I'm praying that he's too distracted to remember that information at the moment.

We pass Nordhoff Street and my shoulders begin to relax ever so slightly.

'Okay. Time to make a decision,' I tell him.

He stews over it for a second before answering. 'All right. Take the next exit.'

I turn on the blinker again and we exit at Devonshire Street.

At the bottom of the ramp, I turn right toward a shopping plaza and spot the perfect opportunity; an ARCO station right before the next stoplight. It's well-lit and even now, at 10:20 p.m., it's busy with people gassing up and going in and out of the building.

I take my foot off the gas as we approach, readying for the turn, and immediately feel the still-warm barrel of Damon's gun press against my ear.

'Nope,' he says through gritted teeth.

'What do you mean?' I ask, leaning away from the gun. 'You said to get gas.'

'Not here,' Damon replies, lowering the gun so that it's out of view of the surrounding drivers. 'Get your blinker off.'

I flip the lever down, shutting off the turn signal, and stop at the red light.

'What is wrong with you?' I ask, slightly rotating my head in his direction but careful not to turn around.

'We're not stopping at a gas station like that,' Damon says.

'Like what?' I ask, trying to play dumb.

'A lot of light. A lot of people.'

'I thought you said you weren't worried about being spotted.'

'I said I wasn't worried. I didn't say I would be stupid about it.'

With my head slightly turned, the gas station is visible through the passenger window. People are filling up at the pumps, while others exit the convenience store with a snack or energy drink for the ride home. They're going about their evening, oblivious to the fact that only a few yards away a man is pointing a gun at my head, just out of view.

Have I ever been that oblivious? Have I ever been mere feet away from someone who needed help and not known?

'The light's green,' Damon says behind me. 'Keep going and I'll tell you where to get gas.'

*

We spend the next few minutes continuing on, passing multiple gas stations that are all apparently too risky for Damon, but at least we're getting further and further away from Julia.

Eventually, Damon has me turn onto a secondary street. There's less traffic, but there are still gas stations every couple blocks.

Finally, he leans forward and points. 'There.'

I have to follow his finger because I don't even see it at first.

The large sign above the gas station is only sporadically lit by a malfunctioning bulb. The same goes for the sign closer to the ground which displays the prices per gallon. The prices seem cheap but then, in one of the flickerings, I catch the small print stating that there's a surcharge of a dollar twenty-five if you're using a debit or credit card. There are only four pumps. A large white van sits at one. The other three are empty. There's not even a convenience store, only a small brick booth that has been painted white. Inside sits a cashier behind a plexiglass window.

'Turn in there,' Damon says.

I make the turn and the car gently bounces as we pull into the gas station.

'Pump number four,' Damon says.

His thinking is obvious. Pump four is the furthest from the small building that houses the cashier.

I stop next to the pump, hit the button to open the gas tank door, and make a move to get out.

'Stop.'

I look at Damon in the rearview mirror.

'Before you get out, I need you to roll down the windows. That way I can hear you if you try to get someone's attention, like Mr. Repairman over at pump two,' Damon says with a nod.

I glance over to see the older, overweight man filling the tank of the white van, the side of which is stenciled with the logo of a smiling plumber. I roll down the three remaining windows, since Damon shot out the one behind me.

'Good,' Damon says. 'Now, I've still got the keys, so if you try anything, I'm climbing into the front seat, and heading to Julia. I've got your phone, so you won't be able to call her. You'll have to convince somebody, who will think you're crazy at first, and by the time—'

'Yeah. I got it,' I snap in frustration.

Damon waits a few moments for me to calm down. 'So long as you know that this gun is still pointed at you.'

'Great. Are you done? Because I thought you said we needed to keep moving.'

He glares at me, not liking my back talk. 'Twenty-five dollars. That's all we'll need. And make sure I can see your hands at all times.'

'How am I supposed to do that?'

'By doing it. Now, go on.'

As I step out of the car, my nostrils are assaulted by the smell of gasoline laced with the stench from the overflowing trash can sitting between the pumps. There's also a squeegee resting in a container of filthy blue water. Dirty paper towels litter the ground nearby. I keep my body open to the back seat so that he can see my hands, but my head is above the car. I can't see his face, but he can't see mine, either.

I take the opportunity to discreetly search for anything that could help me and spot the security cameras mounted over each pump.

I take out my wallet and extract my credit card but freeze. A crazy plan is rapidly forming in my brain. I switch my credit card for my debit card. I insert it into the slot next to the display and glance over the top of the pump toward the cashier behind the plexiglass. He's sitting in a chair, scrolling through his phone. I can't make out his features. He's little more than a silhouette.

Please be paying attention.

Once my card is inserted, the display on the pump asks for my PIN.

I hold my breath and tap the four buttons. Each one brings a short blip.

The screen blinks: AUTHORIZING . . . AUTHORIZING . . . BEEEEEEEEEEEP!!!

Shit!

INVALID PIN, the screen announces.

'Lucas?' Damon asks from inside the car.

'It's fine. I just— I hit the wrong button.'

I glance down through the open window. Damon is quiet and unmoving. From this angle, I can see that he's still holding the gun in his hand.

'Get it right, this time,' he says, just loud enough for me to hear.

'Yeah.'

I start the process over.

Entering the wrong PIN had been intentional. I'm hoping it gets the cashier's attention. What I hadn't planned on was that painfully loud beep, possibly alerting Damon to my plan.

As I enter my PIN, correctly this time, I cast my eyes to the shadowed figure of the cashier behind the window of the booth.

He's no longer looking at his phone. He's looking at something below and in front of him. Did it work? Is he looking at the security camera feed?

He looks up and out the window. He could be looking in our direction but I can't be sure.

However, it's over in a second and he goes back to looking at whatever is in front of him. I lift the nozzle from the pump, place it into the opening of the gas tank, and press the handle. As the gas begins flowing from the pump and the display starts tallying, I look up at the security camera overhead. I've heard urban legends that most of the security cameras you see don't actually work and are only for show.

I hope that's not true. I need this camera to be working and please, *please*, Mr. Cashier. Please be looking at this one.

Looking up toward the camera, I begin slowly mouthing the words. *Help me . . . Call the police . . . Help me.*

The gas continues flowing into the car as I repeat my message over and over, willing myself, through the camera, to get the cashier's attention. *Help me . . . Call the police . . . Help me . . . Call the p—*

'Okay. That's enough,' Damon says, causing my heart to stop. Did he see what I was doing?

'Get in,' he says.

It takes a second for me to understand that his 'that's enough' was in response to the gas, not my efforts to get the cashier's attention. I look down to the open window. Damon hasn't moved. I can't see his face, but the gun is still in his hand.

I check the total on the pump display. 'I've only put eighteen dollars—'

'I said that's enough. Get back in the car.'

I return the nozzle to the pump and take one last opportunity to look at the cashier.

He's not there.

Is he calling the cops? Or did he just go to the bathroom? Did he even see any of that? Or was the risk I just took all for nothing?

'Back in the car, Lucas.'

I replace the gas cap, close the hatch, and get back behind the wheel.

'Who forgets their PIN?' Damon warily asks, as I start the engine.

'The guy who's had a gun pointed at him all night by a man who's forcing him to drive around so he can murder people,' I answer.

'Don't mess with me, Lucas.'

'I did what you told me to do. Sorry if my brain glitched.'

He takes a moment, weighing my response before reaching a conclusion.

'Don't let anything like that happen again. Now, we need to get back on the road.'

I take my foot off the brake pull forward, and exit the gas station.

Chapter 17

All it took was three months of being back in Millersburg; three months of being right back where we started, of seeing friends we had grown up with who had gone to other colleges, returning and settling in as if they had never left. Of seeing the same sights. Of having the same options for entertainment, culture, food, that we had grown up with and we both knew we couldn't stay.

And then there was our families. Dad was still shut down. I hated moving back in and dreamed of living somewhere, anywhere else.

Julia's situation was even worse. Her parents' divorce was messy and she was being pulled in both directions. There was nothing joyous for us in the town where we grew up.

One weekend, we drove up into the surrounding hills and parked on an empty overlook that offered a view of the valley below. Millersburg was laid out before us. There was the Kroger and the hardware store that was dying a slow death. There was the small police station and smaller library. Further out, nestled in the trees, were the decaying smokestacks of the steel mill that had closed down decades ago. Julia and I had just had sex in the back seat and were now sitting up front, staring out at the town.

It was depressing to contemplate how much of our lives'

memories had taken place within this one field of view.

'If you could move anywhere, where would it be?' I asked her.

It was something that we had poked at, but had never spoken of seriously.

In the faint glow of the moonlight, I could see Julia purse her lips as she considered. 'Are we talking *anywhere*? Like in the world?'

'Well, let's keep it in the States.'

'Okay . . . Not New York or Chicago.'

'Why not?'

'Couldn't do the cold,' she answered. 'If I'm moving, I don't want the weather to be the same as it is where I'm moving from.'

'So, someplace like Miami?'

She wrinkled her nose. 'Oh God. No. My grandparents retired to Florida and that place is insane.' She thought about it a little longer. 'You know what? I think I'd do Los Angeles.'

'Really?'

'Yeah.'

'Have you ever been to Los Angeles?'

'Nope,' she said. 'But if we're just playing around.'

I turned to stare out at the town.

Los Angeles. It was the furthest you could get from our town. I thought of what it would be like. Being a big movie buff, I wanted to see Hollywood. I wondered what it would be like to live near the ocean? The more I thought about it, the more I wanted it. The more I wanted to get out of this town and get our lives started.

'What if we weren't?'

'Weren't what?' she asked.

'Playing around.'

Julia shrugged. 'Then, yes. I would say Los Angeles.'

She was thinking it was a hypothetical.

The more I turned the idea over in my mind, the more it took hold. The adventure. The boldness. The certainty that it was the right decision and that everything would work out. Julia and I could make it work.

'Let's do it,' I said.

'Do what?' she asked.

'Move to Los Angeles.'

She laughed as she turned to look at me . . . and then stopped laughing.

'Are you serious?'

'Yeah,' I told her. 'There is nothing for us here anymore. I don't want to live the rest of my life in this town. Let's go. Let's do it.'

She laughed in disbelief but slowly realized that I was in fact being serious. She turned to look out at the town and grew quiet. I could tell the idea was taking hold of her as well.

'What do you say?' I asked.

She fought a smile of disbelief, held up her hand, and extended her pinky finger.

I hooked mine in hers.

That was that.

Chapter 18

I think I'm in the clear.

If Damon had any suspicions about what I was doing at the gas station, he would have said something by now. He would have said 'strike two' or whatever, but we're getting back on the Interstate, heading north, and he hasn't said a thing.

He's handed over the reins to the automated voice from my phone to guide us while he tends to the contents of the backpack. Now and again, there's that slight *clink* of something metal.

What is in that backpack? Maybe if I know what's inside, it could give me clues as to what Damon has planned.

Keeping one eye on the road, I strain to look in the rearview mirror.

In the regular intervals that we pass under streetlamps, I can see the zip ties and more manila envelopes, but I also spot what appears to be some sort of black cylinder. I crane my head slightly to get a better look when—

Ding-ding-ding.

The text alert causes me to quickly get my eyes back on the road, as if I've been focusing on the traffic and not spying on Damon.

The display screen on the center console reads: *INCOMING TEXT: JULIA*

'*Hey,*' the automated voice reads out. '*Wondered if you had any updates. I didn't hear anything after the last text. Not being nosy. Just want to know you're okay.*'

Damon picks up my phone from where it's been resting on the back seat next to him.

'Anything you want to say?' he asks.

My mind starts racing. Is there some sort of codeword, some inside joke that only Julia and I know that would make her think, *Hmm. That's a strange thing for Lucas to say. I wonder if he's trying to tell me something?*

'Lucas?' Damon asks, expectantly.

The moment to come up with a coded message to warn Julia has passed. If I try anything now, Damon will see right through it.

'Tell her that I love her and I'll be home as soon as I can.'

Damon considers and then begins typing, reading aloud as he does so. '*Still at the office but trying to wrap things up. I'll let you know as soon as I'm on my way* . . . aaaaaaaand send.' He dramatically taps the screen.

'You forgot the part where I told her I loved her.'

He shakes his head. 'Nope. I didn't forget it. I'm worried that it might sound odd, like you might not text that to each other all the time, but I have a feeling that if we wait a sec, it'll sort itself out.' He sits patiently with the phone in his hand and a smile on his face.

Seconds later, another text arrives and is read out over the speakers.

'*Roger that. Sophie and I will be waiting. I love you.*'

Damon's smile brightens. 'There? See? Now we can let her know.' He begins typing. '*Love you, too . . .*' He pauses and then rolls his eyes as he resumes typing. 'Kissy-face emoji . . . aaaaaaand send.'

After hitting the button, Damon puts my phone back on the seat.

'So, tell me about you and Julia. What's the story with you two?

Why does she think you're at work? What happened?'

'Why would I tell you anything about us?'

Damon shrugs. 'I'm trying to make conversation. I don't need to. I already know everything I need to know about her to make you do what I say. I know where she is, that you've got a baby on the way, and that you're lying to her about what you're doing. I find that very interesting. I want to hear your story, but if you prefer, we can turn on the radio like you normally do with your rides.'

I don't want to tell him anything else for fear that I'll give away more about Julia and me, but he's right. At this point, he knows everything he needs to use her as leverage against me. Maybe I can protect Julia and Sophie by getting him to see them as real, innocent people who have nothing to do with whatever his plans are.

'Julia and I grew up together in a really small town in Pennsylvania called Millersburg,' I begin. 'We met at the local pool when we were ten and became best friends. I always had a crush on her but never did anything about it.'

Damon smiles. 'Oh no. Were you one of those lovesick teens who always carried a flame for her?'

'Something like that.'

'She didn't feel the same?'

'We just never got the timing right.'

Damon gives me a look. 'Ummmm . . . apparently you did.'

'Well, yeah. Eventually. After high school, we ended up going to the same college. We didn't plan on that. It was just something that happened and things finally clicked our junior year.'

'Where was college?' Damon asks.

'Allegheny College. It's a small school in a place called Meadville.'

'So, what the hell are the two of you doing in Los Angeles?' He suddenly has an unpleasant thought. 'Please tell me you didn't come out here to be actors.'

'No. I majored in English.'

'English? What were you planning to do with that?'

'I don't know. I thought I maybe wanted to become a teacher.'

Damon nods. 'And Julia? What was her major?'

'Julia majored in business.'

'And her plans?'

'She wanted to get into marketing. Anyway, after graduation, Julia and I came home to Millersburg. We were both only children and the situation with our parents wasn't really the best. After a few months of watching all our friends settle back into that small town for the rest of their lives, we decided that wasn't for us. Don't get me wrong,' I quickly add. 'We love our parents, and Millersburg was a great little town to grow up in, but we wanted something more. We wanted to see more of the world.'

Although I'm telling Damon the truth, it sounds so corny and naive. I'm half-expecting him to laugh but he's quiet. I look in the rearview mirror to find him staring at the back of the passenger seat with a strange, sad smile on his face.

'And what did your parents think?' he asks.

'They hated it, of course. Her parents were in the middle of a nasty divorce. Julia was kind of caught in the middle and her parents tried to talk her out of moving. My father . . .' I hesitate. The only other person who really knows this story is Julia. 'Well, my father isn't much of a talker. All he said was that we were making a stupid, childish mistake and that he would be waiting when we came crawling back to Millersburg after a few months.'

Damon gets a pained expression. 'And your mom? What did she think about your decision?'

'Mom died my sophomore year of high school. Ovarian and uterine cancer.'

'Oh . . . I'm sorry.'

'Thanks?' I can't help the upward inflection. Nearly every person I've told about my mother's death over the years has said 'I'm sorry.' I always appreciate it, but this is the first time I'm hearing sympathy from someone who has killed people and shot cops.

'That must have been difficult,' Damon adds.

'Yeah . . . She . . . One day, she had some pain in her stomach, so she went to urgent care. Two weeks after that, she was diagnosed. Then, two weeks after that, it was over. That's how fast it went. It had been growing in her for years, undetected. By the time they found it, there was nothing they could do . . . It broke my dad. I mean, I get it. Mom's death wasn't fair. It made no sense, but Mom wouldn't have wanted us to shut down our lives because of what happened to her. I grieved for a while, I still do, but Julia helped me through it . . . My dad never got over it. He's never even tried.'

'Is that why the two of you don't talk?' Damon asks.

'Yeah . . . I kept telling him he had to try to move on. I was young and devastated, but I know now that I didn't appreciate what he was going through. I wish I had done things differently. I wish I would have just told him . . .'

My voice trails off.

'*Take exit two-three-four and head west on one eighteen and continue for one-point-seven miles,*' the automated voice says.

It's only now that I realize how quickly my brain shifted to talk about something, anything, other than what is happening, even if it's to talk about the worst time in my life with a killer in my back seat.

I maneuver into the far-right lane, guide the car through the gentle curve of the ramp, and merge into traffic, heading toward Granada Hills.

'Please,' Damon says. 'Continue.'

It takes me a second to pick up my train of thought and I decide to skip ahead a little.

'So, after college when Julia and I realized that we didn't want to stay in Pennsylvania, we started talking about moving. At first, it was kind of a joke, you know? Where we'd live, what we would do . . . and then one day it wasn't a joke anymore. We made a plan and pulled the trigger.'

'Just like that?' Damon asks, with what sounds like a mild sense of awe.

'Yeah. Just like that.'

He smiles. 'Two kids on an adventure, huh?'

'Something like that.'

'Let me ask you this,' Damon says, leaning forward slightly. 'If you could go back in time, would you try to stop yourself from moving out here?'

I think about it for a second and then answer honestly.

'No.'

'Really?'

'I might warn myself not to pick up anyone in the Hollywood Hills, but yeah, I think we'd still come out here. I guess if I was going to give my younger self some advice, it would be to come out and visit first, get the lay of the land, find a place to live, and maybe scope out the job market and try to get hired before hitting the road.'

'Things didn't go according to your plan?'

'No. Not really,' I answer, matching his hint of sarcasm.

'What happened?'

'Our ideas of what we thought this city would be ran into reality. We crashed at a really crappy motel out here in the valley while we looked for jobs.'

'How'd that go?'

'Awful,' I scoff with a shake of my head, recalling those days and nights where Julia and I came to grips with how rash our decision had been and how unprepared we were. 'We lived there for a month, trying to get jobs while the money we'd saved dried up fast. We stopped looking for jobs we might like and hunted for any jobs we could get. She finally had to get a gig at Target. I was lucky. I got a job as an assistant to an asshole at a tech company in West Los Angeles. They weren't our dream jobs and they didn't pay all that well, but we needed something.'

'Why do you call it lucky if your boss was an asshole?'

'I was lucky to get the job. My boss was an asshole because he was a nepo-baby. That's when someone is born int—'

Damon holds up his hand. 'Lucas, I'm old but not *that* old. I'm familiar with the term "nepo-baby."'

'Sorry. Anyway, he thought he was this hotshot tech bro when in reality, he had his job because his uncle was the CEO of the company. The guy couldn't schedule a video conference call without me.'

Damon lets out a light laugh. 'Then what happened?'

'Once we had the jobs, we needed a place to live, and of course, we came to Los Angeles at the height of the housing market. Rents had doubled in the past three years, but anything was better than that motel. We found the studio in Van Nuys that we could barely afford and told ourselves that it was just a start.' I almost panic at accidentally mentioning the apartment and quickly move on. 'Once we got promotions and raises, we'd trade up . . . and then . . .'

Damon grimaces. 'Oh, man. Here it comes.'

'Yeah,' I answer, not enjoying how much *he's* enjoying this. 'We were being careful but apparently not careful enough. We got pregnant.'

'Two kids on an adventure,' he says again, but there's no mockery or sarcasm.

'Yep.'

'Wow . . .' he says with a shake of his head.

'*Exit at Alviso Ave,*' the automated voice instructs.

We exit the highway, descend into Granada Hills, and then begin heading north, toward the large houses in the foothills that overlook the valley.

'What do you think of Los Angeles?' Damon asks.

'I hated it at first, but we're starting to adapt.'

'Really?'

'Yeah. I think it's like anything. We had our expectations and it was really tough to discover that they were way off, but that kind of made us find the things we do enjoy. It's a big city. It's not just Hollywood or Beverly Hills. There's a lot to explore.'

'Would you ever go back to your home town?'

'No,' I answer without hesitation.

Damon nods, seemingly genuinely impressed with my answer.

'Can I ask you something a little more personal, Lucas?'

'Do I have a choice?'

'You do. You can choose not to answer and I will not hold it against you,' he says, with a sincerity that feels odd.

'Uh, okay. What?'

'You and Julia are in your early twenties, right?'

'Yes.'

'You're broke, you're thousands of miles from your families, you're both working crappy jobs, in a crappy apartment—'

'What's your question?'

'Wouldn't the best option be to terminate the pregnancy? Are the two of you religious?'

'No. No, we're not religious. Julia and I talked about it and all the options were on the table. We saw everything clearly. We knew we were broke. We knew our jobs sucked. We knew all of that.'

'And?'

'. . . We really wanted to have a baby.'

'My God,' Damon says in disbelief. 'Two kids on an adventure *and* really in love.'

'We were in love before we left Pennsylvania but us coming out here together, being the only ones we could count on in this city, being each other's support, it really solidified us.'

'And what did her parents and your dad say about the new development? About being pregnant?'

'Her parents freaked out a little – can't say that I blame them. But after a couple months, they've accepted it. They're supportive.'

'And your dad?'

I sigh. 'Not so much. I called to give him the news. He thought

I was telling him that we were coming back to Pennsylvania. The old man started gloating. He said that he had tried to warn me. Then he said that Julia and I could stay at his house until we were on our feet.'

'I guess that was nice of him.'

I can't tell if he's joking.

'I guess, but I told him we weren't coming back. I just wanted him to know that he was going to be a grandfather. I hung up and that was the last time I spoke to him.'

Damon nods.

We continue in silence and I take in the surroundings. The palm-tree-lined streets. The fancy houses. We're on an incline as we travel up into the foothills and the higher we go, the more opulent the houses become.

'Are you afraid?' Damon asks.

'You have a gun. Of course, I'm afraid.'

'No. I mean, are you afraid about becoming a dad?'

'. . . No,' I lie.

'You're not?' he asks suspiciously.

'I'll figure it out, you know? I know it's going to be hard, but Julia and I can do it.'

Damon looks out at the passing houses with a knowing smile. 'Well, at least you're doing it the right way.'

'Which is?'

'Totally unprepared.'

'Why is that the right way?'

'Because if you knew what you were getting into, you'd be freaking out,' he says, as he continues to watch the houses. 'What happened then?'

'What do you mean?'

Damon gestures around the car. 'This? How did this happen? Why does she think you're still at the tech company?'

'Oh. Well, Target would only let her work part time so they wouldn't have to provide health insurance. Julia and I got married so she could get on the insurance plan offered by the tech company. She and I were going to get married at some point, when we were more settled, but this kind of forced our hand. We went to the county clerk, filled out the paperwork, and like a lot of stuff, we said we'd do it right later. We were saving every penny but when she hit the third trimester, she had to quit the job. Then . . . well, remember my asshole boss?'

'Yep.'

'His incompetence caught up with him. His whole department was fired.'

'Was he fired?' Damon asks.

I snort in derision. 'Come on. He was the nephew of the CEO. He got promoted but everyone who worked for him was let go. No severance. No insurance. Nothing.'

'And you didn't tell Julia?'

I shake my head, half in reply and half in disapproval of myself. 'I panicked. I was afraid of what the stress might do to her and Sophie. I didn't mean to lie to her—' I catch myself. Why am I trying to avoid accepting blame for my actions to this guy? 'No, I did lie to her. I made the choice to do it. I hate myself for doing it, but I thought I could fix things and she wouldn't have to know . . . and I didn't want her to think of me as a failure.' My admission, saying it out loud to another person, hits me like a ton of bricks. 'I know it was stupid, so stupid, but I was *so* scared. I would go out in the morning as if I was going to work, and spend the day submitting résumés and trying to get interviews. I ran up a couple thousand dollars of credit card debt for some short-term health insurance. I submitted for anything and everything, but couldn't get a job. One afternoon, I was sitting in the car, sending out résumés through my phone, listening to music, when an ad came on for rideshare driving. I figured it was a way to have at least something coming in, but I'm not an idiot. I knew it wasn't going to get me out of the hole. I just needed more time . . .' I stare at the road. 'I hate lying to Julia. I really do. It's the worst thing

I've ever done, and I don't know how to fix this, but I'm trying . . . So, I guess I should change my answer to your question. Am I scared about becoming a father? I wasn't before, but now that it's almost here, yes, I'm worried. I'm terrified, and not just about the money stuff. I'm worried that I'm not going to be enough for our daughter. I'm worried that I'm not going to be enough for Julia. I'm worried about all of it . . . I guess I am freaking out.'

Damon is silent. When I glance at him in the rearview mirror, he's staring out the window with a thoughtful expression.

'Lying to her was stupid but she might understand. And freaking out is totally normal. It's good. It shows that you care.' He takes a breath. 'Okay. Pull over.'

'Why?' I ask.

The automated voice comes over the speakers.

'*You have arrived at your destination.*'

Chapter 19

Damon's staring at a large, white, two-story house with a wraparound porch. There are hedge walls marking the edges of the property and the lawn slopes gently down to the road, offering a spectacular view of the San Fernando Valley over the roof of the one-story ranch house across the street. The surrounding houses are spaced further apart than any other neighborhood I've seen in Los Angeles.

'All right, Lucas. This is going to be tricky, but because of your little escape attempt at the last house, you have to come in with me.'

'No. You don't need to do that,' I plead. 'I'll stay in the trunk.'

'Not a chance. We're going to have to move fast this time, because this neighborhood has regular patrols every twenty minutes.'

'You know the timing of the patrols?'

'Yes. I told you; I've been planning this for a long time. And since you're coming with me, I'm going to use you to help me solve a problem for this particular stop.' He pulls a couple zip ties from the backpack and stuffs them in his back pocket, but holds on to one. 'Now, put your wrists together.'

'Why?'

'I've gotta zip-tie your hands and put tape over your mouth.'

'No! No, no, no. Please. I can't breathe—'

His tone darkens. 'Lucas: I don't want to have to hurt you, again.'

My head is still throbbing from where he hit me earlier as a reminder of what happens when I resist. I don't see any way to fight him and I'll need all my wits if an opportunity to escape presents itself.

I turn my back to him, lean forward, and press my wrists together behind me.

'No,' Damon says. 'Put your hands in front of you.'

'Why?'

'*Put your hands in front of you,*' he commands.

I twist to face him, press my wrists together, and offer them up.

Damon loops a zip tie around them and cinches it tight. Once again, the plastic sinks into my flesh, which is still red and raw from before, but the difference in having my wrists bound in front of me, rather than behind my back, is night and day. Once my wrists are secure, he rips off a strip of duct tape.

'Deep breaths,' he says. 'Oxygenate your body.'

He waits while I take a series of deep breaths.

'Ready?'

I reluctantly nod.

Damon places the strip over my mouth and smooths it out to make sure it's sealed.

Unlike the last stop, where he smashed the base of my skull so hard I almost passed out, yanked on my hair to get the tape on my mouth, and nearly dislocated my shoulders to get me to stop resisting, this is totally different. My senses still freak out from my mouth being covered and my wrists being bound, but it's nothing like the overwhelming panic I experienced before. Is Damon being nice? Is this some sort of reward for cooperating? Isn't that what torturers do? They show some slight kindness to their hostages, which makes them easier to—

'All right, Lucas. Once we get out of the car, we're going to move fast. The gun is still in my hand and it'll be pointed at you at all times. Got it?'

I nod, again.

Damon threads his arms through the straps of the backpack and exits the car. Keeping the gun close to his hip, he quickly walks around to my door and opens it.

'Come on.'

He grabs my wrists to help me out and then quietly closes the car door.

'We need to stay low,' he says, and places his free hand on my shoulder to guide me toward the house. His head is on a swivel as he scans back and forth, watching for any signs of life from the other houses or an approaching car from down the street. The house glows under the white lights. The lawn is like a putting green. We start making our way up the driveway, at the head of which is a black McLaren parked next to the house. Damon keeps us close to the tall hedge that marks the edge of the property and stop once we reach the car. The stone path leading to the porch is across the driveway and there's a tall fence with a gate leading to the backyard on our right. Damon studies the house, listening intently for any sounds from the backyard on the other side of the fence, but there are none.

Once he's satisfied, he guides me across the driveway to the stone path. We're moving faster and I nearly stumble trying to get up the handful of stairs to the porch, but Damon catches me and helps me up the last few stairs.

The front door is only feet away. There's an intercom mounted next to the doorframe.

Damon positions me next to the porch railing.

'Face the street!' he hisses.

I begin to turn but it's not fast enough for him. Damon grabs my shoulders and spins me around so that my back is to the front door. He quickly takes a few more zip ties from his pocket. Before I realize what's happening, he secures my bound wrists to the cool metal of the porch railing. He then quickly drops to a knee and secures both of my ankles to the bottom railing, rendering me completely immobile.

'Do not move and do not make a sound,' he says, as he stands.

Damon presses the doorbell. He then sprints off the porch and disappears around to the side of the house, leaving me alone, bound to the railing.

The silence is unnerving.

Am I really alone? Is Damon watching somewhere from the shadows? No. He ran like he had somewhere to be.

I pull at my restraints, testing them, because now would be the time to escape, but as before in the trunk, these zip ties around my wrists and ankles aren't going anywhere. I raise my eyes to the street, hoping someone in one of these houses will look out one of their massive windows, or that someone on a walk, catching some night air, will come down the street and see me bound to the porch railing with tape over my mouth.

There! The house across the street. Through the large front window, there's a man standing in the living room. He's illuminated by the flickering light of a television and a dim table lamp beside him. He points a remote at the television and it goes dark, but I can still see him by the light of the table lamp. He walks over to the window. I thrash as much as I can, hoping my movement will catch his attention, but he reaches over, pulls a cord next to the window, and disappears behind a set of descending blinds.

I scream against the tape, but there's no way he can hear my muffled screaming all the way over th—

'Hello?' a voice asks through the intercom behind me, but I can hear the owner of the voice speaking. He's on the other side of the door.

I need to warn him. I grunt and pull against the zip ties, trying to turn my body enough for him to see the tape over my mouth, alerting him to the danger.

'Can I help you?' he asks.

I'm straining to contort my body, but can barely move.

'Are you okay?'

No! And neither are you!

I grunt as loudly as I can, hoping he can hear me.

'Hey. You need to get off my porch.' There's uncertainty in his voice because who wouldn't be creeped out by a stranger ringing your doorbell at this hour and standing there with their back to the door, not speaking to you?

'Okay. Listen, buddy. I don't know what your deal is. I don't know what you want, but if you don't leave right now, I'm calling the cops.'

I do the only thing I can and start frantically nodding.

'Wait . . . Do you— You want me to call the cops?'

I nod again and strain with everything I've got. Pulling at my wrists, I manage to rotate my torso and crane my neck around just enough for the camera in the intercom to see the tape over my mouth.

'Holy shit. Do you need h—?'

The intercom cuts out as something slams against the other side of the wall next to the door. The man cries out and there are the sounds of a scuffle.

I begin desperately pulling against the zip ties with renewed energy as the struggle inside the house continues. I lean back, using all my weight in an attempt to break the plastic. It feels like my hands are about to fly off my wrists as the front door is flung open. Damon rushes out, knife in hand, and cuts the ties to the porch railing. Once I'm free, he throws an arm around my chest, drags me backwards, and then flings me through the open door and into the house.

I stagger backwards into the foyer. I stumble as my feet hit something. I topple backwards and land flat on my back. The air is knocked out of me. I close my eyes against the pain and turn onto my side as my breath slowly returns.

The front door closes and the lock is engaged.

I open my eyes to find myself staring into the face of the man

I just tripped over, lying on the floor. His wrists are bound behind his back and there's tape over his mouth. He looks to be in his mid-forties with thinning hair. His eyes are wide with terror behind the thin lenses of his glasses.

Suddenly, Damon steps over me, grabs the back of the man's shirt, and begins dragging him away toward the interior of the house, which opens to a vast space. On one side is the kitchen with an island counter surrounded by tall chairs. The other side of the space is a living room with a fireplace, sectional sofa, and a large television on the wall. There is a hallway that leads into darkness at the far end of the room.

As they pass the island counter, Damon sets the backpack down and takes one of the chairs. The gun is tucked into the back of his waistband. He drags the man and the chair a few more steps, stops, and sets the chair. He then hauls the man up and drops him into it before taking two zip ties from his back pocket and binding the man's ankles to the legs of the chair.

Once he's secured, Damon goes through the man's pockets and pulls out his phone. He rips the tape from the man's mouth, pulls up the lockscreen on the phone, and holds it in front of the man's face.

'What's the code?' he asks.

The man can only stare at him in shock.

'What is the code?' Damon asks, again, louder.

The man looks at the phone, then at Damon, and then quickly inhales to scream.

'HELP M—!'

Damon slaps him across the face. Hard. The impact sounds like a thunderclap and the chair nearly topples over. The man's head is wrenched to the side. His glasses go flying. His mouth contorts in surprise and pain.

Damon grabs his hair and forces him to look at the phone.

'What is the code for this phone?!' Damon roars.

Still disoriented, the man blinks and begins to sputter. 'I – I don't know what you—'

Damon lets go of his hair and winds up to hit him again, which brings the man halfway back to his senses. He turns his head to avoid the impact and whimpers.

Damon gets right in his face. 'THE CODE! NOW!'

'Okay! Please! Okay! One, zero, eight, seven!' the man cries.

Damon punches the numbers into the phone, unlocking it, and then takes a second to adjust the settings as the man moves his jaw back and forth, willing it to work again.

Once Damon is finished, he returns to the backpack lying on the counter. As he opens it, the man looks at me and then back at Damon.

'Okay. Okay. Listen,' he sputters. 'I don't know you. Okay?'

'That's okay,' Damon says, slipping the man's phone into the backpack. 'Because I know you . . . Patrick Henford.'

The fact that Damon knows his name causes Henford to shrink and clam up for a few seconds before finding his voice, again.

'I – I don't know what this is about, but if it's money or something, I can get you whatever you want. I know people who can—'

Damon turns and silences him with an icy stare.

Henford watches as Damon pulls one of the manila envelopes from the backpack. He walks back to Henford, picks up his glasses from the floor, and places them on his face.

Unsettled by the gesture, Henford begins speaking rapidly. 'I – I – I mean it. I don't know what is – I don't know what you want, but whatever it is, I promise, I can get it. I know people. They can get you whatever you want!'

Damon opens the flap on the manila envelope and pulls out a stack of about a dozen or so sturdy sheets of paper. From my vantage point, lying on the floor twenty feet away, all I can see is the plain white back of the last sheet.

Damon holds the stack in front of Henford.

'Do you remember?' Damon asks.

Henford stares at the paper. His brow wrinkles in confusion.

'N-no. I have no idea wh—'

Damon flips to the next sheet.

There's a moment . . . and then horror spreads across Henford's face. His eyes widen. His lips tremble. Damon flips to the next page and the horror deepens.

'You remember now, don't you?' Damon confidently asks.

A realization finds its way into Henford's face, as though he's seeing Damon for the first time, and his horror quickly becomes abject terror.

Tears begin pouring down Henford's cheeks. 'Please! Please! I'm sorry! I'm sorry, okay? Okay?! Please! It's just a thing! You don't understand! It's just this stupid thing – I – I – I – I didn't even want to be a part of it, but I had to!'

Judging by Damon's expression, that was exactly the wrong thing to say.

He drops the papers to the floor and grabs the roll of duct tape.

'No! No! No! Wait! Please! WAIT!!!' Henford pleads.

Damon pulls the loose end of the tape and begins wrapping it around his head, gagging him. Damon steps back, pulls the gun from his waistband, and puts the barrel to Henford's temple, who begins choking and gagging as he attempts to scream.

My pulse races at the realization that I'm about to watch a man be murdered right in front of me. I grunt against the tape over my own mouth and struggle to turn my head. Unable to completely turn away, I finally curl into a ball and press my eyes shut.

Henford continues to blubber and whine.

I tense my entire body, waiting for the gunshot . . . but it doesn't come.

Henford is still whimpering.

I slowly uncurl and open my eyes.

Henford is alive but appears to have shut down.

Damon still holds the gun to Henford's temple but he's looking right at me, as if struggling with a decision.

My stomach plummets. Was he waiting for me to open my eyes so that I would have to see this?

Suddenly, Damon lowers the gun and tucks it back into his waistband. He quickly steps behind the chair, tips it back, and drags Henford toward the darkened hallway at the far end of the open space.

Henford is woken from his stupor and resumes struggling.

As Damon drags him away, Henford and I lock eyes. He's pleading for help. He knows he's being dragged to his death.

Damon and Henford disappear into the shadows. His muted grunts fade. Somewhere in the darkness of the hallway, a door closes, completely cutting off the sound of Henford's struggles.

There's a pause, filled only by the hum of the refrigerator and my breathing.

Gunshot.

Silence.

I lie on the floor of the entranceway, unable to move.

The papers are scattered across the floor. The backpack is on the counter.

In the darkness of the hallway, a door opens. Moments later, Damon appears from the shadows. He collects the papers from the floor, puts them back in the manila envelope, and sets the folder on the counter. He pulls his phone from the backpack and dials.

'Send the police to three-seven-eight-seven Doheny,' he says, zipping the backpack closed. 'They'll find Patrick Henford's body in the laundry room and the reason why in an envelope on the kitchen counter.'

Damon hangs up. He puts his phone in the backpack, puts his arms through the straps, and steps away from the counter, leaving the manila envelope where it is.

He quickly strides over, crouches down, and pulls me up by my wrists to get me to my feet.

'Time to go.'

Chapter 20

'*In half a mile, turn left onto Interstate four-oh-five South,*' the automated voice says.

My knuckles are white on the steering wheel. My shoulders are so tense, they cramp as they lock my arms in place.

All I can see are Henford's eyes pleading for help as Damon dragged him into the shadows. They were the eyes of a man who knew he was about to die.

And I couldn't do a thing.

I was lying bound and gagged on the floor, helplessly forced to watch.

No. I wasn't just helpless.

I was bait.

'Did you say something?' Damon asks from the back seat.

Did I say that out loud?

I didn't mean to, and I can avoid a conversation by responding with, 'No, I didn't say anything,' but I'm too pissed to let it go.

'I said, "You used me as bait,"' I angrily mutter.

'What are you talking about?'

'You used me as bait!' I snap at Damon's reflection in the rearview mirror.

'What's your point?'

'You used me as bait *to kill a man*!'

Damon calmly stares back at me in the mirror before repeating with emphasis, 'What. Is. Your. Point. Lucas?'

'It's not enough that you're making me drive you around to murder people? Did you have to use me as a part of your plan?'

'What about the first house where I killed someone while you were trying to escape?' he asks with a shrug.

'What about it?'

'You drove me there. Doesn't that mean you were already helping me kill people? Why are you so upset now?'

'Because this is different!'

'How?'

'Because it is and you know it!'

We stop at the red light and wait for the green arrow to turn left to take the ramp back on to Interstate 405. There are no other cars around.

I can tell from Damon's expression in the mirror that he knows I'm right but he's not going to leave it at that.

'I wouldn't have used you as bait if you had just stayed in the trunk,' he says. 'That's your fault. If you had trusted me, I wouldn't have had to bring you inside.'

He's speaking to me as if he's addressing an unruly child. It's infuriating but all I can do is shake my head.

'Okay. You need to feel better about yourself?' Damon asks. 'Fine. Would it help you to know that Henford was not an innocent man? No one we're visiting tonight is. Far from it.'

'No,' I answer, still fuming. 'It doesn't make me feel better.'

'Why not?'

'Because I'm not going to take your word for it. You don't get to decide that and then kill them.'

Damon's expression hardens. 'I am the only one who's going to decide that.'

'Then tell me: what did they do?'

Damon pauses, as though he's about to do so, but stops and

shakes his head. 'Something unforgivable.'

'That's not good enough.'

He cocks his head. 'Oh. I'm sorry. Do you think I owe you an explanation? And if you're not happy with my explanation, if it doesn't meet *your* standards, should I stop what I'm doing?'

'You said that they did something "unforgivable",' I argue. 'I want to know what was so bad that you would make me help you kill them.'

Damon rolls his eyes. 'You didn't help me do anything.'

'You used me as bait! You tied me to that porch railing to get him to the front door so you could sneak up behind him. He was going to help me and you needed him to be focused on me so that you could—'

'You haven't helped me do anything, Lucas!' Damon erupts. 'I didn't give you a choice. Do you hear yourself? I strapped you to that railing. I put duct tape over your mouth. That's like, I don't know, a worm on a hook feeling guilty when someone catches a fish.' He shakes his head in frustration and disbelief. 'How can I make you understand that this has nothing to do with you? I'm the monster tonight and you're just some kid from Pennsylvania. You're no one.'

'Maybe not to you!' I fire back. 'But I've got someone who loves me and a daughter on the way. What about you? Are you someone to anybody?'

Damon stares at me coldly in the mirror but doesn't answer.

Finally, we get the green arrow.

I turn left, crossing the opposite lane, and climb the ramp back onto the Interstate.

'You made me a part of what you're doing,' I say, under my breath, but loud enough for him to hear. 'I'm going to see that guy's face every night when I try to go to sleep.'

Damon's expression changes. 'Fine. You want proof that you didn't help me? I can clear your conscience. I wasn't going to bring it up, but I can tell you why you shouldn't feel like you were bait . . . but it will cost you.'

I fidget between the road and his face in the mirror.

'Cost me what?'

Damon shakes his head. 'No. How important is it to know you had nothing to do with what happened?'

My teeth sink into my lower lip. Then, the image of Henford's pleading eyes flashes across my mind.

'Tell me.'

Damon sighs and gives me a pitying look before speaking. 'When I came through the back door, I heard him speaking to you.'

'Yes . . .'

'He said that he was going to call the cops. Do you remember?'

'. . . Yes.'

'And then he said, "Wait. Do you want me to call the cops?" Do you remember that?'

'Yes . . .'

'So, that means that you were trying to communicate with him.' Damon leans forward. 'Were you trying to warn him, Lucas? With your hands and ankles zip-tied to the porch railing and with duct tape over your mouth, were you trying to tell him that he should call the police, even when I told you not to move or make a sound, just like I told you to stay in the trunk?'

I stare out at the road.

'Answer my question, Lucas.'

'. . . Yes.'

'"Yes" what?'

'. . . I was telling him to call the cops.'

Damon nods. 'Then there it is. You tried to save him. You did your best to stop me, after I warned you that there would be consequences. Congratulations. Your conscience is clear. I hope it makes you feel better.'

It doesn't. My stomach is turning at his pitying smile.

Damon then sits back, picks up my phone from the seat, and unlocks it.

'What are you doing?' I ask.

'I told you that there would be a cost,' he says, tapping away on the screen.

My skin ripples. 'What is it? Strike two?'

Damon scoffs. 'No, no, no. You've shown that you're not a huge fan of baseball and we are past strike two.'

He gives one final tap on the screen.

A moment later, the automated voice comes over the speakers. *'Exit at Nordhoff . . .'*

Chapter 21

We need to talk.

In the thirty seconds it took me to reach the empty stairwell, my mind envisioned a million scenarios for why Julia would send a cryptic text that said we needed to talk, and each scenario was more terrible than the last.

I reached the stairwell and made sure the door was closed behind me before dialing her number.

'Julia? What's wr—?'

'I'm pregnant,' she said before I finish asking.

I sank down, sat on the landing, and stared straight ahead. The hum of the halogen lights in the stairwell filling the silence that followed is a sound I'll never forget.

That was the moment that time began to pass differently. I could feel it speeding up, hurtling forward.

'Lucas?'

'I'm here.'

'I got sick at work,' she said. 'I thought it was a stomach bug or something, but then I realized I was late and I got a pregnancy test and—' Her voice cracked and I heard her sniffle through the phone. 'Can you come home?'

'I'm on my way.'

*

'You can't leave for the day. I need you here,' Adrian, my boss said, from behind the desk in his office. The walls were adorned with photos of celebrities he had met. Behind him was a bookshelf full of books about business, power, and how to be successful, none of which, I was sure, he had ever read.

'Adrian, a family thing came up. I have to take care of it. I'll be back first thing tomorrow.'

He sat back and stared at me with something halfway between sorrow and disappointment. 'All right, but if you ever want to sit behind a desk like this, in an office like this, you have to get your priorities straight, even when it involves family. And this decision you're making right now?' He leaned forward and tapped his temple. 'It stays right here when I make future decisions about this company. Understand?'

I could have pointed out that, in regards to his mention of 'family,' his uncle was the CEO of the company, but I needed to be with Julia.

'I understand,' I said.

I wasn't worried about being fired. Adrian talked a big game but the guy was lost without me.

*

I arrived back at the studio apartment to find Julia curled up on the couch, staring at the opposite wall. I sat next to her. Without a word, she leaned into me and I wrapped my arms around her.

For a time, neither one of us said a word, but as we sat there, I could still feel time speeding up.

'You okay?' I finally asked.

She nodded, but I knew her answer was relative.

'What do you need right now?' I asked.

'. . . I don't know.'

123

Another long silence.

She sighed. 'What are we gonna do?'

'What do you want to do?'

'No, no,' she quietly replied. 'I asked you first. And all options are on the table.'

It was my turn to grow silent, because I had been turning it over in my head the whole drive back to the apartment. We had talked about kids, but it was always in the abstract. It was something for down the road, when all our ducks were in a row and in our current situation, even ducks were a luxury we couldn't afford. I knew what our circumstances dictated; we both did . . . but still . . .

'Okay,' I said, taking a deep breath to brace myself for the insanity I was about to put out into the universe. 'I know we're not in the best spot, but, Julia . . . I want to do it. I want us to have a baby.'

She spun around to look at me, her eyes starting to brim. I was ready for an outburst, but instead, she had the most beautiful smile I had ever seen.

'Yeah?' she asked.

'Yeah.'

She threw her arms around me and we held each other, trying to contain our excitement.

She pulled away to look me in the eye. 'If it's a girl, I think we should name her Sophia.'

That was where I almost lost it.

I was afraid, excited, every conceivable emotion, but when Julia suggested my mother's name if we had a daughter, everything fell away. No matter how hard things had been for us, I knew we had made every right decision because there was no place I'd rather be and no other person I would rather have been with.

I kissed her again and then we sat there with our foreheads together, neither speaking until I had a thought.

'Wait. What if it's a boy?' I asked.

'I've been thinking about that, too,' she said through a sniff.

'And?'

'We should name him Sophia.'

I laughed and kissed her, again.

We spent the rest of the day on the couch, just holding each other, talking about the future; the fun parts and the parts we knew would be a struggle. I held her the whole time, promising her and myself that I was never going to let her go and that I was going to do everything to keep her and our baby safe.

Chapter 22

Julia's silhouette passes across the second-floor window.

'I need you to listen, Lucas, because this is how I will kill her,' Damon says, leaning forward from the back seat and speaking into my ear as we both stare through the windshield to the apartment building. We're parked on the street about fifty yards away.

'The second floor makes things a little harder,' Damon continues. 'And you said it's a studio apartment, right?'

He waits for a reply but I say nothing.

Julia walks past the window, again. She's pacing around the apartment. She's at the stage of the pregnancy where no position is comfortable. Recently, whenever we've tried to sit down to watch a movie, twenty minutes in, she'll get up and start walking around while trying to watch the show.

'A studio apartment also presents a problem. See, if you're breaking into an apartment, the best window to go through is the bedroom window. It's the room where we spend the least amount of time. Well, the least amount of time that we're awake. You go in through the bedroom window because there is the smallest chance of being spotted if someone is in the apartment.'

I don't know how he knows this and I don't care.

Julia once again passes by the window. Her hand is pressed

against her back, trying to counter her expanded belly. She's backlit by the Christmas lights we hung in the apartment to brighten the place up a bit. We call it our 'poor man's track lighting.'

'Studio apartment. Second floor. It would have to be a smash job. I'd simply walk up and kick in the door. The doors on these types of buildings are usually decades old. A few swift kicks and you're inside. You don't even have to worry about the lock. Once inside, I would use something like a baseball bat. A gun would be too loud and she might not die right away when she is shot. She could scream. Bludgeoning would work better. One hit to silence her and then you can make sure the job is done . . . And then, I would disappear. I'd be gone before any of your neighbors called nine-one-one.' He's suddenly struck by a thought. 'Do you think they even would? Are you friends with your neighbors? Or, like everyone else in Los Angeles, if they heard Julia scream, do you think they would simply turn up their televisions and not get involved?'

Actually, yes. We are friends with our neighbors. Well, one of them, at least. There's an old Hispanic man that lives in the apartment below us named Mr. Herrera. He barely speaks any English and we don't know what he does for a living, but he always waves and says 'hello' when he sees us. He left us a plate of homemade tamales the day we moved in. When Julia started to show, he began making regular appearances with plates of food, which we appreciated not only because we were saving every penny, but also because Mr. Herrera is one hell of a cook. One evening, while Julia was sleeping, I stepped outside to get some air. He spotted me, and waved me down to his apartment. He sat me down at the small metal table outside his door, and celebrated Little Sophie's upcoming arrival with some of the best tequila I've ever had. Between his limited English and my almost non-existent Spanish, it was a great, and oftentimes hysterical evening.

But I'm not telling Damon any of this.

He's waiting for me to tearfully plead for Julia and Sophie's safety like I did earlier, but that was a lifetime ago. It was before he held a bloody blade to my throat. It was before he shot a cop and it was before he made me watch as he dragged a man away to be executed. That was before he had us park here to threaten Julia. He thought it would break any resistance I had left.

He was wrong.

Instead, there's a rage growing in me I've never felt before. You would think a rage like this would burn white-hot, but it doesn't. It's cold. It's blood congealing into ice. It's splinters of glass moving through my veins. There is still fear, fear of what will happen to Julia and Sophie, but that fear has been pushed to the back, replaced by a determination to keep them safe.

'That's what will happen, Lucas,' Damon continues, still trying to get a reaction. 'It will be quick. It will be brutal, and I will disappear. Julia doesn't know it, but she and Little Sophie are now counting on you. Your life and theirs, depends on you understanding that those are the stakes. You obviously are not getting it, so I want you to take a good look. This is how close I can get and neither you, nor the police, will be able to stop me—'

'This is the closest you will ever get to them.'

My voice is calm and even. My eyes are still on the window. My life is not in this car. It is in that apartment.

'I beg your pardon?' Damon asks.

'This is the closest you will ever get to them,' I quietly repeat.

'Lucas,' Damon says with a sigh. 'I know you're young and think you're invincible, and that you might be able to figure something out, but you need to grow up. You need to think of what is best for Julia and your daughter, and that is no more escape attempts and no more trying to interfere with my work. You need to do that for their sake. Do you understand?'

'This is the closest you will ever get to them.'

My eyes never leave the window but I can feel Damon looking at me. I can feel his sudden uncertainty, possibly realizing he's made a mistake by bringing us here.

'All right,' he says with a shrug. 'As long as you understand that it's up to you.' He checks the time on my phone, winces, unlocks the screen, and begins typing.

'*Continue straight,*' the automated voice says a moment later.

I take one last look at the window.

Julia walks by once again.

'Let's go,' Damon says.

I take my foot off the brake and pull away from the curb.

All Damon's done is bring everything into focus.

I know how this night has to end.

It can't end with him completing his work, because what would stop him from killing me and then Julia to make sure there are no loose ends? It can't end with him completing his work and then disappearing. Every day for the rest of our lives, I would worry about him returning.

The only way this night ends is with the knowledge that he can never harm Julia. Whether that means he's in custody or dead.

But that means I have to walk a very fine line. I have to stay with him until one of those things happens. I have to work against him. I have to delay and stall, but I can't be obvious about it because he'll kill me and I have no doubt that he'll then kill Julia.

I have to stay with him until he's either captured or dead, even if it means staying with him while he does his work.

If that's what it takes to keep Julia and Sophie safe, that is what I have to do.

Chapter 23

That cold ball of rage hasn't dissipated one degree by the time we reach Sherman Way and begin heading east, cutting across the valley.

As we pass the strip malls, liquor stores, and car repair shops, my certainty only grows that this night ends with Damon either captured or dead, and I need to start working to make that happen now.

I need to know what his plans are. Before we stopped at the apartment, I was too busy being afraid, cowering, begging, and pleading for the safety of Julia and myself. I only asked questions here and there. I need to know what's happening but I can't flat out ask. I have to walk that fine line of stopping him without him suspecting what I'm up to. Asking where we're going or who he's going to kill will only set off alarms.

A quick glance in the rearview mirror shows Damon typing on the phone that he took from Henford before he killed him. There is the faint clicking sound effect as his fingers tap the screen and then the *whoosh* when he hits send. He then sits back and stares intently at the phone. I assume he's waiting for a response.

I can't ask him where we're going or who he's killing. He's not going to tell me, which leaves only one other option.

'Why are you doing this?' I ask.

He looks up from the screen. His eyes narrow. 'I thought you didn't want to get involved in what I'm doing. You just paid a hell of a price for me to clear your conscience.'

'That's the point. I want to know why it's so important that you're threatening to kill the wife and unborn daughter of someone you just met if they don't do what you say.'

I'm trying to still sound a little scared, but after what I told him at the apartment, I'm not sure he's buying it. His eyes narrow further.

Our standoff is broken by the playful *whoosh* of an incoming text from the dead man's phone in his hand.

Damon reads it. Whatever it says causes him equal parts satisfaction and revulsion. He angrily taps out a reply, hits send, and then tosses the phone onto the seat.

'Who are you talking to?' I ask.

He stares at me in annoyance, still stewing from whatever text conversation he was just having.

'I'm not sure I like this new interest in what I'm doing tonight, Lucas.'

I shrug. 'Okay . . .'

He sits back to watch the passing assortment of random stores and bland apartment buildings.

'Who are you texting?' I ask before he can get comfortable.

A flicker of shock crosses his face. It's only a second and his annoyed expression returns.

'*In half a mile, turn right onto Highway one-seventy South,*' the automated voice reads.

'Focus on the road,' Damon finally says. 'All you have to do is drive.'

I guide the car off of Sherman Way and onto the ramp to join the flow of traffic heading back toward the city.

'So, why are you doing this? Why are you killing these people?' I ask, as the skyline of the Hollywood Hills grows in the distance.

He's about to snap at me but stops. He takes a moment to collect himself and replies as calmly as he can: 'I'm not telling you anything about what I'm doing tonight. You need to focus on driving. By now, the police have found the cop.'

'The one you shot?' I ask, rhetorically.

'I told you: he's going to be fine. He's going to have a hell of a bruise and I'm sure it wasn't very pleasant, and they've probably found him by now, which means almost every cop in the city is going to be looking for us. For this car. That's why we need to keep moving. You do not need to know my motives.'

The idea that the cops are looking for us gives me a faint glimmer of hope, but it's tempered by the knowledge that Honda Civics are one of the most common vehicles on the road. Even the color of mine, metallic gray, is run-of-the-mill. A quick scan of the surrounding cars finds two that are similar to mine.

There's a buzzing sound from the back seat. The car's speakers come to life with the purr of a ringtone. The display on the center console changes. *INCOMING CALL: JULIA*

The breath catches in my chest. Instinctively, my thumb moves to hit the answer button on the steering wheel.

'Stop!' Damon shouts.

I freeze, my thumb hovering above the answer button while the phone continues to ring.

'That is my wife,' I argue. 'She's almost nine months pregnant. I'm going to answer this call to make sure she's okay.'

Damon hesitates as if he's uncertain as the ringing continues.

'I'm not going to tell her what's happening,' I continue, 'but if I don't answer, she *will* think something is wrong.'

Damon grits his teeth in resignation. 'Okay, but you better be good at lying.'

'Been doing it for two months,' I mumble, and press the answer button. 'Julia?'

'Oh, hey. I thought it might go to voicemail.'

It's there in her voice; the fatigue, the restlessness. They've been growing these last few weeks. She's ready for Little Sophie to get this show on the road. She's been handling it like a trooper, but she hasn't had a good night's sleep in over a month.

'Is everything okay?' I ask.

'Yeah. Everything is fine,' Julia says. 'Sorry to keep bugging you.'

'You're not bugging me at all,' I answer, honestly, while Damon watches me intently from the back seat, waiting for me to screw up.

'I was—' She stops. 'Wait. Are you on your way home? It sounds like you're in the car.'

Damon raises his eyebrows expectantly as I frantically search for an answer.

'No. Not yet. I just stepped outside to take the call. There's a lot of traffic on the street,' I say with a wince, hoping I sold it.

'Oh,' she answers, disappointed. 'I don't want to interrupt work. Like I said, I thought it would go to voicemail.'

'It's totally fine. I needed to get out of there, anyway.' I stare directly at Damon in the rearview mirror. 'My boss is being an asshole.'

Cute, he sarcastically mouths.

'Ugh,' Julia groans. 'When are they going to fire that guy?'

'Never. CEO's nephew.'

'Do you think you'll be much longer?'

'I hope not.' My eyes stay on Damon. 'We're adding the final touches before we deliver to the client tonight.'

'Okay,' she says, clearly bummed.

'But you're sure everything's okay?'

'Yeah. Sophie's turning cartwheels but it's getting late and I wanted to let you know that I'm going to bed soon. I made spaghetti. There's a plate waiting for you in the fridge.'

All I've had to eat in the last ten hours was a peanut butter sandwich; the mention of spaghetti causes my stomach to sit up and roar. I also check the time on the center console. It's 11:04 p.m.

'Thank you. I'll be extra quiet when I get home so I don't wake you up.'

'I'm not sure this kid will let me sleep.'

'If you're still awake when I get home, I'll give you a foot rub.'

'Mmmmmm . . . Pinky swear?' she asks.

I can hear her smiling.

'Pinky swear.'

'Okay,' Julia sighs. 'I'll let you get back to it. I'm sure you don't want to keep Adrian waiting.'

'Probably not,' I reply, my heart sinking.

'Get home safe.'

'I will. I love you.'

'Love you, too.'

Julia hangs up.

Neither I nor Damon speak for a few moments.

The Hollywood Hills continue to grow in the distance. The other side of the hill has the Hollywood sign. The brightest lights on this side of the hills are the glow of Universal Studios.

Talking to Julia was like an oasis. For those brief minutes, everything was almost normal.

'You're good at that,' Damon finally says.

'Good at what?'

'Lying to her.'

He's stating a simple fact, but my guilt makes it feel like he's judging me.

'As I said, I've been doing it for two months.'

'*In one mile, stay right onto Highway one-oh-one South,*' the automated voice says.

'What's with the "pinky swear" thing?' Damon asks.

'It's just something we do.'

Damon shakes his head. 'Two kids on an adventure . . .'

We merge onto the Hollywood Freeway. The traffic grows. We pass the congested exit to Universal Studios and continue on, emerging out of the pass to the other side of the Hollywood Hills. The lights of Los Angeles are spread out before us, scattering my thoughts of Julia and reminding me of the present situation.

'Where are we going?' I ask.

'We're almost there,' he murmurs.

The automated voice comes over the speakers. '*In half a mile, turn right onto Hollywood Boulevard.*'

'And you still won't tell me why you're killing these people?'

'We're almost there,' Damon quietly repeats, as he stares out the window.

Chapter 24

Even at this relatively late time of night, Hollywood Boulevard is its usual mix of tourists, club-goers, and vagrants.

We pass the new apartment buildings that are attempting to gentrify a storied part of Los Angeles that had become rundown. We drive by the Pantages Theatre, which is adorned with banners and signs announcing the season's run of Broadway shows.

The further west we head, the thicker the traffic becomes, both on the road and on the sidewalks, where people are crouching down to take photos with the star of their favorite celebrity on the Walk of Fame. Souvenir stores begin popping up, still open to accommodate the late-night shoppers.

By the time we reach the Chinese Theatre, traffic has slowed to a crawl. Outside it there are people dressed as movie characters, charging tourists five bucks a pop for a photo. Other tourists are pressing their hands and feet into the hand- and footprints of legendary celebrities on the concrete slabs that make up the plaza of the theater.

Los Angeles held a lot of disappointment for Julia and I when we arrived. It took us a while to find the things we liked about the city, but the Grauman's Chinese Theatre has always held a special place for me. One night, despite our financial woes, Julia and I decided to splurge and have an old-fashioned 'Hollywood Date Night.' We ate dinner at a restaurant off of Hollywood & Vine. Later, we had drinks at one of those ultra-cool bars that didn't have a sign out front. A friend at work told me about it. The entrance was simply a door in an alley. After that, we attended a special midnight screening of *Casablanca* at the Chinese Theatre. The place was packed with people who loved the movie just as much as Julia and I do. The interior of the theater, with its red and golds and massive chandelier, was stunning. I imagined that this was how *Casablanca* had its Los Angeles première back in 1942. It's my favorite night that Julia and I have spent in Los Angeles. I'm also pretty sure it was the night that Sophie was conceived.

For a moment, I forget about what's happening. I forget about the killer in my back seat. I forget that I should be trying to get information from our surroundings and from Damon as to what his plans are and how I can stop him and reminisce about that night.

But I'm snapped back to the car because the nostalgia I'm feeling is the opposite of whatever Damon is experiencing. He is radiating hatred from the back seat.

It might be that the double-decker bus in front of us, which is full of people on a sightseeing tour, is going too slow. It might be the glaring lights. Or it could be the noise. With one of the windows shot out, the sounds of Hollywood Boulevard find their way into the car; the honking, the thumping music from one of the nearby cars, the laughter and cries from tourists posing for photos, the guy on the corner, drumming away on plastic buckets as people occasionally drop a dollar or two into the upturned hat lying on the sidewalk in front of him.

Whatever it is, it's clear that Damon would rather be anywhere else.

He grunts and checks the directions on my phone.

'Turn left up here. Sunset will be faster.'

Following his instructions, I turn at the next intersection. We head south for two blocks to Sunset Boulevard, where there's only slightly less traffic.

I don't think Damon wanted to save time. For whatever reason, he couldn't stand to be on Hollywood Boulevard.

Are his feelings about our surroundings tied to why he's murdering people? Or is he just anxious to get to his next kill?

My mind starts drawing wild conclusions until we make the turn onto Sunset Boulevard and I'm struck by a thought.

My God.

Has it only been a few hours since I picked up Keith outside the club a few blocks from here? A glance at the clock on the dashboard shows that it's a little after 11 p.m.

I shake it off as we pass the bars, restaurants, and nightclubs.

We drive by the legendary Chateau Marmont. Julia and I had talked about doing a weekend getaway there, that is until we found out that the cheapest room was eight hundred dollars a night on the weekends. After that, we decided that we would check out the lobby and grounds, but now, it's just another item on our long list of things we said we'd do one day.

There's a line of people outside the Comedy Store, waiting to get inside.

A few minutes later, we pass the black facade of the Viper Room. People stand in clusters of two or three near the door, smoking cigarettes or vaping as they chat.

Even growing up in small-town Pennsylvania, Julia and I had heard the epic stories about the Viper Room; the wild parties, the rockstar performances. I don't know what I was expecting the first time I saw it when Julia and I did our 'Welcome to Los Angeles' tour, but it wasn't a small building sandwiched between two liquor stores and a place across the street advertising Tarot card readings for five dollars, but it only added to the mystique; that so many stories happened in such a small, nondescript building. We were also surprised that the equally famous Whiskey a Go-Go was practically across the street; the place where so many famous bands got their first br—

There's a muted *whoosh* from the back seat.

Damon takes out Henford's phone. He looks at the screen and then out the windshield to the horizon. I try to follow his gaze. There's a cluster of office high-rises growing in the distance. Damon looks down and begins typing on Henford's phone. As before, he doesn't look happy. He makes one final tap and the phone emits that playful *whoosh* as the message is sent. Damon then stares at the phone and waits . . . and waits . . .

Another text arrives.

Damon reads it and then stuffs the phone into his pocket with a sense of finality before opening the backpack. He extracts a couple zip ties and shoves them deep into the pocket of his hoodie.

'*In one quarter mile, your destination will be on your right*,' the voice announces over the speakers.

I glance up ahead to the cluster of high-rises Damon was looking at a moment ago.

That must be where we're going; the tall, angular building silhouetted against the backdrop of glittering lights.

'All right, Lucas,' Damon says, slipping into game mode as we approach. 'This is going to be different. You're coming in with me and I can't zip-tie your hands or duct-tape your mouth. You have to stay by my side at all times and prove that you can follow directions, because if you try anything in here, I will have no choice but to kill you. There will be other people around and if you mess with my plans, not only will I kill you, I will have to kill others – and I promise you, they won't be wearing bulletproof vests. Got it?'

It's not an idle threat and that feeling – that conclusion I reached as we drove away from the apartment – hasn't gone away. I'm not leaving his side until I know he can't threaten Julia or Sophie ever again. But does that mean I'm okay standing by as he kills whoever he's here to kill? And if there's a chance at any point to stop him, I have to take it, but am I willing to sacrifice others?

'Got it?' he asks, again.

'Yeah.'

The entrance to the parking garage at the base of the building is coming up on our right.

'Good. Now, once we turn in here and reach security, you let me do the talking.'

'Security? You're going to try to talk your way inside?'

'No. I won't have to.'

'Why not?'

'Because they're expecting us.'

Chapter 25

I crane my neck to see the top floor as we pull through the intersection. The nightclubs that Sunset is famous for are behind us and we've reached the upscale business end of the boulevard. A quick inventory of the neighboring buildings yields an expensive sushi restaurant, a boutique furniture store, and a two-story building that houses a car dealership for exotic imports. Two sports cars, whose brands I don't recognize, gleam in the front window but none of this tells me anything about the building we're about to enter.

I flip on my blinker and turn into the parking garage. We descend toward a tinted-glass booth next to the gate.

'Remember,' Damon says, as I apply the brakes. 'Let me do the talking.'

We pull even with the booth and stop.

Inside the booth is an older man wearing a crisply pressed white shirt, black vest, and black pants. He's seated on a stool in front of a computer. On the desk next to the computer monitor is a handheld radio spouting a talk show. A phone is mounted to the wall of the booth.

'Good evening,' the old man says. 'How can I help you, gentlemen?'

'Hi. Patrick Henford here to see Julian Walsh up on fourteen. He's expecting me,' Damon cheerily answers and then nods to me. 'And a guest.'

I have no idea who Julian Walsh is. I've never heard of him but the old man nods.

'Do you have your ID handy?' he asks.

Damon gets a pained expression and turns on that dangerous charm he's used throughout the night. 'This was sort of a spur-of-the-moment thing and I left it at home, but if you want to give him a call, Julian can vouch for me.'

'Sure,' the man says with a smile. 'Give me one sec.'

The man turns to his computer and begins pecking on the keyboard with his index fingers. He pulls up a screen and leans in close to read it. He finds what he's looking for and lifts the phone from its cradle on the wall to punch in some numbers. There's an awkward pause as the man waits with the phone pressed to his ear.

'Mr. Walsh?' he finally asks into the line. 'It's Jimmy down in the garage. How are you this evening? . . . Good. Listen, I have a Patrick Henford here to see you. He also has a guest. Unfortunately, Mr. Henford left his identification at home but he said you would vouch for them? . . . Uh-huh . . . Yes . . .' The man wrinkles his nose in uncomfortable confusion and looks at me. 'Well . . . I mean . . . I'm not sure it's for me to say . . . I suppose so . . .'

Why do I appear to be the subject of their conversation?

'. . . All right. Yes, sir . . .' Jimmy finally says. 'Of course, Mr. Walsh. I'll send them on up and let the front desk know. You have a good night.'

Jimmy hangs up the phone, seemingly glad that his exchange with Julian Walsh is over. He reaches back into the booth and presses a button, causing the arm of the parking gate to rise.

'You're all set. Feel free to park in any space down on the second level that is not marked "Reserved."'

'Thank you, Jimmy,' Damon says with a wave.

Jimmy returns the gesture and gives me a weird side-eye as we drive under the raised arm of the parking gate.

*

The first level is practically empty but all the spots are marked 'Reserved.' We follow the signs for 'Additional Parking' down to the second level. The squeal of the tires echoes as we descend and take a hard right.

There are more cars here, but not many.

'Park as close to the stairwell as you can,' Damon says, pointing across the parking level.

I head down the aisle and maneuver into a spot a few yards away from the stairwell doors.

'Okay,' Damon says, as I kill the engine. 'One last time. You're going to stay by my side and keep your mouth shut.' Damon shows me the gun. 'This is going to be in my pocket with my finger on the trigger. Got it?'

'Yeah. I told you: I got it.'

'Pinky swear?' he asks with a sarcastic smile.

I stare at him.

'Sorry, Lucas. Was that too soon?'

'Let's get this over with.'

*

Damon stays uncomfortably close as we enter the stairwell and ascend to the lobby.

Once we reach the door, I grasp the handle and pull it open.

The walls of the lobby are black marble, as is the floor, causing our footsteps to echo in the vaulted ceiling as we cross toward the reception desk. Beyond the reception desk are two security guards, stationed by the elevators. I steal a glance at the directory on the wall, trying to find out anything I can, but it's filled with dozens of names and businesses.

'Hi,' Damon says to the young woman behind the security desk as we approach. He keeps his voice down but it still manages to bounce off the walls and ceiling. 'I'm Patrick Henford with a guest to see Julian Walsh. Did Jimmy let you know we were on our way up?'

'He did,' she replies, not looking up from her computer. 'You know where you're going?'

'Sure do.'

'Elevators are right over there,' she says with the slightest gesture over her shoulder. I look past her to the elevators, where the two security guards are chatting away about something that's apparently really funny.

'Thank you,' Damon replies, and gives me a look that says 'start walking.'

The security guards halt their discussion as we near the elevator. Damon nods hello, which they return.

I try to make eye contact to get their attention. I can't say 'This man has a gun!' because Damon's got his finger on the trigger in his pocket, but I'm hoping I can give them a look to let them know something is wrong, but they go back to their conversation without noticing me as Damon presses the button.

The elevator doors open and we step inside.

Chapter 26

The elevator opens to a hallway lined with doors extending to our left and right.

Standing behind me, Damon places a hand on my shoulder, guides me out of the elevator, and stops. We stand on the thick carpeting of the hallway and wait. The only immediate sound is that of the air conditioning flowing from the vents overhead, keeping the temperature somewhere just above freezing.

Damon takes a second to make sure the hallway is clear, and then looks over my shoulder to consult the directory mounted on the wall opposite the elevator. I scan it as quickly as I can, hoping for some information about Walsh. The directory lists CPAs, lawyers, and consulting firms. I spot Walsh's name near the bottom, but there's no title or company name. Just the number of his office. Damon sees it, too.

'This way,' he says, and we begin moving to our right.

He keeps his hand on my shoulder as we pass door after door. There is an occasional voice or ringing of a telephone, but it's almost midnight and most of the offices are silent.

We finally reach the door to Walsh's office at the end of the hall, where Damon pulls me to a stop. He steps forward and tests the door handle to see if it's locked. It isn't. He slowly pushes it open, and then nods for me to go inside and whispers, 'Quietly.'

The temperature in the small lobby is only a few degrees warmer than the hallway outside. One wall of the lobby is a massive window overlooking Sunset Boulevard. Across the lobby is a large reception desk, the front of which has what I assume is Walsh's signature etched into it. Next to the desk is the opening to a hallway.

Damon has me take a few more steps into the lobby and then closes the door behind us.

'Is that you, Henford?' a voice calls out from the hallway. 'Get your ass down here. I want to meet this guest that you brought.'

Damon pulls the gun from the pocket of his hoodie and instead of placing his hand on my shoulder, he firmly grasps the back of my neck, aims the gun over my shoulder toward the hallway, and guides me to it.

The hallway is short, consisting of three doors, the last of which is slightly open. Damon silently navigates us toward it but stops when we're a few feet away.

'Open it, slowly,' Damon whispers in my ear, keeping the gun over my shoulder and aiming it toward the door.

I reach out and slowly push the door open. Damon prods me forward and we step inside.

The walls of the office are lined with framed posters of blockbuster films and arthouse flicks, most of which I've seen. There are shelves with awards and photos. There's also a massive TV mounted to the wall. Across the office are two chairs situated in front of a large desk that is a replica of the one in the lobby. Behind the desk sits a man in his early forties who I can only assume is Julian Walsh. His hair is slicked back. His face is angular with high cheekbones. He could be a movie star himself. Behind Walsh is a glass wall that offers a stunning view of Los Angeles with the Hollywood sign floating on the hillside in the distance. We've interrupted him in the middle of pouring himself a drink as he's holding a decanter filled with an amber liquid over a glass.

He stares at us for a moment. 'Who the fuck are you?' he asks, seemingly oblivious to the fact that Damon is aiming a gun at him. 'Where's Henford?'

'He's not coming,' Damon says darkly.

Walsh isn't scared. He's not trembling. More than anything, he appears curious.

'Huh . . .' he says and then shrugs. 'Then I'm guessing you were the one that was texting me from Henford's phone, telling me to come to the office?'

'Correct,' Damon answers.

Walsh looks at me and then back to Damon. 'And this is your plus one? The one I said I was hoping would be a tight piece of ass?'

Damon nods.

'But there is no tight piece of ass?'

Damon shakes his head. 'No, there is not.'

Walsh shrugs. 'Well, I guess that explains why Jimmy down in the garage was so cagey when I asked if your guest was "hot."' Walsh addresses me. 'Don't get me wrong, kid, I'm sure you're a lot of fun, but you're not my type.' He smiles, waiting for either Damon or myself to appreciate his joke. Neither one of us do. 'All right. Obviously, there's something you want to discuss with me. So, let's discuss.' He finishes pouring the whiskey into the glass and extends the bottle to Damon. 'Can I offer you a drink?'

Damon doesn't acknowledge the bottle. He only stares at Walsh while keeping the gun aimed at him.

Walsh realizes he's not going to get an answer and offers the bottle in my direction. 'How about you, kid? You look like you could use something to take the edge off.'

'You're not talking to him,' Damon says. 'You're only talking to me.'

Walsh meets my eyes one more time before returning his focus to Damon. 'All right. What can I do for you, Mr. Man with the Gun?'

Keeping the gun aimed at Walsh's head, Damon sets the

backpack on the floor, and removes a set of zip ties from his back pocket. 'First, you're going to put your hands behind your back. I'm going to bind them, and then we're going to talk.'

Walsh considers Damon's proposal and shakes his head. 'Nah. I'm not doing that.'

'I beg your pardon?' Damon asks.

'I said I'm not doing that.'

'And why not?'

'Because whatever you've got to say to me, whatever you got to do, you can do it without my hands behind my back. You want to talk? Talk. You want to shoot me? Then shoot me. But I'm not putting my hands behind my back and I'm not letting you put those things on me.'

I've seen Damon hesitate at certain points this evening, but this is the first time I've seen him knocked completely off his game, unsure how to handle it. Walsh sees it, and presses on.

'Look, I respect what you're doing. I do. You fooled me into coming here all alone. You arrived with a gun and a hostage of some sort,' he says with a wave in my direction. 'So, you're obviously intelligent and you've got something *very* important on your mind that you want to talk about. I totally respect that because, and I don't know if you know this, but my job, what I do, *all* that I do, is negotiate highly stressful situations. It's what I am best at. It's what I was born for, okay? Now, I'll grant you that the negotiations normally don't involve someone aiming a gun at me, but it's not all that different from hundred-million-dollar deals, am I right?'

He spreads his arms and smiles, once again waiting for a reaction from Damon but gets none. Walsh exhales in resignation. 'All right. Whatever. Why don't the two of you have a seat? Let's talk this out like civilized individuals. There has to be something I can do for you.'

Walsh's confident, relaxed demeanor in the face of Damon's gun is somehow reassuring and I take a step toward the chair.

'Lucas,' Damon says, stopping me in my tracks. His eyes and aim never leave Walsh. 'Go stand by the wall.'

Walsh perks up. 'Lucas? Is that your name, kid? Nice to meet you. My name is Julian Walsh. You may have heard of me. If you haven't, that's fine, because I know you've seen some of the films that I've put togeth—'

'I told you,' Damon hisses, his tone deepening. 'You're not talking to him. You're talking to me.'

'Okay, okay, okay,' Walsh says, rolling his eyes. 'Tough crowd, am I right, Lucas?' he asks, but the question wasn't for me. He's taunting Damon, directly defying his command and testing the boundaries, but Damon isn't taking the bait. 'Okay. Let's talk. You and me. Whatever's bugging you, we can work something out.'

'I really don't think we can,' Damon says.

'Look, scary man, I told you; this is what I do, okay? I find solutions. I find ways to make it work. I have dealt with every type of human being imaginable.'

'I promise that you have never dealt with anything like me,' Damon coldly replies.

A small crack forms in Walsh's calm, reassuring facade. It takes a second for him to patch it and match Damon's tone. 'Okay. You obviously think you're some kind of commando, but I have handled some of the biggest stars in the world.' Walsh continues speaking as Damon crouches down, opens the backpack, and pulls out one of the manila envelopes. 'I negotiate deals that lead to billion-dollar blockbusters. I get it done. I'm "that guy." I am *the* guy. Do you understand? Do you get that? I'm th—'

Damon tosses the manila envelope onto the desk in front of Walsh, halting his speech.

'What is that?' Walsh asks.

Damon nods. 'Open it.'

Walsh stares at Damon and then down at the envelope as though it's a coiled snake ready to strike. He anxiously licks his lips, deciding if he's going to do what Damon is telling him. He finally picks up the envelope and begins to slowly lift the flap but stops. 'I don't know what this is, but you've got to promise me that when I open this, anthrax isn't going to come flying out, okay?' Walsh forces a laugh that dies a slow death as a bead of sweat rolls down his temple.

'All right. Fine. This is fine,' he says, frustration creeping into his tone. 'But I'm telling you, whatever this is, there's some way that we can work it out.' He finishes opening the flap and reaches into the envelope. 'We can reach a deal, some sort of understanding.' He's talking more to himself than to Damon as he pulls out the papers. 'You tell me what you want. I'm the guy who can get it done, you know? I'm the guy. I'm the . . . guy . . .' His voice trails off as he sees the first sheet. His chiseled jaw, which has been working at lightning speed, slows to a stop and hangs open. He flips to the next sheet . . . and the next . . . and the next . . . His eyes grow wider and his complexion paler with each passing piece of paper. Then, just like Henford, Walsh is hit with a horrible realization. He slowly looks up at Damon who nods in return as if to say 'yes.'

'Okay . . . Okay . . .' Walsh sputters, trying to play it cool while swallowing the lump in his throat. He returns the papers to the envelope but it takes a few tries because his hands are shaking. He lays the envelope on the desk and taps it with his finger. 'This is – uh—' He puts up his hands. 'Look, this is bad. There is no getting around that. I know it's bad. I want you to know that I understand that, but I'm *telling* you; we can – I can work something out for you—'

'You asked me what I wanted,' Damon says, keeping the gun leveled at Walsh's head.

Walsh claps his hands. 'Yes! Yes. You want something and that is *totally* understandable after what happened with—' He begins to motion to the envelope but realizes that's a bad idea. He comes to a full stop, takes a deep breath, and centers himself. 'Tell me what it's going to take to make this right and, no matter what it is, I will make it happen.'

'Anything?' Damon asks.

'Anything,' Walsh confidently answers. 'You name it.'

Damon nods to the wall of glass behind him. 'I want your brains on that window.'

That crack in his persona forms again and Walsh's fear is plain, but it's only for a second. His composure returns.

Damon waits for his answer, but he becomes a little unnerved as Walsh studies him.

Something changes. Walsh's confidence returns. A smile splits his face as if he's suddenly figured something out.

'Hey, kid? Lucas, right?' he asks in my direction but not looking away from Damon. 'This guy has put you through hell tonight, hasn't he?'

'Do not talk to him,' Damon says to Walsh before I have a chance to respond.

'He has Henford's phone,' Walsh says, ignoring Damon's warning 'Tell me, Lucas – did he kill him?'

'Don't answer him,' Damon says, matching Walsh's stare.

'I'll take that as a yes,' Walsh continues. 'Has he killed anyone else?'

I don't answer but Walsh can see it in my face.

'I'll take that as another yes.' He puts his eyes back on Damon while still talking to me. 'Listen to me, Lucas; this asshole is killing people. Now, he's going to kill me, and make no mistake – at the end of the night, when he's done killing people, no matter what he's promised you . . . he's going to kill you, too.'

'Do not talk to h—'

'Think about it, Lucas! After he's done, why would he leave you alive?'

Walsh allows me to process what he's said before continuing. 'You know I'm right, Lucas.' Incredibly, Walsh slowly rises from his chair and begins working his way around the side of the desk. Damon tenses, unsure of what to do. Walsh is moving slowly

151

enough that he's not a direct threat, but the fact that he's moving at all has Damon on his heels. 'He's keeping you around for a reason, but when he's done . . .' Walsh clears the side of the desk and stops. 'You're just as dead as I am.'

'Don't listen to him, Lucas.'

The two men stare each other down.

'Lucas,' Walsh says, still focusing on Damon. 'The best bet to stay alive, the best bet for *both of us* . . . is to rush him. Right now. Odds are that he might shoot one of us, but if we work together, we can take him.'

'Stay right where you are, both of you,' Damon warns.

'He's telling you everything you need to know, Lucas. Listen to him. He knows he's losing control. You can hear it in his voice. He knows that if we rush him, we have a chance.'

'Shut up!' Damon rages.

'Do the math, Lucas!' Walsh fires back. 'It's either he kills us both, me now and you later, or we take the chance, right here and we can—'

The gun erupts in Damon's hand and the glass behind Walsh becomes a spider's web of cracks, radiating outwards from the bullet hole behind and just to the side of Walsh's head.

Walsh recoils and throws his arms over his face. I fall back against the wall.

Walsh slowly lowers his arms to find Damon is still aiming the smoking gun. He takes a quick glance over his shoulder at the fractured glass and turns back to Damon. Instead of withering, Walsh's confidence only grows.

'There it is,' Walsh says. 'He did that because he knows I'm right. He tried to shut me up because what I told you is the truth and I guarantee you that someone on this floor heard that shot. They're going to come looking, and if that happens, things will really get out of hand. We need to do this right now. If we work together, he loses. It's you and me, Lucas. What do you say?'

A horrible thought seeps into my mind; Walsh is right.

Isn't he? He's saying the things I've been suspecting all night. Why would Damon keep me alive when all this is over? Can he even keep me alive? He shot a cop. I don't care if the cop lives and when the police catch up to us, they won't care, either. Is Damon planning on dying in a hail of bullets? He said that his survival wasn't part of his plan, so what good are any of his promises if I'm right next to him when the shooting starts?

Damon casts a sideways glance in my direction. 'Lucas, stay right where you are.'

Walsh leers at Damon and begins setting his feet. 'It's now or never, kid. On three . . . One . . .'

This is the opportunity I've been waiting for ever since we left the apartment. This might be the only chance to see Julia and Sophie. I'm taking it. The strength slowly returns to my legs. My weight shifts to the balls of my feet.

'Two . . .'

Damon's eyes dart in my direction.

His look is not a warning. It's not a threat. It's a message: *Don't trust him.*

It stops me in my tracks.

It's insane that I would consider such a thought, especially coming from Damon, but that look makes me realize exactly what is about to happen. My weight transfers back to my heels, keeping me against the wall, just as Walsh shouts.

'THREE!'

Walsh charges forward but instead of rushing to attack Damon, he goes straight for the open office door. As he runs, he turns his head in my direction for a split second and his face drops. He was going to screw me over and make a run for it while I attacked Damon.

Instead of shooting him, Damon throws out his free arm and hooks it around Walsh's throat as he attempts to get by. He spins Walsh to the floor, dropping him on to his stomach. Damon then plants his knee squarely on Walsh's back, pinning him down.

'What the fuck, kid?!!!' Walsh screams.

He struggles to get out from under Damon's knee but he isn't going anywhere.

Damon tucks the gun into his waistband, pulls out another zip tie from the pocket of his hoodie, and grabs Walsh's wrists.

'Ow! Goddammit!' Walsh cries out, as Damon tightens the zip tie around his wrists.

Damon takes his knee off Walsh's spine and stands.

Walsh begins flopping around, attempting to turn himself over. 'All right! All right!' he rages and is finally successful in flipping over to stare up defiantly at Damon. 'Fine. You got me, asshole. Congratulations. Now what are you going to do? You gonna shoot me?'

A wicked smile plays across Damon's face as he looms over him. 'Actually, I've got a much better idea.'

Damon crouches down and pulls the roll of duct tape from the backpack.

Walsh is seized with panic. 'Hey! Come on! We can sti—'

Damon pulls a piece of tape loose, presses it over Walsh's mouth and then wraps the tape several times around his head, gagging him. Damon maneuvers himself over Walsh's shoulders, hooks his hands under his armpits, and drags him across the floor, back toward the opaque, cracked wall of glass. He lets Walsh go and picks up the heavy chair that Walsh was sitting in. Damon winds up and roars as he swings the chair into the already fractured glass. There's a crunch and crackling as the cracks grow. Walsh attempts to scream against the tape, but there's almost no sound. Damon winds up again and slams the chair into the window.

It gives way. Countless bits of tempered glass fall to the floor in a loud, high-pitched crash. Cool night air rushes in and swirls around the office, accompanied by the sounds of the city below.

Out of breath, Damon drops the chair and stands over Walsh, who is silently sobbing against the tape.

Damon stops and looks at me.

My legs start to buckle. I'm about to watch my second murder in less than two hours.

Damon breaks eye contact, bends over, and grabs Walsh.

I turn away from the window and collapse against the wall, shutting my eyes tight, and throwing my hands over my ears, futilely attempting to block out the sounds of Damon's struggles as he drags Walsh to the ledge. There's an interminable pause, a pause that feels like a lifetime, and then, through my hands over my ears, Damon emits a growl that turns into a roar of physical effort.

Seconds pass. I finally lower my hands from my ears and glance over my shoulder.

Damon is standing on the ledge, behind the desk, looking down. His shoulders rise and fall with labored breaths. He takes one last inhale, looks around the city, and then turns to me, his eyes filled with a savage satisfaction.

He quickly moves around the large desk, leaving the manila envelope on the desktop, and snatches the backpack from the floor. He grabs the collar of my shirt, and pulls me to my feet.

'We have to go. Now.'

Chapter 27

Damon grips the back of my neck, not only to guide me, but to keep me on my feet as we hustle out of the office and into the shortened hallway. We reach the small lobby where he suddenly stops.

There are voices out in the hall, accompanied by the squawk of a radio.

'Shit,' Damon says under his breath.

He quickly walks us across the lobby, where he pushes me up against the wall next to the door. There's a sharp pain as my sternum hits the small square panel that houses the switch for the fire alarm, causing me to groan with pain.

'Shut up,' he insists, and then cautiously opens the door just an inch to peer into the hallway.

From my angle with my face pushed up against the wall, I can see over his head.

The two security guards from the lobby are opening doors to the offices, talking to the people inside. They're only a few doors down from us.

Damon quickly draws back and quietly closes the door just as the guards are about to turn in our direction to continue their search. He pulls me off of the wall and then hits the switch to turn off the lights. We go back across the lobby, where he pushes me down under the desk. His thinking is clear; he wants to make it look like the office is unoccupied, but he's forgotten about Walsh's office at the end of the hall. The door is still open and light is spilling through. Damon curses, caught between trying to run for Walsh's office to turn off the light or running back across the lobby when the voices of the security guards arrive just outside the door.

Gun still in hand, Damon dives under the desk and crouches in the space next to me as the security guards open the door.

'Hello?' a voice asks.

A flashlight beam cuts through shadows and hits the wall behind the reception desk before pointing toward the opening of the hallway.

'Anyone in here?'

Damon presses the gun against my head. In the ambient light coming through the glass wall, I can see his expression. He's daring me to call out.

I could yell, alerting the guards, but Damon will kill me. I only caught a glimpse of the security guards in the hallway but I don't think they have guns. I'm pretty sure Damon will have enough bullets after killing me to take care of them.

I'm trying to control my breathing. There's no tape over my mouth but the gun against my head is causing my breath to come in spasms through my nose.

The light from the flashlight leaves the opening to the hallway and stops on the wall across from us, just above the level of the desk.

'Hello?' one of the security guards calls out.

Damon slowly puts a finger to his lips.

The gesture is so unsettling, it freezes me in place.

The beam of light hangs there, waiting, as if they know we're here.

With his finger still pressed to his lips, Damon casts a furtive glance back toward the hallway, where the light from Walsh's office still burns.

'Is someone back there?' the security guard asks.

The light contracts a fraction of an inch and there's the sound of a footstep as the security guard takes a step into the reception area.

Damon slowly pulls the gun away from my head and readies himself. He positions his feet underneath him, preparing to stand.

He's made his decision; he's going to shoot his way out.

Without thinking, I pull in a breath. I'm going to yell to warn the security guards before Damon shoots them. Damon hears me as he starts to stand and it causes him to hesitate, just as the silence is cut by the jarring squawk of the security guard's radio.

'Chip? Glen? You copy?' a loud, fuzzy voice asks, as Damon returns to my side, under the desk.

'We're almost done with floor fourteen,' the guard replies. 'Then, we'll head up to fifteen.'

'Negative,' the voice on the radio responds. 'LAPD are here in the lobby. They want you to come down. They're having us tell everyone to lock themselves in their office and hang tight. They'll finish sweeping the building.'

An interminable silence follows.

'Copy that,' the guard says with relief. 'We're on our way down.'

The circle from the flashlight on the wall in front of us cuts out and the door to the hallway closes.

I turn my head to look at Damon.

He has a thousand-yard stare as he contemplates the wall where the beam from the flashlight burned only moments ago.

'They've locked down the building,' I say quietly. 'They're going to find us.'

Damon snaps out of his stupor. He scrambles out from under the desk and stands. He reaches down, pulls me out, and drags me over to the windowed wall to stare down to the street below.

There are four police cars in front of the building and two more at each end of the block, preventing traffic from getting any closer. Their red and blue flashing lights alternate across the surrounding buildings. I crane my neck to the side. There are more police cars approaching.

A sliver of hope begins to burn in my chest.

'It's over,' I say.

Damon turns to me.

The resignation or acceptance that I was hoping to see isn't there. Only defiance.

He grabs me by the collar and pulls me back across the lobby.

'What are you doing?!' I cry, trying to pry his hand away, but his grip is unbreakable.

He slams me against the wall, next to the door.

'Lucas,' he seethes. 'There is something you need to understand.'

He reaches out to the square panel in the wall next to me and pulls the fire alarm.

A shrill, staccato alarm starts screeching and the white reflector light mounted in the corner of the ceiling begins to flash.

'This is over when I say it's over.'

Chapter 28

Damon opens the door to the hallway an inch or two, and waits as the alarms and flashing lights continue.

A handful of doors in the hallway open and people begin spilling out. They look back and forth in confusion before making their way to the stairwell at the far end back by the elevators.

'Okay,' Damon says, amid the lights and alarm. 'Once we go through this door, we are just as confused and concerned as everyone else. We are going to the stairwell and then to the parking garage. I'm going to be right behind you. This gun will be in my pocket, pointed at your back and my finger will be on the trigger. Do not try to run and do not try to warn anyone. Got it?'

I nod in defeat.

'Good. Let's go.'

Damon pulls the door open and we step into the hall to join the flow of humanity heading for the stairs. There's not a ton of people but there are more people than I would expect this late at night.

As we make our way down the hall, one of the office doors opens and a guy pokes his head out.

'What's going on?' he asks a passing woman. 'The security guards called us and said to stay inside because of the gunshots.'

'Yeah, but . . . you know . . . fire alarm,' she answers with a helpless shrug and continues walking toward the stairwell. The guy steps out of the office and falls in with the rest of us.

Another door opens as we pass and a man and woman exit, smoothing out their clothes. The man zips up his fly as he and the woman awkwardly avoid eye contact.

We reach the end of the hallway, where an older man with a beard is holding open the door to the stairwell for everyone to pass through.

Damon and I join the stream of people descending the stairs.

The sound of the alarm is even more punishing in the cramped stairwell as it ricochets off the concrete walls. The cascade of footsteps on the metal stairs sounds like a thundering downpour. Everyone has formed a single-file line with one hand on the railing as we make our way to the ground floor. No one is running. No one is panicking.

'Did you hear the gunshots?' someone asks.

'Is that what's going on?'

'That's why they were telling everyone to stay in the office,' someone else responds.

'Now there's a fire?'

'I have no idea.'

The questions are being asked somewhere above and behind us but I don't want to look for fear of attracting attention. I can feel Damon's eyes boring into the back of my head.

'How long do you think until they let us go back in?'

'Don't know that either.'

'Will they let us back in if there's a fire?'

'There's never a fire.'

'I'm just going to my car and getting out of here. Otherwise, we'll be here all night.'

My feet tangle and I'm almost sent tumbling into the woman walking in front of me, but I grab the rail and keep my balance.

That was Damon.

'Will they let us go to our cars?' a woman asks.

'Will they let us out of the garage?' someone asks.

'They have to,' Damon says. 'When a fire alarm goes off, they open the gates of the parking garage so that people can get out.'

I can't tell if Damon is lying but there are murmurs around us and a few mutterings of 'good idea' as we approach the ground floor.

Quickly leaning over the rail, I can see people exiting into the lobby. As we reach the last few stairs, between the alarm and thunder of footsteps, there's a voice echoing from the lobby into the stairwell, 'This way, folks. Please come this way. We need you to exit right through here.'

No sooner does my foot hit the concrete landing than Damon puts his hand squarely on my back. He's so close, I can practically feel his breath on my ear.

'Keep moving,' he says.

We emerge into the lobby. The drum of footsteps is less than what it was in the stairwell. There's the occasional squeak of a rubber-soled shoe on the marble floor. The red and blue lights of the numerous police cars outside flash through the space. Straight ahead, through the glass wall, I can see that the police cars have been joined by a fire truck. The emergency exits next to the revolving door leading to the street have been thrown open. There are firemen standing next to them, waving the line of people outside to the sidewalk.

I'm about to follow the crowd through the lobby to the exit when Damon grips the back of my shirt.

'Left. Left. Left,' he urges under his breath. 'Same way we came in.'

Damon steers me out of the flow of people toward the door leading to the parking garage.

'Excuse me! Guys!' one of the firemen calls from the front of the lobby. 'We need you to exit this way!'

I turn my head. The fireman stationed next to the door is

staring at us. He takes a few steps away from the door in our direction.

'Don't look,' Damon insists. 'Keep going.'

'Gentlemen, you have to— No! Wait! Everyone! Do not go to the parking garage! We need you to exit this way!'

Voices erupt behind us.

'Go, go, go!'

'Hurry!'

'Keep going!'

It's not the police or firemen. People are falling in behind us as we hustle to the parking garage stairwell.

'Ladies and gentlemen! Please!' the fireman implores, but it's too late.

I press on the crash-bar and the door flies open.

'Go!' Damon shouts.

I begin descending the stairs as quickly as possible.

Behind us, the stairwell fills with the sound of voices and footsteps.

We hit the landing with the door marked 'Level 1' and continue down.

At the next landing, I grab the handle to the door marked 'Level 2' and fling it open.

My car waits only a few steps away.

'Get in!' Damon shouts as he takes out the key fob and hits the unlock button.

I reach the driver door just as he reaches the back door. He tosses the backpack inside and follows it in as I fasten my seatbelt. I look toward the stairwell we just exited. People are pouring out and scrambling for their cars. The whole scene has the resemblance of a jail break.

I hit the ignition, bringing the car to life. We back out of the space and I line up the car to head down the aisle. People cut in and out of our headlights as they bolt for their cars.

'Try not to hit anyone,' Damon says, pulling his phone from

the backpack. 'But if you do, don't stop.'

'. . . right,' I reply, putting the car in drive and heading toward the incline to the first level.

Most of the people running for their cars stay out of our way but I'm forced to hit the brakes once or twice. We head up to the first level, where there are even more people scrambling to get to their cars. I can see the parking gate up ahead. Jimmy, the parking attendant, is gone but sure enough, just as Damon said it would be, the arm of the gate is raised, allowing cars to leave freely.

We drive under the arm and head toward the street but are forced to stop just short of the entrance.

There's a sedan and then an SUV stopped directly in front of us. They're being held up by a policeman who stands with his arms raised.

Damon curses. 'There has to be another way out of the garage. Back up and we'll see if we can—'

A car emerges from the parking garage behind us. It stops right on my rear bumper to the point that the impact sensor starts beeping. More cars fall in behind, creating a line snaking back down into the garage.

We're trapped.

'What do we do?' I ask.

Damon looks back and forth. 'You're going to have to ram him.'

'What?!'

'Ram the car ahead of us! Push them out of the way and then head to the left. We'll make a break for it and try to get back to the highway.'

I motion toward the SUV in front of us. 'I can't push them out of the way!'

'Do it!'

My car is not going to be able to move that SUV, but if we don't get out of here, Damon might decide his only option is to start shooting. There must be more than a dozen cops on the street and they will shoot back.

'Lucas?!'

I can't think of any way to argue. In desperation, I get ready to hit the gas, but stop at the sound of something echoing behind us.

It's the sound of horns.

'Lucas, I told you to—'

'Wait!'

The sound steadily builds, like an approaching train. It reaches the car behind us, and they begin to lay on their horn, as does the car and SUV in front of us.

'What are you waiting for?!' Damon asks. 'Ram him!'

'Hold on!'

The cop holding us up is trying to placate the driver of the sedan, insisting that they can't leave.

The chorus of horns behind us continues to build and is suddenly reinforced by angry voices.

'Come on! Let us go!'

I glance in the side-view mirror. People are leaning out of their windows, yelling at the cop.

'What the hell are you doing?' the driver behind us rages. 'Get out of the way!'

'You're really trying to keep us in a building where there's a fire?' someone further back screams, amplified by the concrete walls, ceiling, and floor.

'We need everyone to sit tight!' the cop implores.

Damon rolls down his window and sticks his head out. 'Come on! Just let us out!'

The poor cop turns toward the knot of officers standing on the sidewalk, next to the exit of the parking garage and gestures, asking for guidance.

One of the officers, a man with a gray mustache, glares at the line of cars and throws up his hands as if to say, 'We don't have time for this.' He motions for the cop to stand aside.

The now grateful cop takes a step back to allow the lead car to pull forward and then instructs them to head left.

Possibly worried that someone in charge might change their mind, the lead car hits the gas and lurches forward, causing the tires to squeal and the cop to flinch. The car makes the turn left and heads down the street. It has to stop as the two cop cars blocking off the end of the street move apart, allowing them to pass. The SUV in front of us follows suit.

We pull forward for our turn to exit, and my headlights illuminate the cop's tired face.

I want to point at Damon and yell, 'This is the guy you're looking for! He's right here!' but I know his gun is still pointed at me. Instead, I mouth 'thank you,' as we make the turn out of the garage.

He gives me a wan smile and a tight nod, looking appreciative that someone showed him a kindness amid the mess.

We slowly pass between the two cop cars at the intersection. The officers step out of their cars and stare back at the building, taking no note of us.

My shoulders sag. We made it out without Damon killing anyone else, but he did kill Walsh and I helped him escape. Does that make me an accomplice? Should I feel guilty or should I feel satisfied that I stopped him from killing anyone else?

It's only after we've gone a few blocks, when the lights from the police cars and fire trucks are no longer visible and traffic begins to build, that I realize Damon hasn't said a word.

I find him in the rearview mirror. He's got the gun in one hand and his phone in the other, but he's staring at me with unbridled rage.

'Pull over.'

Chapter 29

My moral dilemma is over, replaced by a simple, furious question: Why is he pissed at me now?

I didn't go along with Walsh's plan to rush him. Granted, that wasn't really his plan. He intended for me to rush Damon while he made a break for it. I had thought about it, but in the end, I didn't do it. I didn't get in his way when he killed Walsh. I stood against the wall as he threw him out the window. Well, to be clear, I didn't stand against the wall. I crouched down, turned away, and had my hands over my ears, but the point is, I didn't try to stop him. Also, I didn't try to warn anybody as we made our escape through the hall, down the stairs, across the lobby, and out of the parking garage. I kept my mouth shut and did as he said.

So, what exactly is his problem?

I turn at the next intersection onto a side street and slow as I search for a parking spot.

'No! Not here,' Damon bites out.

'You told me to pull over!'

'Not here! Keep heading north.'

'Make up your mind!' I rage. 'Do you want me to pull over or keep—'

'Just follow my instructions, Lucas.'

'I am, goddammit!' I shout. 'What the fuck is wrong with you?!'

We have a brief standoff as we stare at one another in the rearview mirror. He's still got the gun in one hand and his phone in the other.

Damon grits his teeth. 'Go north two more blocks and we'll find a place.'

I turn left at the next intersection, taking us off of Sunset, and head north.

'Turn right up here,' Damon instructs.

I didn't catch the name of the street, but it holds more gas stations and liquor stores. You would never guess that we were only two blocks north of Sunset Boulevard.

We've only gone a few yards when Damon suddenly erupts, 'Here! Turn here and pull over!'

His instructions are so sudden that I have to wrench the wheel over before I can hit the brakes. Damon is nearly thrown across the back seat and the tires squeal in protest, but we make the turn onto the empty, darkened street. It's not much more than an alley.

'Stop the car!'

I stomp on the brake, causing the anti-lock brake system to engage. My seatbelt catches and throws me back. Just as before, the unbuckled Damon hits the back of the seat behind me. It wasn't my intention to do that, but I'll take it.

'Cut the engine,' Damon says, after collecting himself.

I press the button and the engine stops.

'Now get out of the car!' Damon rages.

I unclip my belt and fling it away with such force that when it smacks into the window next to me, I'm worried it cracked, but a momentary inspection shows it's still intact. I grab the handle on the door, throw it open, and storm out.

Damon exits from the back seat, still holding the gun and his phone, and joins me in the alley. I stand next to the car while he takes a few steps, turns, and aims the gun at me.

'You were going to do it,' he says, tightly gripping the gun.

'Do what?!'

'You were going to rush me, like Walsh told you to do!'

'No, I wasn't!' I lie.

'You were going to!'

'No, I wasn't and in case you haven't noticed: I DIDN'T!'

He laughs in disbelief.

Walsh's words ring in my head; he's losing control.

'And the security guards?' Damon asks. 'Are you going to tell me that you weren't about to warn them before the radio went off?'

'But I didn't!' It takes me a second longer to respond, because he's right, so I add, 'And I got us out of the parking garage.'

'What are you talking about?'

'That SUV in front of us. We were stuck. You wanted me to ram him but I told you to wait. If I had done what you told me to do, we would both be dead right now.'

'Oh, please. We would have—'

'There were a dozen cops on that street!' I shout, the words pouring out of me, fueled by anger and adrenaline. 'There's no way we would have made it out. If I'd have done what you told me to do and rammed that SUV, they would have found you, and they would have shot you, and probably me, too! I got us out of there! I saved you, dammit! And you lied to me!'

'I never lied to y—'

'You used me as bait, again! You told Walsh you were bringing someone.'

'I had to say there was a plus one to get you through security! I couldn't leave you in the car! I never said I was bringing him someone to have sex with! He just assumed it because that's what these guys do!'

We stare at one another.

I need him to acknowledge that I got us out of the garage. I need him to acknowledge that I'm going along with his plan and that I'm keeping Julia and Sophia safe. I need to hear that from him right now.

Instead, he sighs in frustration and motions with the gun. 'Turn around.'

'What?'

'Turn around and put your hands on the roof of the car.'

'What are you going to do?' I ask, my blood still boiling. 'Shoot me?'

'No, Lucas. I'm not going to shoot you. I'm going to make a phone call. Now, turn around and put your hands on the roof. I've still got the keys, so don't try to go anywhere.'

I furiously stare at him.

He starts to dial but sees that I haven't moved. 'Get your hands on the fucking roof!'

My whole body is shaking as I turn and place my hands on the roof of the car.

Damon moves behind me. I look over my shoulder to see that he's taken a few steps away, as if he'd like some privacy for whatever call he's making.

'Yes,' Damon says, quietly into the phone. 'I'm calling about the shooting in the building on Sunset Boulevard . . . Yes, I know the police are already there, but you need to send them to the fourteenth floor, office number one-four-three-five . . .'

I want to correct him and say that they'll find Walsh on the sidewalk below, but stop.

There, through the window that's still open from when Damon yelled at the cop at the entrance to the parking garage, lying on the back seat, is the open backpack, and inside are the two remaining envelopes.

I don't give a damn about his warnings. He can threaten me all he wants but I need to know what's in them. I need to know why he's killing these men. I need to know why my family is in danger.

I quickly reach my hand through the open window and into the backpack. I pull out one of the envelopes, open the flap, reach inside, and extract the stack of papers. Although the alley is dim, there's more than enough ambient light from the surrounding buildings, streetlamps, and signs to see clearly.

The stack clears the envelope and I stare at the first page.

It's an actor's headshot. The image of a young woman. If I had to guess, I'd say she's in her very early twenties. Her raven black hair cascades down over her shoulders. Her eyes are a piercing blue. Her smile is vibrant, joyous, and playful.

She's impossibly beautiful.

With Damon still speaking quietly behind me, I quickly flip to the next page.

It's another photo, but of lesser quality, like it's been blown up from a phone. It's the same young woman, but she's posing with a group of men. I recognize Henford and Walsh. They look to be in a massive living room with white stucco walls, red-tiled floor, and leather couches. There's a coffee table in front of them with bottles of booze.

I flip to the next paper and my heart stops.

The young woman is naked. The awkwardness, fear, and unease are apparent in her face despite her attempt at a smile. The men are all still standing around her, posing with ludicrous smiles and thumbs-up, like it's some college spring break picture.

I flip to the next picture.

It's her on her knees in front of Walsh, whose pants are down.

Revolted, I flip to the next picture, which I immediately regret.

Now, she's with two of the men who I don't recognize. Bodies exposed. Limbs tangled with the girl. The men are flushed, smiling at the camera.

I hurriedly flip, again.

It's her and another man, but I stop . . . because I recognize him. I'm not sure there are many people on this planet who wouldn't recognize him with that trademark mop of blond hair. He's now in command. Just him and the woman. He's completely nude. His expression is savage, as is what he's doing. In the background is the figure of an older man, sitting on one of the couches, watching, clearly entertained.

My stomach flips as I go to the next image. My brain doesn't realize that I can just stop looking. Each page just brings more and more flesh and more and more degradation but what brings on the strongest sense of horror isn't the acts in each successive image.

It's her eyes.

It's the sadness. The fear. The surrender.

I finally reach the end and those eyes are staring back at me, pleading, sad, helpless.

That's when it hits me. I understand and am hit by the same horrible realization that came to Walsh and Henford.

I flip back to the headshot.

The hair. The eyes. The jawline.

This young woman could be the daughter of only one person.

No sooner have I connected the dots than Damon emits something between a roar and a primal scream.

A hand grabs my shoulder and spins me around. A fist slams into my jaw with such force that my knees buckle. The photos fall from my hand and scatter across the alley.

I slide down against the car and collapse on the asphalt.

I'm looking up at the stars but my vision is swimming until Damon is standing over me.

His eyes are crazed and his teeth are bared as he forcefully presses the gun to my forehead.

He's going to shoot me.

In that moment, as my senses flail, still trying to recover from Damon's punch, I look up at him, past the gun, and I see the eyes of someone I've only seen once before. They're the eyes of someone who has endured a loss with which they cannot come to grips nor can they move on. Before, I was too young to recognize it, but now, I know. All I can think to say are the words I wish I would have said when I saw that in my father.

'I'm so sorry.'

Damon's expression eases and he and I see each other.

He slowly pulls the gun away from my forehead. He's staring

at me in shock and bewilderment, as though he's never heard those words before.

The rest of my senses are starting to return. The left side of my face feels tight as I try to work my chin back and forth.

Our attentions are suddenly ripped away by the sound of approaching sirens.

Damon looks back toward the opening to the alley.

The sirens build and the walls at the opening to the alley are faintly illuminated by flashing red and blue lights. Damon takes a few steps toward the opening. He plants his feet and raises the gun as the sound of the sirens grows.

The flashing lights intensify. The sirens are almost on top of us.

I pull myself into a sitting position and try to stand but my balance isn't working just yet. I'm forced to crawl to the front of the car, away from Damon and the approaching sirens. If he intends to make a last stand, here in this alley, I have to find cover before the bullets start flying.

I get myself around the front of the car and look back toward Damon, who is standing motionless with the gun raised.

The first cop car appears, but only as a blur as it rockets past the entrance to the alley, followed by three more cop cars, also racing by.

The lights and the sirens quickly fade.

Damon is frozen, still aiming the gun down the alley.

He lowers the gun. He turns and walks back toward me as I use the car to steady myself and stand. He collects the photos from the ground and returns them to the envelope. He reaches in through the open window, grabs the backpack, stuffs the envelope inside, and throws it back through the window onto the back seat before turning to me.

I'm still a little woozy, but my feet are solid beneath me.

Damon watches me for a moment.

'Are you okay to drive?' he asks.

I briefly consider saying no in the hope that he'll leave me here, but then I remember that I have to stay with him for Julia and Sophie.

'If you can't drive,' Damon continues, 'I'm going to have to zip-tie your wrists again and put you in the backsea—'

'I'm fine. I can drive,' I quickly answer. I need to stay as mobile as possible. I'm still hoping for the chance to stop him in a way that won't get me killed or give him the chance to escape.

'Are you sure?' he asks.

'Yeah,' I reply, rubbing my aching jaw.

Damon is about to say something. Maybe even apologize. It's right there in his face but instead he says, 'Okay. Let's keep moving.'

He turns and opens the driver door for me before getting into the back seat.

I guess it's the closest to an apology that I'm going to get.

Chapter 30

It's midnight. We're back on the road heading west, but keeping to the side streets to avoid any encounters with the police. The trade-off is that we're moving at a crawl. Every intersection brings a stop sign or traffic light. On the occasion that we fall in behind someone, there's no opportunity to pass. We have to adjust to their speed until they turn off our route.

And Damon is rattled.

For the first couple minutes after exiting the alley, every time we stopped at a stop sign or traffic light, he would peer in every direction, searching for police cars. He would have me wait until he deemed that the coast was clear, but as we've put more distance between us and the building on Sunset, he's grown quiet and his paranoia has lessened.

Now, he's just staring out the window.

Every few moments, he'll shake his head, as though denying a memory. Other times, his lips will purse and his face will tighten in a flash of anger.

Wherever his mind is, it's a very, *very* dark place.

I know he didn't want me to see those photos. He wouldn't want anyone to see those photos, except for the men he's punishing to confront them with what they did, but I can't stop thinking about them. The cruelty and horror of those images are seared into my brain; the savage joy of the men and the sadness and hopelessness in the eyes of the young girl is burned into my mind.

I also can't get past the fact that I recognized the man with the mop of blond hair. He appeared to be the ringleader, making the most appearances in the photos, and relishing his demeaning acts upon her.

His name is Alex Northrup – Hollywood's new wunderkind director. He burst onto the scene a few years ago after a short film he wrote and directed won nearly every award at Cannes. Since then, he's won two Oscars for a film he wrote and directed called *Paper Cut*. He's been praised for being bold and edgy. One prominent film critic called him 'a new voice that forces us to recontextualize the use of violence in cinema,' or something like that. In the interviews I've seen, he's always brash and egotistical, quick to give his unflattering opinion of other directors. Lots of people love the few films he's made while others loathe him. I thought they were pretty good, but now, all I can see is the face in those photos.

And that girl.

More than the acts I saw in those pictures, I will see those eyes.

Before, I wanted to know what Damon was doing and why in the hope that it would help me work against him. That's still the case, but now, a part of me simply needs to know.

'Who is she?' I finally ask.

Damon, his face still toward the window, doesn't answer. He merely closes his eyes.

That's when I understand and have to correct my question.

'Who was she?'

He sighs and slowly opens his eyes.

'Chloe . . . Her name was Chloe . . .' Damon says, a sad smile pulling at the corner of his lips and adds, 'She was named after her grandmother.' There's nothing threatening about Damon in this moment. Only sadness. His eyes are still toward the window, but

176

that's not what he's seeing. He's watching memories and snapshots in his head. 'That little girl meant everything to me. You hear all these corny, sappy clichés about having a child, stuff like "it's your heart walking around outside your body" or "you never knew you could feel a love like that" . . . They *are* corny, but damn, are they true.'

'What happened?' I ask.

He hesitates, unsure about continuing, but then leans back.

'Her mother left us when she was two. I was a single dad, raising a daughter on a cop's salary . . .'

He pauses and a lot of my questions are answered as the pieces fall into place: his knowledge of break-ins, that the parking gate would open during a fire alarm, his use of firearms and how to subdue Walsh.

'Is that what you meant before?' I ask. 'About being Sherlock Holmes in another life?'

'Yeah, but I may have been giving myself a little too much credit. I was just your average cop . . . But being a cop, you see people at their absolute worst. You can get jaded real quick, but raising Chloe changed me. She taught me to have more empathy, to have more patience . . .' Damon smiles. 'Unless she told me that someone at school was picking on her. Then I would burn the world down to find them.' His smile fades. 'Raising her was the craziest, most frustrating, most humbling, most amazing thing I've ever done. I wanted to protect her from everything in this world . . . and even some of the things at home.'

'What do you mean?'

'We were broke. I loved being a cop, but it's not like the money was pouring in. I needed to start saving up for her college, and everything else. I wanted to give her everything she wanted. I put in a ton of overtime. I was constantly pleading with babysitters because of the hours I worked. I pulled in every favor I could. Like I said, I loved my job, but I tried to get into some other line of work with better pay so I could have more time with Chloe while still giving her everything she wanted, but in the end, I wasn't cut out for anything else. Hell, I couldn't even take a day off.' He shakes his head. 'But even though the pay was shit, the benefits were pretty good. I mean, when Chloe was twelve, her appendix ruptured. She started to go septic and there were a couple hours where the doctors didn't know if it would go one way or the other and I . . .' The words catch in his throat. 'That was the most terrifying night of my life.' Damon has to collect himself before he shakes it off. 'That's the one thing the sappy clichés don't mention.'

'What's that?'

'Yes, it's like your heart walking around outside your body and yes, you've never felt the love that you will feel for your child, but if they're in danger and there's nothing you can do for them, you'll experience fear and helplessness that you never knew was possible.'

He remains silent for a few seconds.

'Where were you from?' I ask.

'Minnesota,' Damon answers, looking out toward the passing apartment buildings that are gradually being replaced by houses. 'She loved the snow . . . And she loved to play. That girl had the craziest imagination. The places, the characters, the *ideas* she would come up with. You would not believe that she was only five years old. I never felt luckier than when she asked me to play with her. I got to be monsters. I got to be princes and kings. I got to go to space. I got to visit other worlds. I was a hero all because she wanted to play. That was her escape. It was mine, too.'

It's as if Damon's forgotten where we are, where we're heading, and what he's done. He's just a father, bragging about his child. Then, he leans slightly forward as he has a thought.

'And she was beautiful. I know every parent says that about their child, and sure, all children are beautiful, but I knew when Chloe was about ten. I said to myself, "Oh no. She's going to be stunning." I dreaded her growing up for all the normal reasons a parent dreads it, but I began to live in mortal fear of the day she discovered boys . . . and the day they discovered her.'

I'm caught between listening to his story and watching the road. He's distracted and now could be the perfect time if we came across a police car, but Damon's plan of keeping to the side roads to avoid them is working.

'But that imagination of hers? It never went away,' he continues. 'Chloe loved to read. She loved writing little stories. She kept playing pretend even after her friends grew out of it. Then, when she was fourteen, I took her to see a production of *Cinderella* . . . and that was it. She knew right then and there what she wanted to be. From that moment on, Chloe was going to be an actress. She—' His throat catches, again. 'I was so happy. I was so happy that *she* was happy and excited and ambitious and I encouraged her, but man, those fears in me started to grow. I got her acting lessons. We went to more plays, but all the while, I kept praying that it was just a phase. That at some point, acting would be downgraded to a hobby, but it wasn't. She took to acting like a duck to water. From then on, she was cast in the lead of all her school plays. She would film movies on her phone. All the while, she was growing into a beautiful young woman . . . but to me, she was always going to be my little girl.'

The automated voice comes over the speakers, instructing me to turn at the next intersection, which I do. The houses are growing larger and more lavish.

The interruption breaks Damon's narrative and he checks my phone. I want to keep him talking not only so that he's distracted, but because I honestly want to know more.

'How did she end up out here, in Los Angeles?' I ask.

'When it was time for her to go to college, she wanted to major in acting but I told her she had to double-major in something else, too, just to be safe. I had no problem paying for it. I mean, what's a couple more tens of thousands of dollars of debt when it's for your child's dream, right?' Damon's voice lowers. 'Chloe thought I was insisting on her getting a double-major because I didn't believe in her. I told her that wasn't it at all. I tried to explain that I was doing it to protect her. I tried to get her to understand how hard it was to become an actor, but she wouldn't listen. It was the first time we really fought. I mean, we had fought before over things like curfews and when she couldn't have boys over, but this was real. I couldn't make her see that I was trying to do what was best for her . . . Maybe that was a mistake. Maybe if I had just let her major in acting, none of this would have happened, but I couldn't back down.

'So she went off to college and, just like high school, she was cast in everything. She was surrounded by people telling her how great she was and that she was going to be an actress or a model. That she had *it*. Her junior year, she started talking about dropping out of college and moving to Los Angeles. I told her absolutely not. She had to wait until she graduated. After that, she could do whatever she wanted. She argued with me, asking why she couldn't do it now? I told her again about the odds against making it as an actress, but she still thought it was because I didn't believe in her.' He's forced to stop and collect himself. 'It's really hard when your child, who you've invested everything in, who you have sacrificed so much for, is upset because they think you don't believe in them.

'She kept telling me that everyone at school said she was going to be a great actress and in a moment of frustration, I said, "Yes – everyone in Minnesota."' Damon has become more animated as he's been speaking, but now it's as if he suddenly deflates. 'That was it. There was no coming back from that. I had really hurt her. I didn't mean to. I was trying to protect her, but she couldn't see that . . .'

The automated voice has me turning back onto Sunset Boulevard. Damon is either too distracted or maybe he no longer cares that we're back on a main road. I glance around for any police cars but there are none to be seen as we pass the sign announcing our entrance into Beverly Hills.

'Her junior year, we were talking less and less,' Damon continues, seemingly lost in thought. 'She spent the next summer at a repertory theater in upstate New York. She didn't give me any updates, but I finally was able to take some time off of work and I went to see her play Viola in *Twelfth Night.*' He beams at the memory. 'She was so great. She was alive on that stage and I was so proud of her. I brought her this huge bouquet of flowers and waited after the show, but she . . . She wasn't happy to see me. She didn't want the flowers. She told me that I shouldn't have come if I didn't think she could make it as an actress. That was the breaking point. After everything I had done, the debts I had run up paying for her college, and after all the times I tried to explain to her that I was only trying to protect her – and then she says that to me? I was so angry . . . Kids will do that to you, sometimes.' He lightly laughs and grows quiet. 'We had a massive blowout. I said things I shouldn't have. Things I couldn't take back. She said some things, but that doesn't matter. I was her father and I screwed up.

'She didn't come home before going back to college for her senior year. And for the first time since she started college, she didn't come home for Thanksgiving. I didn't push it because I was still trying to apologize for what had happened. I thought it might be best to give her some space. It got to the point that we were hardly talking at all, and when I asked how school was going, she would get really quiet and evasive . . .' Damon takes a deep breath. 'Then, about a week before Christmas, she called me. She was sobbing. She told me that she hadn't gone back to school. She was here, in Los Angeles. She had dropped out and run away to become an actress. She was renting a room in an apartment with two other girls. She had gotten some headshots and was submitting for auditions. I didn't know how she was getting by. She didn't tell me, but she'd connected with a manager who told her that he could get her a part in a new movie with a famous director and producer . . . but there was something she had to do. Something she had to do for him and for the agent and the writer of the movie and the producer and the director, as well. Something that was just part of the business in Hollywood. All the young starlets did it and if Chloe did it, she would be a star in this new movie . . . So, she did . . . Only to find out afterwards that there was no movie. It was just a game these guys played with young women who were hoping for their big break . . . and they took photos. They sent her the photos and said that if she ever told anyone, they would release the pictures . . .

'That's when she called me. To hear your little girl so hurt and so sad . . . She apologized to me. She apologized for being so stupid and she apologized for how disappointed I must be in her. I told her that I wasn't disappointed in her and that I loved her and that everything was going to be okay . . . but her voice – I knew . . . I knew what she was thinking of doing and I told her that I'd be on the next flight to Los Angeles and to wait but by the time I got here, my girl was gone . . .

'To everyone else in this town, she was one more dreamer who didn't make it. A failure that makes everyone else who succeeds that much more special . . .' Damon's face darkens. 'But I had her phone. I had the photos. It took me two years to identify everyone in them. Can you imagine that? Can you imagine having to look at those photos every day for two years? Every day, looking at what they did to her? What I'm doing tonight is two years of tracking down these guys and planning. It became the only thing in my life that mattered.'

The automated voice has me turn north from Sunset Boulevard and into the mansions that make up Beverly Hills.

But something isn't making sense.

'I . . . There's something I don't understand.'

Damon comes back to the present. 'What?'

'You said two writers, the agent, producer, and director . . .'

'Yes.'

'That's five people.'

'Your point?' Damon asks.

'You killed three people where I picked you up, and you've killed three more, and now we're heading to—'

'There are more people involved, Lucas. I'm sorry if I only gave you the abbreviated version of the story,' he says. He's not really sorry, just dismissive.

'But . . . Why would they send her photos with their faces?'

'That was a screw-up by the manager,' Damon says. 'Guy named R.J. Castillo. He was our stop in Mar Vista where you were in the trunk. He was supposed to crop out the faces of everyone involved except Chloe, but he had a bit of a drinking problem and sent the photos to Chloe unedited. When the rest of the guys found out, they stepped up the threats against her, letting her know what would happen if she didn't keep quiet.'

'And the house where I picked you up?' I ask. 'Who was there?'

Damon sighs. 'The writer. Well, one of them, anyway. A guy named Scott Graham.'

We're now deep into Beverly Hills. These are the palaces and mansions people think of when they hear the name.

I know I shouldn't say a thing, but I can't take the silence and there's a thought that's eating at me.

'Look, I'm not going to even pretend to know what something like this does to a father, but these guys, yes, they're horrible and they should be in prison but you're *murdering* them.'

'Are you saying they don't deserve it?' Damon asks.

'I don't know. I just think—'

'Wait about two weeks.'

'Why? What happens in two weeks?'

'You'll have a daughter.'

'You suddenly care about that?' I ask. 'You suddenly care whether I get to meet my daughter?'

The sadness that's been haunting Damon as he's told his story fades away and he glares at me. 'That is up to you, Lucas. It's been up to you all night.'

'Says the guy who a few minutes ago was going to shoot me in the head while I lay on the ground in an alley.'

'Yes, I was – and I still will if you screw this up.' He leans forward. 'Let me make this clear, Lucas: we did not just share a moment. I did not want to tell you what happened to my daughter, but now that you know, you should more clearly understand what I am willing to do to make sure these guys pay. Earlier, you accused me of being one of those people who will go through anyone to get what I want, and yes, I am. I have become that kind of person and I will go through you if I have to.'

He sits back.

I keep my focus on the road ahead. There is a long silence.

'The photos . . .'

'What about them?' he asks.

'I recognized Walsh and Henford . . . But one of the others . . . I recognized him. That's Alex Northrup. The director?'

'Yes,' Damon says, and begins prepping by going through the backpack. 'And he's our next stop.'

'Who's the older guy in the background?' I ask. 'The one who is just sitting there the whole time?'

'He's not just sitting there,' Damon says. 'And let's worry about one stop at a time.'

Chapter 31

The Mission-style mansion, with its stucco walls and red clay tiled roof, is massive, spanning nearly the entire width of the property.

It's illuminated from below by lights hidden in the bushes, giving the house the look of a fortress, but as Damon and I stare across the wide, manicured lawn to the house, I can tell he senses the same thing I do. Something is wrong.

While the accent lights in the bushes are glowing, there's not a single light on in the house.

'All right,' Damon finally says. 'Hands behind your back.'

I snap out of staring at the house. 'What?'

'Get your hands behind your back. I need to bind your wrists.'

'You don't need to do that,' I protest.

'Yes, I do. I made the mistake of letting it slide with Walsh. I'm not making that mistake again.'

I look down at the waiting zip tie in his hand. I can try to fight him, but I don't want him to hit me. My head still hurts from our first stop when he smacked the back of my head with the gun to get the zip ties on my wrists. My face is throbbing from the punch he delivered to my jaw, which suddenly reminds me of what comes after he zip-ties my wrists.

'No duct tape,' I suddenly blurt out.

'Excuse me?'

'I'll let you zip-tie my wrists, but no duct tape over my mouth this time. I need to be able to breathe.'

My attempt to bargain leaves him momentarily speechless.

'Fine. I don't have time to beat you into submission again and I need you to be able to walk. Let's go. Wrists behind your back.'

I lean forward, twist my torso, and press my wrists together behind my back, which causes me to face the house as Damon secures the zip tie.

'Are you sure he's even here?' I ask.

'Trust me,' Damon says, pulling the tab to tighten the plastic around my wrists. 'He's in there.'

Damon checks that the zip tie is secure, grabs the backpack, and exits the car. He opens my door and helps me out into the street.

After closing the car doors, he clamps his hand on the back of my neck, plants the gun in the small of my back, and we begin making our way across the lawn.

As the structure looms larger, the feeling that something is off only grows.

Halfway across the lawn, Damon suddenly pulls me to a stop.

Every suspicion I have is confirmed as I follow his gaze and see that the heavy front door to the house is wide open, waiting for us.

Damon peers into the darkness beyond the door and scans the lifeless windows of the house.

'We can't go in there,' I say.

Damon stares intently at the door.

'That? That right there?' I say, nodding. 'That is a trap.'

Damon surveys the house one last time, resolutely sets his jaw and says, 'I know.'

He reapplies the pressure to my neck and digs the gun into my back, prodding me forward.

We finish crossing the lawn, step onto the porch, and slowly pass through the door into darkness.

Once inside, Damon applies more pressure, forcing me into a

semi-crouch while aiming the gun over my shoulder. He waits, listening for any sign of life. He then quickly closes the door behind us and throws the deadbolt, locking us in. The sound echoes through the entrance hall, off the tile floor, and into the pitch-black overhead. His message to whoever is waiting for us is clear: *You're locked in with me.*

As we wait for the sound to fade, the cavernous space comes into shadowed focus. There are staircases to the left and right, curving graciously up to a walkway on the second floor. The staircases form an arched entrance that leads to a larger space, where I can make out a faint, flickering light being cast from somewhere off to the left.

Damon waits a few moments longer, but the house remains still. He uses the hand on the back of my neck to keep me in that semi-crouch while once again aiming the gun over my shoulder as he guides me at an agonizingly slow pace toward the entranceway formed by the staircases.

My eyes continue to adjust to the darkness and as we get closer to the entranceway, I can see that there are shelves on either side, upon which rest the two Oscars Alex Northrup won for *Paper Cut*. There are also a few Golden Globes and countless other awards that I don't recognize.

We pass under the staircases into a large sitting area. I can make out plush couches, chairs, and statues. The space is open to the second level and there are hallways going off to the left and right. Straight ahead, the back wall is one massive window, looking out to the pool in the backyard. The only sound is that of my breathing, which I'm trying to stifle. If this is a trap, Damon is my best and only protection.

We stop in the center of the space and it hits me. I recognize where we are. This is where it happened. This is the room from the photos. Damon keeps sweeping the walls and the walkway that lines the upper level with the gun. Once he's satisfied that there's no one above us, he focuses on the hallways that go off to our left and right. The one to the right is pitch black. There is a faint, flickering glow coming from the hallway on the left.

Damon moves us through the leather couches, chairs, and tables toward the hallway with the faint light. Every few steps, he'll look back to prevent anyone from sneaking up behind us. As we pass between the last leather couch and table before we reach the entrance to the hall, he performs another quick check while keeping his hand on my back. I'm still crouch-walking with my hands bound behind my back and his quick turn causes me to stumble. My shin slams into the corner of the heavy table. It sounds like a car crash in the silent house. A cry nearly escapes my lips but Damon quickly throws his hand over my mouth and uses the leverage to keep me from falling. I sink my teeth into my bottom lip and fight the scream of pain back into my chest as my shin throbs.

Damon doesn't move. He keeps his hand on my mouth and the gun aimed down the hallway toward the flickering light as he waits for me to collect myself.

Finally, I nod to let him know I've got it under control.

He slowly releases his hand from my mouth and returns it to my back as I take a few silent breaths. I reflexively look down at my shin, as if there's more information it'll tell me, and notice the table. I motion to Damon and he looks down, as well.

The flickering light is reflected in a large mirrored tray sitting on the table. Resting on the tray is a razor blade, a metal straw, a baggie, and multiple lines of white powder. It's clear from the arrangement of the lines that there used to be more.

Someone was having a hell of a party before we arrived.

Damon tenses behind me. He does another quick sweep of the surrounding shadows, tightens his grip, and resumes guiding me to the hall.

The hallway goes on for thirty or so feet before turning to the right. That's where the light is coming from. The flickering light makes it easier to see, but there's not much to take in; only the closed doors that line this section of the hall.

Damon slows me down as we pass the doors, aiming the gun at each, waiting for someone to throw them open and attack, but they remain closed.

He has us stop before we make the turn and silently pushes me up against the wall. He then moves ahead, pressing his back against the wall next to me as he carefully leans his head around the corner. He does it one more time, taking a longer look, before finally stepping away from the wall and into the open, aiming the gun somewhere I can't see. He remains motionless for a few seconds and then pulls me away from the wall and over to him. He gets me back in the semi-crouch position and I can now see that the flickering light is coming from a partially open door at the end of the hall.

We resume slowly moving forward. Damon grips the back of my neck and keeps me crouched. He continues to check behind us as the door with the light grows nearer.

We finally arrive at the door and stop. Damon listens intently but there isn't a sound as the light continues to flicker.

He waits for a second longer and then kicks the door open. He applies more pressure and pushes me down further with one hand while sweeping the interior of the room with the gun in the other before guiding me inside.

It's a home theater, but not like the kind you'd find in someone's living room or basement. It's a scaled-down theater in this man's home. There are about a dozen rows of oversized plush leather recliners with small tables in between them. Art deco sconces line the walls and red curtains frame the screen at the front of the room.

But none of this registers.

All I can see is the screen, upon which are projected the photos from the envelope; the photos of what they did to Chloe. They're cycling through, one after the other in a nightmarish presentation.

Damon's eyes are wide and full of hate and revulsion as he

guides me down the aisle next to the wall, past the rows of recliners. We stop in front of the screen. Our shadows block out a small portion of the projection. It's sickening to know that, because of where we're standing, the images are being projected on us. Damon stares in horror at the screen. His pain is evident.

I cast my eyes down to the floor. I don't want to see these images again. Ever. Once was a million times too many.

Damon's breath quickens as he comes out of his stupor. 'We need to g—'

Suddenly, a third shadow rises, nearly blotting out the entire screen. It's accompanied by the unmistakable sound of the racking of a shotgun.

Damon shoves me to the ground and dives in the opposite direction just as the blast fills the theater and the section of screen where we were standing is ripped to shreds by buckshot.

'THAT'S RIGHT, MOTHERFUCKERS!' roars a voice from the back of the theater. 'YOU THINK YOU CAN COME INTO MY HOUSE AND FUCK WITH ME?!!! YOU THINK YOU CAN FUCK WITH ALEX FUCKING NORTHRUP?!!!'

The voice is screeching, hysterical, and has started moving down the aisle toward me.

'COME ON! LET'S DO THIS!!!' Northrup shrieks. 'YOU CAME TO DANCE?!!! LET'S FUCKING DANCE!!!'

There's another eruption from the shotgun and the top of the recliner above me is ripped away. Shreds of stuffing fall to the ground and dust kicks out of the wall behind me.

I look across the floor just in time to see Damon, gun in hand and backpack across his back, arm-crawl around the opposite corner of the recliners and disappear, leaving me lying on the floor, wrists bound behind my back, as this coked-up psychopath approaches.

'Get out here!' Northrup shouts as he continues moving down the aisle where Damon and I walked moments ago.

There's another rack of the shotgun.

'COME ON, YOU PIECE OF SHIT!!!'

He stops. There's no sound.

Then, Northrup's voice drops to a menacing growl.

'I know who you are, shitbird. You're the dad, right?'

He's getting closer. I try to quietly wriggle away across the floor to follow Damon around the far corner, but I'll never make it before Northrup reaches the front of the theater. He's going to find me.

'You think you're some kind of badass?' Northrup asks, closer still. 'Would it piss you off to know that your little girl was nothing special? I don't even remember her name. I've had dozens. More of them arrive in this city every fucking day. Don't get me wrong, she was good, but it's going to be so much more fun blowing your fucking head off . . .'

He's at the next to last row. His mop of blond hair appears above the recliner. I'm on my back, trying lamely to slide away across the carpeted floor.

Suddenly, Northrup whips around the last row of recliners, swinging the shotgun to his shoulder. His eyes are wild. His breathing is rapid.

The barrel of the shotgun is pointing right at my face. Dust plays through the rays of light as the images continue cycling on the screen and across Northrup's upper torso.

'Who the fuck are you?' he asks, and then notices that my hands are behind my back. 'You're the dude he's got tied up, aren't you?'

I forget everything that is happening and stare at him in shock. How does he know who I am? How does he know who Damon is? How did he know we were coming?

'Where is he?' Northrup asks.

'I – I – I don't know!'

Northrup brings the gun to his shoulder, looks down the barrel at me, and screams, 'WHERE IS HE?!!! And don't lie to me or I'll blow your fucking face off, man!!!'

'I'm telling you, I don't know!' I plead.

His mouth splits into a mocking sneer. 'You don't know?' he scoffs. 'Then what good are you?'

He sights down the barrel and is about to pull the trigger when there's a sound at the back of the theater.

Northrup spins toward the sound and fires the shot that was meant for me.

Just as the gun kicks against his shoulder, there's a flash of movement behind him. I barely make out Damon's face as he emerges from the darkness behind the row of recliners. A split second later, he's on Northrup. Damon grabs the barrel of the shotgun and wrenches it to the side. Northrup screams and tries to turn to face him. Damon turns with him, attempting to keep the gun away as they draw in close together. They're suddenly face to face with the shotgun pinned between them. There's another blast. One of them lets out a sharp cry, but I can't tell who as they're pressed together. Northrup is fueled by cocaine, but Damon knows every pressure point. He's able to use Northrup's own thrashing movements against him. Northrup tries to swing the butt of the shotgun at Damon's face, but he easily avoids it and counters by striking his thumb into Northrup's eye. Northrup cries out and the shotgun clatters to the floor.

In one swift motion, Damon moves to Northrup's side, raises his foot, and slams his heel into the side of Northrup's knee. There's a sickening *pop* and the knee bends sideways. Northrup bellows in pain and drops to the floor. Damon doesn't lose an instant. He gets Northrup on his back, grabs the mop of blond hair, tilts his head back, and then delivers a forceful strike with the heel of his palm to Northrup's exposed windpipe. Northrup's cries are instantly reduced to wet choking gasps. He no longer cares about his knee or his eye or even Damon as he struggles to breathe. Damon takes a second to steady himself. He pins Northrup's shoulders with his knees, takes a breath, looks down into Northrup's bulging eyes, and then proceeds to methodically pound his fists into Northrup's face. Northrup is too busy fighting for air to put up any resistance as the punches land. Damon's expression is stone-like, even as the blood erupting from Northrup's nose spatters his face. He continues striking until his fists come away slick with blood that catches the light from the projector as it's flung from his fist onto the screen. Damon's hoodie becomes covered in blood as he continues to strike.

Finally, Damon stops. Out of breath, he looks down at Northrup's bloody, shattered face. Northrup lets out a low, mangled groan. Damon winds up and delivers one last ferocious blow. Northrup goes limp. Damon sits back on his heels and breathes. He turns his head to look up at the images on the screen. Then, he looks back at the unrecognizable Alex Northrup. His face is swollen and seeping blood, but he's still breathing, as evidenced by the blood bubbling at his lips and the slow rise and fall of his chest.

It's only then that Damon remembers I'm just a few feet away.

He gets to his feet and walks over.

He hooks my arm and pulls me to my feet without saying a word.

I'm too numb with shock to resist as he leads me to the back of the theater. There, he retrieves the backpack from the floor where he must have thrown it to distract Northrup the second before he shot me.

Damon shoves me into one of the recliners in the last row.

'Sit here and do not move,' he says, out of breath.

He takes the backpack and begins walking to the front of the theater.

'He was going to kill me!' I yell, finally finding my voice. 'Why didn't you shoot him?!'

'Because that's not how I want it,' Damon replies. But something is different. His voice wavers.

He disappears behind the first row of recliners and sets to work on Alex Northrup. There's the sound of zip ties being applied. Moments later, Damon rises with a manila envelope in one hand and the gun in the other. He glances at the envelope and then the screen.

'Looks like I don't need these,' he says, indicating the envelope while staring down at the floor. 'You've already got a copy . . .'

He furiously hurls the envelope down at Northrup, who emits a barely audible wet groan.

'Yeah, I know,' Damon says. 'You're the great director, Alex Northrup. You will be missed . . . but don't worry; more directors arrive in this city every fucking day.'

Damon aims the gun and fires.

I thrash in my seat. 'Goddammit!!! You ca—!'

'I said to sit there and shut up!' he snaps at me, the words coming out between ragged breaths.

He bends down, once again disappearing from my view. When he reappears, he has the backpack in one hand and is holding his phone to his ear with the other.

'Send the police to three-five-oh-seven La Vista Verde. You'll find the body of Alex Northrup in the theater . . . He was watching a movie,' Damon adds before hanging up.

I can't do this. I know I have to stay with Damon until I'm certain he'll never hurt Julia or Sophie, but I can't be in this room. Not with the images on that screen. Not after being almost killed with a shotgun and not with the man Damon just murdered only a few feet away from me.

Without thinking, I press myself out of the seat and walk across the back of the theater to the door.

'LUCAS!'

I stagger out of the theater and into the hall. Seconds later, I'm moving through the massive seating area. I can hear Damon's footsteps on the tiled floor of the hallway as he chases me, but his steps are heavy and uncertain.

I have to get outside.

I pinball it off one of the couches and reach the entrance formed by the staircases.

'STOP!'

I keep moving, stumbling through the entranceway formed by the stairs and past the award shelves. The front door is in sight. I have to turn my back to open it, since Damon closed it and locked the deadbolt when we entered. As I turn and my hands fumble for the deadbolt, Damon comes lumbering out of the darkness under the stairs like an animal, the gun still in his hand.

My fingers are finally able to turn the deadbolt and then go for the door handle. I push the handle and pull the door open. I can taste the night air. I spin to run outside, but Damon crashes into the door, slamming it shut.

He raises the gun to my face. His breath is labored and he has to lean against the door for support, but his eyes are livid.

'We're not done yet,' he says.

'I can't do this anymore.'

'One more stop,' he says. 'One more stop and it's over.' He stands upright, pushing himself away from the door, but there's a red smear from where his body was pressed against it.

We both notice it and look down.

Blood is slowly seeping from the shotgun wound in his side, soaking into his hoodie and jeans and mingling with Northrup's blood.

I look up into Damon's face.

He winces but it appears more in disappointment than pain.

'You have to get to a hospital,' I tell him.

Damon shakes his head. 'No. We're finishing this.' He winces in pain. 'And now, I really need you to drive.'

Chapter 32

Damon keeps the gun in the small of my back and his other hand clamped at the base of my neck as we exit the house and cross the lawn to the waiting car, but his pace is uneven, his grip is less vise-like. Every few strides he has to suppress a grunt of pain.

My mind is reeling with one question – one question that is overshadowing the fact that, moments ago, a coked-up man who is now dead was firing a shotgun at me.

Once we reach the street, Damon opens the driver's door.

'Get in.'

I climb behind the wheel.

'Now, give me your wrists,' Damon says.

I hold out my wrists. He takes the knife from his pocket, unfolds the blade, and cuts the zip ties. All the while, I'm staring back at the house.

Damon slams my door shut and then opens the rear door, slings the backpack across the seat, and follows it inside. Crouching down to enter the car causes him to be rocked by a jolt of pain and he nearly cries out.

'Start the car,' he commands, as he pulls out my phone.

The question is still tumbling through my mind. I hit the button, bringing the engine to life while Damon hurriedly mashes the screen on my phone with shaking fingers.

'*Continue straight on La Vista Verde for one mile . . .*' the automated voice says.

Damon drops the phone and pulls the small first aid kit out of the backpack. He begins rifling through the kit before simply dumping its contents onto the seat.

I'm still staring back at the house, remembering Northrup's words; 'You're the dad,' 'you're the dude he's got tied up.'

Damon grabs what's left of the gauze from earlier, unrolls it, and goes to lift his hoodie and shirt to dress his wound when he realizes we're not moving.

'Lucas?' he asks through painful breaths. 'What are you waiting for?'

'How did he know we were coming?' I ask, quietly.

'What?' Damon asks, hissing as he lifts his shirt.

'He knew who you were. He knew who I was. How could he have known that?' I ask, louder this time, still staring at the house.

'We have to keep moving, Lucas.'

His attempt to dodge my question only fuels my insistence.

'*How did he know we were coming?*'

Damon pauses and stares at me.

'It's been a long night, Lucas. I don't have an answer for you. Now, drive.'

I turn away from the house and twist so that I can look him in the eye.

'You're lying.'

He freezes, holding the gauze to his wound.

I'm not accusing him of lying. He *is* lying.

'You know exactly how he knew. Now tell me: how did he know that we were coming?'

Damon's pain and impatience grow as he returns my stare.

'I explained this to you before we went inside: there is more to it than what I've told you. It's complicated. We have one more stop, and if Northrup knew we were coming, there's a chance our last stop knows it, too.' His voice continues rising in speed and intensity. 'We've hit too many snags tonight that have slowed us down, which is why we need to move fast. I have planned this night for years and there is one last person we need to visit, *so drive the damn car!*'

I turn around to stare at the house again and shake my head. 'No. Not until you tell me how he knew. Not until you tell me what is waiting for us wherever we're go—'

BANG!

The gun erupts next to my ear and the window next to my head is obliterated.

I can't hear a thing over the high-pitched ringing, not even my own screams of pain and shock as I clap my hand over my ear and throw myself forward. I frantically work my hand back and forth against the side of my head, trying to physically remove the sound from my skull.

After a few more seconds of writhing, I regain some semblance of control. My mouth is open in a silent scream and there's the acrid taste of gunpowder in the back of my throat. My right ear is starting to register sounds, but it's like I'm under water. There's nothing in my left ear, only ringing and buzzing.

I pull my hand away from my ear and check for blood, but there's none. I sit back in the seat to see Damon in the rearview mirror. The gun is still in his hand. Smoke curls from the barrel, but holding the gun level is taking some effort on Damon's part.

Everything has changed.

The calculating, in-control Damon is gone.

What's staring back at me is a wounded feral animal.

'That is the last time,' he bites out, his face contorting in pain. 'We stand a better chance of finishing this night if you drive, but if you disobey or try to delay me one more time, I will shoot you and take my chances at driving myself. Are we clear?'

I don't have a choice.

Damon is wounded. He might even be dying, but that doesn't

change the fact that I have to make sure, even if he kills me, that he can never get to Julia or Sophia before he bleeds out. If he kills me here, there's a small chance that he may decide the best way to finish what he started is to get medical treatment now, finish the job later, and go after Julia and Sophie out of spite.

I still have to see this through. I have to make sure he's stopped, even if it means he bleeds out in the car, but I can't overtly stall him or he could kill me right now. We have to keep moving.

'Where are we going?' I ask with a sigh, as I put the car in gear.

'Back to where we started,' Damon replies.

Chapter 33

We make our way silently north toward the silhouette of the looming Hollywood Hills. The houses grow even larger and more extravagant as the road begins to gradually incline.

Damon is patching himself up with the meager provisions in the first aid kit, which was clearly intended for cuts and bruises and not shotgun wounds. He grunts in pain every now and again as he applies pressure in an attempt to slow the bleeding.

I try to keep my eyes on the road, anticipating the automated instructions, even though the voice calls them out well in advance.

The incline grows steeper until the road bends to the right, avoiding a straight climb, but continues to rise to the point that the city is now below us with Beverly Hills behind.

I'm startled when Damon lets out a sharp hiss.

I look at him in the rearview mirror but my eyes are drawn over his shoulder and out the back windshield. Silhouetted against the lights of Beverly Hills behind us is the black shape of a police helicopter. It hovers in the air like a backlit wasp. As I watch, it's joined by a second helicopter that drifts past.

This can't be a coincidence.

Damon's been leaving a trail of dead, powerful men all night and calling the police to come find them. He put a block of

Sunset Boulevard on lockdown. We were nearly caught in a trap by Northrup. Damon still hasn't told me how Northrup knew we'd be there, and now there are police helicopters over Beverly Hills.

They have to be after us.

Damon notices that I'm looking past him. He twists in his seat to see for himself, which causes him more pain, but he spots them, too. They're easier to see as we climb higher, putting more lights behind them.

He winces again as he turns and faces forward.

'We just need to stay ahead of them for a little while longer,' Damon says.

We continue along the hillside.

The homes are starting to space out with patches of trees and shrubs between them.

Damon finishes dressing his wound as best as he can. He lowers his shirt and hoodie over the patch job and turns his head to watch the city below. Two of the four side windows are gone, and cool night air blows through the car. Even though the window next to my head is blasted out, I can't hear the wind rushing past my left ear.

I steal another glance at him.

Even after everything that's happened, there is still a part of me that feels for him. It's not that the men he's been killing shouldn't be punished, but as he's been talking about loss, I can't help but hear my father's speech at my mother's funeral; the lament about how unfair and meaningless it was. I know that on some level, Damon's situation is different. He has people upon which to seek retribution. My father was left angry and bewildered with no one to blame but I know that my mother, no matter how senseless, cruel, and random her death was, would never want me or my father to wallow in misery for the rest of our lives because hers had come to an end.

'Do you think this is what she would want?' I ask.

He pulls his attention away from the lights. 'I beg your pardon?'

'Your daughter, Chloe. I know I never met her, but do you think this is what she would want you to do?'

The temperature in the car drops a few degrees, and not from the wind pouring in through the busted windows.

'In case you hadn't noticed, she's no longer here. All I can do is hold the men who drove her to that decision responsible.'

'You didn't answer my question.'

'Because I don't care,' he angrily fires back. 'I know you don't understand that, Lucas. You can't. Maybe one day – if you get to hold Sophie close to you – you will. Then you might understand what it would feel like to have her taken from you, and not only taken from you, but to have someone hurt her so badly, to crush her so completely, that she takes herself away from you.' His rage, his anger, and frustration, have built to a point that the pain in his side flares. He clenches his eyes shut, sits back, and takes a second to breathe. 'I hope you don't. I wouldn't wish it on any father. I hope you never experience a loss like that, but you should know that from the moment that Sophie is born, it will become the greatest fear in your life. It'll haunt you every time she walks out the door. At some point, you can't do anything else but pray . . .'

'Pray for what?'

'That you've done a good job. That you've taught your child to be a good person. That there are terrible people in the world and you can't give in to them, and you should stop them when you can.'

Damon grows quiet.

We approach a three-way intersection, with our road being joined by another, coming up the hillside. The light is red and I begin to slow.

Damon is suddenly alert and brings his face right over my shoulder.

'Whoa, whoa, whoa . . .'

We're alone at the intersection, sitting among the last of the expensive houses before the incline becomes too steep. Damon is staring ahead, through the windshield, to the next intersection in the distance, illuminated by streetlights.

Parked next to the stop sign, under one of the streetlights, are a pair of police cars.

Overhead, the green light for the cross traffic that isn't here, goes yellow.

Our light is about to turn green. If we pull through, we won't be able to turn around without attracting their attention.

'What do you want to do?' I whisper, as if the police cars sitting on the side of the hill nearly a hundred yards away might hear us.

'Turn right,' Damon says, never taking his eyes off the police cars. 'Nice and slow.'

The light above turns green.

I ease my foot off the brake and turn the wheel.

We roll forward and turn south onto the road leading down the hillside, back toward the burning lights of the city.

As I straighten the wheel, Damon gingerly twists in his seat to see if the cops will come after us. He's hoping the cops won't while I'm silently pleading they will, but as we reach the next intersection, disappearing from their view behind the houses, the rearview mirror stays dark.

Damon sits forward, picks up my phone, and begins calculating a new route.

There's no doubt anymore.

Damon's trail of bodies, Northrup's knowledge that we were coming, the helicopters, and now the cop cars waiting in the hills?

They can only mean one thing.

We're being hunted.

Chapter 34

'We're going to have to go the long way around,' Damon says, tapping on my phone. 'We'll head east through the city and then double back up the hill. They think we're coming from the west. We have to stay on the side streets, which is going to slow us down, so you need to make up some time, but don't draw attention to us.'

Everything he's saying is going in one ear and out the other.

'They know where we're going, don't they?' I ask. 'And if they know where we're going, they're going to be ready for us.'

'I don't know,' Damon answers, sounding honest. 'But we need to get there as fast as we can.'

We reach the stop sign of a quiet intersection. The voice from my phone instructs me to go left. We begin running parallel to Santa Monica Boulevard, which is two blocks to the south. At every intersection, Damon takes an inventory of the surrounding streets, searching for any more cop cars.

'We're going after *him*, aren't we?' I ask. 'The guy in the chair? The watcher? He's our last stop, isn't he?'

Damon hesitates, deciding if he's going to ignore my question, but I guess we're beyond that.

'Yes.'

'Who is he?'

'Randall Fletcher,' Damon replies, craning his neck to look up at the night sky for helicopters.

'I know that name.' My brow creases as I try to think. 'Why do I know that name?'

'He's the head of Onyx Pictures.'

The mention of the movie studio causes everything to fall into place.

Onyx Pictures is a production studio that has built its reputation on the magical ability to consistently produce arthouse films that have wide appeal at the box office and then clean up every award season. It was the studio that produced Alex Northrup's *Paper Cut*.

'He lives up in the hills?' I ask.

Damon nods. 'Just above Mulholland Drive.'

I'm trying to picture it in my head. 'If they know we're coming, that place will be locked down. There's no way we c—'

'That's where we're going, Lucas.'

Damon goes back to watching the streets.

I glance out the opening to my left, where the window used to be, and scan the darkened hillside, as if I'm expecting Randall Fletcher's house to have a huge neon sign above it.

They know we're coming. Damon's been killing men and he shot a cop. If they make that connection, they'll be waiting with every gun drawn. If I'm anywhere near Damon, there's no way I'll survive. This has become a suicide mission.

'We're never going to get anywhere near him,' I say, as calmly as I can. 'You've made your point. You called the police and left the photos. Everyone will know. You don't have to do this.'

'We're finishing this, Lucas.'

'There *is* no way to finish this, now. You won't get to him and even if you could . . .' I draw a breath. 'It's not going to bring Chloe back.'

He stops watching our surroundings.

'Do you think my daughter is the only one they did this to?

Do you really think hers is the only life they destroyed?'

I don't answer. There's no need.

'That's what Randall Fletcher does. Not only does he promise hot new directors wealth and fame. He promises them this. He organizes it and covers it up if anyone starts asking questions or threatens to talk. He's been doing it for years. It's not a secret. Everyone in this town knows about it – *everyone* – but no one does a thing about it. They're either afraid of what he'll do to their lives or they go along with it because they want the wealth and the fame. The only ones who don't know are their victims. The young and the naive . . . like my daughter.' He grunts in pain and looks out at the hills. 'Chloe wasn't the first. I'm making damn sure they can never do it again.'

That's it.

Any hope I had of talking him out of it is over and—

The purr of a ringtone fills the car and the center console lights up with a message: *INCOMING CALL: JULIA.*

Instinctively, my thumb goes for the 'answer' button on the steering wheel.

'Don't you dare answer that!' Damon shouts.

I stare at him in the rearview mirror, my thumb over the 'answer' button as the ringing continues.

'This may be my last chance to speak to her. I need to know that she's okay.'

Damon brings up the gun and points it at my head.

'Do not answer that call . . .'

My decision is easy and immediate.

'I'm answering this call. You do what you have to do,' I tell him and hit the button.

He grits his teeth, lowers the gun, and scrambles to find my phone on the back seat. He's going to try to hang up the call, which means I only have a few seconds.

'Julia? Are you—?'

'My water broke!'

206

Damon and I freeze.

'My water broke,' she says again, her voice fearful and trembling. 'Lucas, Sophie is coming.'

I can't move. I can't speak.

'Lucas?'

'I'm here. I'm here,' I'm finally able to sputter.

'Where are you?'

'I – I'm on the road, but I won't be able to get to you in time. Go downstairs and get Mr. Herrera. Wake him up if you have to and he'll take you to the hospital. I'll—'

'No. The police are here. They're going to take me.'

It takes me a second to process. I look at Damon, who is in a similar state of shock.

'The police? What are the police doing there?' I ask.

'They're looking for you.' Julia is on the verge of tears. 'They said something about you at a gas station and you were looking up at the security camera and asking the attendant for help and telling them to call the police. They did but you left and the police didn't know where you went, so they traced your license plate number and came here.' She takes a second to catch her breath. 'Lucas, what's going on? What's happening?'

I steal another look at Damon to see if he's found my phone to end the call, but he's sitting silently, too stunned to react.

'Julia, listen to me. Go with the police to the hospital. They're going to stay with you and I'll be there as soon as I can.'

That brings Damon out of his stupor. He closes his mouth and hangs his head in defeat.

'What's happening?' she asks, again.

I can only imagine that the stress of the police suddenly arriving at our apartment, looking for me, is what sent her into labor. If I tell her what's happening, that I might not be coming home, it might make things so much worse.

'I'm sorry, Julia, but I can't talk right now. Please, just get to the hospital and I'll explain everything when I get there, okay?'

She sniffs. 'Okay. Okay . . . I love you.'

Her tone is clear. She doesn't know what's happening but she knows that we may not see each other again.

'I love you, too, Julia. So much . . . and I'll see you soon, okay?'

She lets out a short laugh of sad disbelief. 'Pinky swear?'

The tears instantly well under my eyes but I can't help but smile. 'Pinky sw—'

The call cuts out.

I look in the rearview mirror just in time to see Damon's thumb come off the screen. His pallid face is almost unreadable. It's frustration, pain, and an odd streak of respect.

'Congratulations,' Damon says. 'You outsmarted me. You protected Julia and Little Sophie. You took them off the board. Well done.'

The relief flowing through me is unbelievable. It's as if I've been holding my breath for hours.

'It's really over,' I quietly say.

'Lucas—?'

'They're safe.' Saying the words is like a stone coming off my shoulders. 'You can't touch them. It's over. You have nothing left to threaten me with.'

'Of course I do,' Damon says. He raises the gun and presses it against the back of my head. 'You want to meet your daughter, don't you?'

My moment of triumph quickly fades.

They're safe for now, but Damon could still win. He could kill me now and possibly survive if he gets help. It's remote but it's a possibility and knowing Sophie will be here in the next few hours, that I've come this far and I still might never hold her causes me physical pain.

'Yeah,' Damon says off my expression. 'I'd say I still have one more card I can play.'

Chapter 35

His point made, Damon lowers the gun with a grimace of pain or frustration or both and checks my phone. The light from the screen causes the sheen of sweat covering his face to glisten.

'This is taking too long,' he says.

'I'm going as fast as I can,' I reply, motioning as we pull up to yet another stop sign. There's one at the end of every block on these side streets. 'And you said not to attract attention,' I add.

He looks up from the phone at me as I pull forward and then turns his head to glance out at the passing apartment buildings, blinking against the air that's blowing in through the windows that are no longer there.

He curses under his breath and then goes back to typing on the phone as we approach another intersection.

'*Turn right,*' the automated voice says over the speakers.

'We're heading back to the main roads,' Damon says. 'They know what kind of car we're driving, but we have to take that chance. Drive fast but yes, do not attract attention.'

I pull the wheel to the right as we roll past the stop sign and through the intersection.

'*In five hundred feet, turn left onto Santa Monica Boulevard,*' the voice says.

As I straighten out, we can see Santa Monica Boulevard up ahead.

'You're not going to get to Fletcher,' I remind him.

'I don't have to get near him. I just have to get close,' Damon says, consulting the phone.

'What do you mean by that?'

'You just worry about the road.'

We reach the stop light at the intersection to Santa Monica Boulevard.

The light is green but my foot stays on the brake and my shoulders tense at an approaching sound.

Moments later, two police cars, their sirens blaring and their lights flashing, come racing down Santa Monica Boulevard from our left. The handful of other cars at the intersection stop. The police cars fly through the intersection and continue on in the direction of Beverly Hills.

'We're right here!' I want to scream. I want to blare my horn and flick my brights to get their attention, but Damon would blow a hole in my head before I knew if I was successful.

The light turns yellow.

'Come on, Lucas,' Damon says. 'Turn before it goes red.'

I make the turn and head east on Santa Monica Boulevard.

We proceed for a couple of blocks in silence. There's this strange feeling of moving through a darkened forest with monsters lurking all around. The stores and shops along the boulevard are closed. The sidewalks are deserted, save for the occasional jogger on a night run or someone in rags pushing a grocery cart overflowing with odds and ends.

We make most of the stoplights, increasing our speed as we continue east. On the rare occasion that we encounter a red light, I keep my eyes straight ahead, not wanting to catch the attention of drivers as they pull up next to us.

Sophie is going to be here in the next few hours. Julia's probably arriving at the hospital right now. At least I hope she is. We tried to have everything planned out. The go bag has been packed and sitting by the door for a week. It was my responsibility to grab it when we left for the hospital. I should have reminded her to take it but now, I won't—

Damon sits up. 'Shit.'

Up ahead, there are more red and blue lights, heading our way.

The cars in the opposite lanes slow to a stop, preparing to allow the cops to pass.

'Pull over,' Damon says.

'Aren't we supposed to just stop?'

'Pull over!' he insists.

I move over into the right lane and stop.

Damon watches intently as the cop cars approach. The sound of their sirens reaches into the car.

I've got about five seconds.

Is there anything I can do to get their attention that Damon won't see? I rapidly scan the console, but don't find an answer by the time the cops sail past, presumably to join the fleet of cops who are already looking for us near Beverly Hills.

Damon takes a second to watch them go. Once they're sufficiently in the distance, he turns back around.

'Okay. Let's keep moving. We're almost far enough east to head back up into the hills.'

I ease the car forward as the rest of the vehicles on the road resume their speed.

I feel like I've missed an opportunity, an opportunity that I'm not getting back.

After a few more blocks, Damon becomes even more paranoid than before, continuously watching our surroundings or the night sky, scanning for helicopters, while blood continues to seep into his hoodie.

'Turn left up here,' he says. 'We're going to go back to Hollywood Boulevard and then head north.'

'There's going to be more traffic than here.'

'We're going to go one block, and then we're heading up.'

I quietly shake my head and plead with him one last time. 'Please, don't do this.'

'We're almost done, Lucas . . . and until then, not another word. Just do what I tell you.'

We head north on Fairfax until we come to Hollywood Boulevard, where I turn right, heading east.

As promised, we only go one block.

'Okay, get in the left-hand lane,' Damon says. 'We're going to take Laurel Canyon.'

We pull up to the red light and prepare to turn onto the twisting road that leads up into the darkness of the hill, when in the distance, there's an increasingly familiar sight. More cop cars are heading in our direction. Three more. The cars around us are already stopping or moving to get out of the way.

The green arrow appears overhead, but the cops are too close. I'm not going to try to turn in front of them. That will definitely grab their attention but Damon would know that was my intent.

'Sit tight,' he says, a hint of tension creeping into his voice. 'Do not turn until they pass.'

As the flashing lights grow closer, my heart sinks. They're not going to see us. These police cars aren't prowling. They've received orders to be somewhere, probably Beverly Hills, as quickly as possible. They're going to run right by us.

Just one. They're looking for the make and model of my car. Let just one of them spot us, sitting here, I pray. *I'll never ask for a cop to notice me ever again. Just this one time!*

The lead cop car flies past us. I catch a glimpse of the officer behind the wheel, facing straight ahead, oblivious that the people he's searching for are only a few feet away. The next two cop cars follow almost simultaneously.

Damon quickly twists in his seat, wincing in pain, to watch them go and make sure we weren't detected.

I have the benefit of the rearview mirror, so I don't have to turn around. I can watch my salvation speed away as I look down Hollywood Boulevard and freeze.

There's another cop car, heading our way. It's traveling almost twice as fast as the previous cop cars, probably trying to catch up.

Damon is still twisted around, watching the first three cars disappear.

This last car isn't going to see us. It's going way too fast.

I have three seconds at most.

This is my last chance. I need to get their attention without Damon knowing.

My finger goes to the lever off the steering wheel, but stops. I can't blink my lights at them. Damon might hear the *click* as I turn the knob.

Two seconds.

I've got it!

I hook my finger around the lever and begin rapidly flicking my high beams, careful not to fully engage them, for fear that Damon might hear that, as well.

My high beams flash off the approaching cop car as it speeds by.

It rockets past just as Damon starts to turn around. He looks relieved that the first cars didn't see us, but this last one takes him by surprise. He turns again to watch it go. He doesn't wait as long to make sure we're in the clear. He turns back to face forward and sees the green turn arrow.

'Okay,' he says with a sigh, settling into his seat. 'Almost there. Let's go.'

That was it. That was my last chance and I failed.

Defeated, I take my foot off the brake and turn the wheel. We accelerate through the intersection and onto Laurel Canyon Road. Almost immediately, I can feel the incline of the road as we begin to climb. There are no stop lights ahead of us. Only darkened road and the shadow of the hill, which is dotted here and there by streetlamps and houses. We're going to Randall Fletcher's house and into what I can only assume will be a gauntlet of well-armed police.

Damon sits forward. 'Once we hit Mulholland, you're going to turn—'

There's a frenzy of movement back at the intersection of Hollywood Boulevard. Red and blue lights flash in the rearview mirror.

Damon spins to look.

One of the cop cars – I'm assuming the last one to pass us – has come back. The red and blue lights on the roof flare and the siren begins to wail. The car swerves through the intersection, points its headlights in our direction, and charges. Moments later, the three other cop cars appear and fall in to join the pursuit.

Damon turns to me, his eyes full of wrath.

'*What did you do?*'

Chapter 36

'I didn't do anything!'

Before the words even leave my mouth, Damon leans forward between the seats to watch the road in front of us. Either he believes me or he knows it doesn't matter.

He points at a rapidly approaching intersection. 'Left! Turn left here!'

I throw the wheel over. The tires scream in protest. The seatbelt is the only thing that keeps me in place. Damon holds onto the back of my seat to keep from being flung against the back passenger door. For a split second, I'm certain we're going to miss the turn and skid into the bushes of the house on the corner, but I'm able to maintain control of the car and straighten out. The cops behind us slam on the brakes in an attempt to follow, but our turn was so abrupt, they slide through the intersection.

'Go! Go! Go!' Damon shouts.

Why am I trying to get away from the police? I should let them catch us.

No sooner does my foot come off the gas than Damon grabs my hair, yanks my head back against the headrest and shoves the gun under my jaw.

'Don't you fucking dare stop this car!'

I'm back to square one. If I let the cops take us, Damon will start shooting. The cops will kill him but I'll most likely be killed in the crossfire, while Damon might take some cops with him. At least I've gotten one step closer: I've alerted the police and Damon hasn't killed me.

But I don't have a plan for what comes next. I just have to keep going.

I press the gas. The motor whines. We rocket past bungalows and small apartment buildings as we ascend the hillside.

Damon releases my hair and quickly checks my phone.

'Up ahead, this will connect with Mulholland. When we get there, go left.'

He turns to look behind us. The cops have regrouped and are back on our tail. Our move has bought us a few seconds, but they're going to catch up with us eventually. It's inevitable. The narrow, twisting roads might work to our advantage for a time, but not forever.

The houses start to thin out as we climb further up the hill. On this incline, my engine is no match for the powerful police cars and they're on our bumper in a matter of seconds.

The lead car behind us suddenly swerves into the oncoming lane and pushes forward, trying to pass us.

'Cut him off!' Damon barks. 'Don't let him pass! Get in the center of the road!'

I pull the wheel, centering us on the painted lane divider and nearly hit the police car, forcing them to fall back.

'Stay right here!' Damon instructs me. 'They won't try to run us off the road. Not when it might send us and them off the side of the hill.'

I've been trying to avoid it, but Damon's words cause me to turn my head and look at the precipitous drop down the hill, back toward the lights of the city. He's right. If they try to run us off the narrow road, it could end in disaster not only for us, but for them, and the danger only grows the higher we climb.

I'm staying in the center of the road, waiting for more instructions from Damon when headlights appear ahead of us, coming our way. There's no red and blue lights. It's just someone on the road.

'Umm . . .' I nervously sputter, causing Damon to turn. He sees the oncoming car.

'Stay right here,' he commands.

'What?!'

'Stay in the center of the road!'

'You want me to play chicken with this guy?'

'Stay here until the last possible second!' Damon barks while switching back and forth between looking back at the cops and looking ahead. 'At the last possible second, get into the right lane. Once they pass, get back to the center.'

The headlights grow closer. The driver begins flashing their high beams.

I need to warn them. I need to tell them what I'm going to do so that they stay in their lane.

I do the only thing I can think of and hit my turn signal, as if I'm going to turn right even though there's no turn to make. Hopefully it's enough to let them know that I'm going to get back in the right lane. I'm praying the police behind us see it, too. Damon is so caught up going back and forth between the cops and the oncoming car that he doesn't hear or doesn't catch the clicking of the turn signal over the whine of the engine and the wind tearing through the car.

We sail toward the oncoming vehicle I'm going about fifty, but it won't matter in a collision that sends us down the hill.

The driver is still flashing their brights as we near and begins laying into their horn.

'Not yet . . .' Damon says.

I grip the wheel and grit my teeth.

'. . . not yet . . .'

The high beams from the oncoming car nearly blind me.

'. . . not y—!'

I can't take it anymore. This feels like the last possible second to me. I turn the wheel, putting us back into the right lane.

Thankfully, the police behind us do so, as well, and the approaching car stays in its lane as they rocket past us. The wind from their wake pulls on the car but I hold it steady.

'Back in the center!' Damon shouts.

I move back over the divider.

The police cars fall in behind us, lights still flashing, sirens still wailing.

If Damon is upset that I moved before he said to, he doesn't have time to reprimand me as he stares up ahead.

'Mulholland should be coming up any second.'

Below us, the lights of the city are growing more distant.

There are no more houses on this road. It's all shrubs and scraggly trees. My headlights only illuminate so far into the distance as we twist and turn. There are also fewer and fewer streetlamps illuminating the road, creating pools of darkness between them.

Finally, up ahead, lined by streetlamps, is a road that runs along the hillside.

'That's it!' Damon says, pointing to the illuminated intersection where the road we're on connects, as well as another road coming up the hill from the opposite direction. 'That's Mulholland!'

In the distance, there are strobing red and blue lights coming up the other road that connects to Mulholland, racing toward the same intersection.

'They're going to try to cut us off,' Damon says. 'We have to get there first. Step on it!'

'If we miss the turn, we're going to slam into the hillside!'

'Just go!'

We hurtle toward the intersection, as does the police car.

'Get ready,' Damon says.

Our headlights illuminate the road, leading us to the

intersection.

'Here we go.'

We're going to arrive at the same time as the cop, which only adds 'collision' to the list of catastrophic outcomes.

My foot stays firmly planted on the gas. Our only advantage is that our road is more level, while the cop is still climbing.

The engine revs as we fly into the intersection. The cop car rises up from the road to block us but we arrive a fraction of a second earlier.

'TURN! NOW!' Damon shouts.

I throw the wheel over to the left but it's too late. We're going to slam into the cop and spin into the hillside, but the driver of the police car hits the brakes, taking what would have been a full-on collision to a light clip of our rear bumper.

Ironically, that clip keeps us from spinning out.

It takes me suddenly pulling the wheel in the other direction, but I'm able to right the car and hit the gas, sending us up Mulholland Drive.

Damon lets out a strangled cry of triumph as he looks back at the tangle of cop cars at the receding intersection.

Which is the precise moment we're suddenly bathed in a circle of white light from the helicopter overhead.

Chapter 37

Damon cranes his head to look up at the helicopter.

'Keep going!' he yells over the thundering rotors. 'The helicopter can't do anything. We just have to keep the cops from getting in front of us to block the road.'

The helicopter has no problem keeping its searchlight on us as we continue up Mulholland Drive.

After a few moments, the road begins to straighten out as it continues to climb. There's nowhere for us to go but upwards. I can push us up to fifty miles per hour, but I'm not going anywhere above that. There are still gentle curves as the road hugs the contours of the hill and the sporadic guardrail to our left offers little comfort.

Behind us, the cops are once again racing to catch up.

Before, when Julia and I would watch clips of police chases, we always wondered why people kept going once the helicopter showed up. At that point, it was over. You can't escape, but now that this is happening to me, I get it. I understand.

It's only over when you stop. You pray for a miracle and the only way to give that miracle a chance is to keep going.

We round a section of the road, revealing a straightaway that continues upwards dotted by occasional streetlamps. Up ahead, there's a spit of land that serves as an overlook of the city before the road disappears behind another contour of hillside, only to reappear and lead directly to a cluster of lights at the top of the hill.

'That's it!' Damon shouts. 'Fletcher's house is up there! Come on, w—!'

Flashing police lights appear out of the cluster of lights he's pointing at. They emerge onto the road and begin to descend the hillside toward us.

I allow the car to roll to a stop. Damon doesn't say a thing.

They've cut us off. There is no way to get to Randall Fletcher now, and we're trapped on this road.

Damon's face is a map of anger, pain, and fatigue.

'That's it,' I say quietly, as exhaustion washes over me. 'I told you we would never get to him.'

Damon stares fixedly ahead.

'Keep going . . .' he snarls.

In the rearview mirror, the police cars are racing up the hill behind us.

I shake my head. 'No. It's over.'

He grabs my hair again and pulls my head back and presses the gun under my jaw, but he has nothing close to the strength he had before.

'I said, keep driving!' he screams, his voice cracking.

He knows he's failed. He knows it's over and the fact he's threatening to kill me when it won't make a difference causes a last surge of adrenaline to flood my body.

'No,' I reply confidently. 'If you have to shoot me, then shoot me, but I will be the last person you kill tonight.'

He lets go of my hair but keeps the gun pointed at my head as he reaches for the backpack. 'No. No, you won't be the last person I kill. If you don't keep going . . .' He pulls out a black metal cylinder – the thing I've been hearing *clink* throughout the night – and holds it close to his chest.

'If you stop,' Damon warns, 'if you let the police catch us before

I can get to Randall Fletcher, when they get close, I will set this off and more people will die. Do you understand me?'

It takes me a second to process but the realization pins me to the seat; we've been driving around all night with a pipe bomb in the car.

I'm staring straight ahead at the road in shock. I glance out to the left at the ground that falls away into the dark abyss before the lights of the city begin. I then look back at the road ahead. The streetlamps illuminate the incline, with the lookout at the end before the road bends around the hillside.

It's not an answer I was hoping for, but it's the answer I've been waiting for.

I told myself that I wouldn't leave Damon's side until I knew he could never threaten Julia or Sophie, again.

Now, in his desperation, he's made it crystal clear. He wants to keep going in the hopes we'll reach Fletcher where he'll detonate the bomb, which will also kill us both. But if I stop, he'll detonate the pipe bomb anyway, killing me and an untold number of police.

Gazing at the overlook, I have a third option.

I'm dead in any of the three scenarios, which makes my choice a simple one.

I grip the wheel and stomp on the gas. The tires screech and the car lurches forward.

Damon watches the pursuing cops, before turning to check the progress of the cops who are coming at us from the other direction. As he does, he notices my expression fixed on the outlook up ahead, and realizes what I'm about to do.

'Lucas?'

'No more . . .' I quietly say.

'Lucas, listen to me—'

'No. I'm not listening to you. You can't threaten me, or my family, or anyone else, tonight.'

Damon's jaw hangs open for a second and then he drops his tone, trying to sound calm. 'Lucas? Lucas, I want yo—'

'No. I'm not letting you kill anyone else tonight.'

Even though the pedal is to the floor, I press harder. The motor revs, pushing us faster and faster toward the lookout and the dark void beyond.

'Lucas,' Damon says, fear creeping into his voice. 'Think about Sophia.'

'I am thinking about Sophia,' I reply, keeping the car aimed straight at the overlook.

His eyes dart between me and the lookout. 'Do you want her to grow up without a father?'

'I'm sure there are parents among the cops behind us, but I'm dead either way. So, I'm making sure you can never threaten her or Julia.'

'Lucas!' he implores, his dread giving way to panic. 'You don't want to do this!'

I shake my head. 'No, I don't, but if I never get to meet my daughter, at least I can teach her the lesson you taught me tonight: that there are terrible people in the world and you can't give in to them . . .' I tighten my grip on the wheel. 'And you have to stop them when you can.'

He stares at me in shock.

'. . . Lucas?'

'No. No more talking. This is how it ends.'

Damon lunges forward, between the seats, attempting to grab the steering wheel, but my grip is iron-tight. I throw my elbow back and connect with his nose. He falls back and I put my hand back on the wheel.

Closer. Closer to the edge.

In these last seconds, I see Julia. I see us in line at the concession stand at the pool. I see us on the shores of the river. I see us at that basketball game. I see us cuddled on the couch that Christmas at Allegheny College. I see us driving across the country, on our way to Los Angeles. I see us holding one another on the couch, talking about life with Sophie. I see birthdays with Sophie. I see

Julia and me, watching her take her first steps. I see us watching her grow. But I know that I won't be there.

'I'm so sorry, Sophie,' I whisper. 'I love you . . . Please, be good.'

I brace myself as we're about to go flying off the overlook.

Suddenly, Damon reappears between the seats, holding the gun. I grip the wheel, ready to hold it firm as we go over the edge, but he aims at the upper corner of the floor of the passenger side and begins firing rapidly.

The car drops a few inches and swerves to the right as the tire shreds.

Despite my grip on the steering wheel, it spins out from under my hands. The friction burns my palms and nearly breaks my fingers. A shower of sparks erupts outside the empty window as the tire shreds away and the metal rims make contact with the road. We rapidly decelerate. The three tires that are still intact scream and the spotlight from the helicopter can't keep up. We slam into the guardrail, which sends us spinning back toward the other side of the road. The outlook disappears. For a split second, we're looking at the hillside, then the pursuing cops, then the lights of Los Angeles, and the outlook, again.

I try to grab the wheel to stop us, but it's no use. We continue to spin.

The last image I see is that of the oncoming light pole just before we sideswipe into it.

There's a horrible impact and a sharp pop as the airbags deploy. I'm pitched violently sideways but held in place by the seatbelt. Small pieces of glass fly across my face. The air rushes out of my lungs and I nearly pass out from the whiplash.

The noise and sensation of the impact feels eternal but is over in an instant.

I slowly come to my senses.

I'm slumped in the driver's seat, still conscious, but shuddering as I fight for breath. There's a hissing sound from under the hood.

Finally, the floodgates in my chest open. I begin to cough as my lungs desperately pull in air.

My eyes open and I frantically look about.

The car is slightly bent around the light pole on the passenger side. We're facing in the opposite direction, looking back down the hill. The windshield and the rest of the windows are gone, scattered across the seats and floor. The airbags are deflating and hang like withered canvas sacks. Suddenly, the car is washed in blinding light as the helicopter finds us, again.

The thumping of the rotors overhead is deafening as they send powerful gusts of air through my decimated car.

Over the sound of the helicopter, a multitude of screeching tires comes to a halt, accompanied by red and blue flashing lights.

Still reeling, I glance to my left, through the window and out to the fleet of cop cars surrounding us. The spotlights mounted to the hoods of their cars flare to life, further blinding me. My vision becomes a rust-colored blur as a trickle of blood runs down my forehead into my eyes. I instinctively wipe it away.

There's a flurry of screamed instructions from the wall of flashing, blinding lights.

'GET YOUR HANDS UP!' 'HANDS!' 'HANDS, NOW!!!' 'GET 'EM UP!'

I hold up my bloodied hands.

There are more screams and barking commands.

'OUT OF THE CAR!' 'GET OUT OF THE CAR, NOW!' 'KEEP YOUR HANDS UP!'

My eyes adjust and I can see the outlines of figures, half-positioned behind the hoods and doors of their cars. All of them have their weapons pointed at me.

Above the shouts and the helicopter overhead, one voice on a bullhorn booms out. 'GET OUT OF THE CAR! AND KEEP YOUR HANDS UP!'

I'm still processing what happened and checking to see if my limbs are still intact.

'OUT OF THE CAR! NOW!'

'Okay! Okay!' I call as loudly as I can.

My hand slowly lowers to the door handle when I feel the now familiar pressure of a gun pressed to the back of my head.

'Do not get out of the car,' Damon says in a strained voice.

There is a renewed burst of commotion outside the car.

I glance in the rearview mirror, the only intact glass left in the car.

'YOU! IN THE BACK SEAT! PUT DOWN THE GUN!'

Damon groans as he leans forward. There's a gash in the side of his head and blood is seeping out. It's taking everything he has to keep the gun pointed at my head. He grimaces again as he shifts his weight to move but it's too much effort. He sits back but continues to aim the gun at my head.

'YOU IN THE BACK! DROP THE GUN!' 'DROP IT, NOW!' 'PUT IT DOWN AND SHOW US YOUR HANDS!!!'

I suddenly remember the pipe bomb in the back seat, which has miraculously not gone off, and turn to the cops.

'Stay back!' I shout. 'Stay back! He's got a bomb!'

The few cops who have started to advance toward the car stop and retreat, all the while keeping their guns aimed in our direction.

I stare at Damon in the rearview mirror.

'Congratulations, Lucas,' he says. 'You did it. You stopped me.' A smile plays on his bloody lips and teeth. 'You were willing to sacrifice yourself to save others . . . I'm actually really proud of you.'

The light from the helicopter and police cars floods the interior of the car, causing the blood smeared across his face to shine.

'You don't have to kill anyone else,' I tell him. 'The police can—'

His smile grows wider and, somehow, sadder.

'Lucas, I haven't killed anyone tonight.'

I turn to look at him, totally forgetting about the gun, which is now pointed at my face, but I don't see it.

'What are you talking about?'

'I said, I haven't killed anyone tonight.'

'What are you talking about?!' I repeat. 'You've been killing people all night!'

'Lucas—'

'The people where I picked you up—!'

'Lucas, you—'

'The house in Mar Vista!'

'Listen to me—'

'You killed Henford and Northrup! You shot Northrup in the—!'

'Lucas!' he snaps, which causes him incredible pain but is successful in shutting me up. 'Think. Have you actually seen me kill anyone, tonight?'

I blink as my mind rapidly replays the events of the evening in my head.

He made the call to the police, telling them that he had killed those people in the Hollywood Hills, but I never actually saw the bodies.

I was in the trunk when he went into the house in Mar Vista.

I remember lying on the floor, bound and gagged at Henford's house. Damon looked at me, as if he was waiting for me to watch . . . and then he dragged Henford into the hallway to shoot him . . . or that's what I believed.

And Walsh. He threw him out the window . . . but I didn't see it.

And Northrup, he shot him in the head . . . Or I thought he did after he dragged me to the back of the theater and put me in the chair . . . where I couldn't see Northrup.

I come out of my memories to find Damon still smiling and aiming the gun at me. He sees the confusion on my face and nods.

'But – in Mar Vista,' I sputter. 'You had blood on your face. Your arm. The knife.'

'It was my blood. I used the knife to threaten Castillo to get him into the chair where I could tie him up, but he struggled. He almost got the knife away from me and as we fought for it, I cut my arm.'

My head is spinning. 'No. No. I heard him cry out!'

'That was me, Lucas.'

I look around in disbelief.

The police are still shouting orders. The helicopter is circling overhead but I'm not aware of any of them.

'You – you threw Walsh out the window,' I say, but my certainty is gone.

Damon shakes his head, once again. 'I didn't want to fire that gun again, because I knew he was right. Someone would come looking. So, I made like I was going to throw him out the window. Then, when you turned around, I tucked him under the desk and just . . .' Damon puts his finger to his lips.

It's the same gesture he gave me as we were hiding under the desk from the security guards. If I had been Walsh and I thought he was going to throw me out a window and Damon gave me that same gesture and stuffed me under a desk, I wouldn't make a sound, either. And now his phone call in the alley makes sense. He told them to go to Walsh's office. I was going to correct him and say that Walsh was on the sidewalk, but he wasn't, and that's when I looked at the photos.

It feels like the car is still spinning as I try to process all of this.

'But . . . the bomb?' I ask.

Keeping the gun on me, Damon leans forward, picks up the bomb from the floor where it fell when we crashed, and hands it to me.

It's a metal water bottle. The kind people bring to the gym.

I look up at him from the water bottle, my mouth hanging open.

He lightly shrugs. 'I told you I was improvising.'

Holding the water bottle in my hands, I'm finally starting to believe him, but I still can't wrap my head around it.

'That's how Northrup knew,' Damon says. 'The fact that he knew proves that I wasn't killing anyone. That was never the plan, but once I called you for a ride, you had to believe that I was killing people. I had the gun to get these assholes to do

228

what I wanted, and I called the police because I didn't want them to form a plan, but with Henford, I had to bring you inside. I wasn't going to kill him, but you had to believe that I did. So I dragged him to the utility room and fired the gun, but he must have gotten free and contacted Northrup. It's the only way he could have known we were coming.'

I stare at him in shock. He's telling me the truth.

'Why?' I plead. 'Why go through all of this?'

'Guys like Walsh and Fletcher? I know what they're like, and the only thing that scares them more than dying is being exposed and having to pay for what they did. And I needed you to believe that I was really killing people or else you wouldn't have done what I needed you to do.' He has to take a breath before continuing. 'But more than any of that . . . Wherever I'm going tonight, I hope I get to see my little girl again, and when I do, I don't want her to see a murderer. I wanted those men to pay for what they did to her. That's why I tied them up, left those envelopes, and called the cops. But I didn't kill them, no matter how badly I wanted to or how badly I think they deserved it.'

'Why not go to the press? Why not tell everyone what happened?'

Damon sighs. 'You know exactly what would happen, Lucas. Chloe would be dragged through the mud. The photos would be all that people would focus on. I couldn't watch what the world would do to her, what they would do to the memory of my little girl. I wanted to light the fuse, but I didn't want to be here when the bomb goes off.'

His arm is shaking as he holds the gun at my head.

'But . . . if you weren't going to kill anyone . . . and you're not going to kill me . . . Why are you pointing a gun at me?'

He inclines his head slightly toward the mayhem outside the car. 'So that they won't shoot. If I lower the gun, they may decide that they have to take a shot before I aim again, and I'm worried you'll catch a stray . . . I know it's hard to believe, but

I'm protecting you. They won't shoot until you're clear of the car . . .' He sighs. 'So, this is where you and I part ways, Lucas. You need to get to Julia and Little Sophie. Trust me: you want to be there when she's born.'

I turn in my seat and stare straight ahead through the wasted remains of the windshield.

He didn't kill anyone. He wanted justice for his daughter. I don't agree with what he's done. I'm not forgiving him, but he doesn't have to die, here.

'Don't do this.'

'It's done, Lucas.'

'Turn yourself in. Make sure these people pay for what they did.'

'I really wanted to make history. I wanted to expose these people and maybe they will be exposed, but I've taken it as far as I can go. If I turn myself in, I become the story . . . No . . . This is where it ends.'

I shake my head. 'No. No, I'm not going to let you do this.'

'Lucas, you really have somewhere else to be. And as a father, I can tell you that you don't want to miss it.'

'Nobody has to die tonight!'

'You can't save me, Lucas. I don't want to be saved.'

'I can try.'

I turn to the flashing lights and screaming voices and hold up my hands.

'GET OUT OF THE CAR!' 'EXIT THE CAR!' 'OUT! NOW!'

'I'm getting out! Don't shoot!' I cry, moving my mouth as dramatically as possible because I don't know if they can hear me over the chaos.

Keeping my right hand up, I slowly reach down for the handle with my left. I pull it and push open the door with my knee while getting my hand back up. The wave of tension that sweeps through the cops as I exit the car is palpable.

'WALK SLOWLY FORWARD!' 'KEEP YOUR HANDS WHERE WE CAN SEE THEM!' 'SLOWLY!'

230

'I will! I will!' I call out. 'Just don't shoot him!'

'WALK FORWARD!'

I do as I'm told but continue shouting, 'Do not shoot! He's not going to kill anyone!'

The perimeter of cops are about ten yards in front of me on the incline. The helicopter hovers overhead. The lights of Los Angeles burn in the distance.

'Please!' I continue calling out. 'Listen to me! Do not shoot him!'

'STOP RIGHT THERE!' 'STOP!'

I can't see who's talking, so I try to address them all.

'He's not going to shoot!'

'STOP RIGHT WHERE YOU ARE!' 'GET YOUR HANDS UP!'

I stop and teeter for a second before finding my balance on the inclined road.

'Please! Don't kill him! He's not—!'

'ON YOUR KNEES, NOW!!!'

'OKAY!' I plead. 'Okay! But listen to me; do not sh—!'

'Lucas?'

The chaos suddenly doubles. More voices begin shouting.

'HEY! HEY! HANDS! SHOW US YOUR HANDS!!!' 'HANDS! GET 'EM UP!!!'

The cops aren't aiming at me anymore. They're aiming past me toward the car.

I turn.

Damon, covered in blood, has emerged from the car but has to lean back on it for support. He's holding the backpack he's been carrying all night in his right hand. His left hand is behind him, hidden within the car.

'DROP THE BAG!' 'DROP IT AND SHOW US YOUR HANDS!!!'

Damon lightly tosses the backpack onto the road where it flops open to reveal the last couple sets of zip ties.

'NOW GET YOUR HANDS UP AND STEP AWAY FROM

THE CAR!'

Damon and I stare at one another.

For a moment, we are the only two people in the world, balanced on the point of a pin.

'I really am sorry, Lucas. I'm sorry about everything . . .' I don't believe the police can hear him. I can barely hear him over the noise. Damon looks around at the chaos, at the helicopter, and the lights of Los Angeles, before returning his attention to me. 'I know I said I didn't believe in fate, but I'm really glad I got to meet you . . .' His balance falters and it takes him a second to steady himself before continuing. 'One day, you may have to make a choice. Whatever you decide is up to you, but I just want you to know that, no matter what you choose, you're going to be one hell of a dad.'

Damon smiles at me. He then lifts his left arm from the car. He's holding the gun in his hand. He aims it at me.

I turn to the wall of policemen and throw out my hands.

'NO!' I scream.

They open fire.

Chapter 38

'I think it's safe to say that it's a total write-off.'

'No shit.'

For a moment, I'm worried that the kind woman from the insurance company will be offended at my involuntary assessment of her conclusion, but I think she gets it.

There's no real reason for either of us to be standing here in this junkyard next to the I-5 in Sunland. She explained that this is part of the process, a formality, but I don't see why it requires me to give up an afternoon to drive out here to come to a conclusion that could have been reached by looking at a photo.

My car is no longer drivable. In fact, it's not even a car anymore. It's closer to a gazebo. A bullet-ridden block of mangled metal.

'We've assessed what the car would have been worth before . . . this,' she says with a slightly baffled wave of her hand, 'and have decided on an amount. If you accept, we can cut you a check that will arrive next week. If you'd like to dispute the amount, we can go to arbitration, per your policy.'

She offers me the clipboard, which holds a form with a dollar amount at the bottom. As I expected, it feels slightly lower than it should, but it'll cover the cost of a car. Not a new car, but a used car, and if a couple hundred dollars is the price I have to pay to finally put this all behind me, so be it.

'That's fine,' I answer.

I've got much more to worry about.

It's been three months since that night.

After Damon was cut down in a hail of bullets, the police put me in handcuffs out of an 'abundance of caution.' Looking back on it, I understand because they didn't know exactly what was happening. I tried to explain to them that at that very moment, my wife was at the hospital, giving birth to our daughter. I pleaded with them to take me to her. They could wait outside the delivery room. Once I knew that Julia and Sophia were safe, I would tell them everything, but first, I had to get to the hospital, the hospital that was part of our 'birth plan,' a phrase which now sounds hilarious to me. Eventually, someone called the hospital to corroborate my story and I got my escort.

I arrived with less than an hour to spare. Julia had a million questions and I couldn't blame her. I looked like I had come from a warzone, which was somewhat true. As with the cops, I told her I would explain everything once we knew that she and Sophia were going to be okay. She kept trying to ask questions until that last half hour of the delivery hit. After that, she could only focus on one thing.

Sophia was born at 2:36 a.m.

She was perfect. She is perfect.

The first time I got to hold her, sitting at Julia's bedside, was another one of those moments where I knew my life had changed. The guy I was five minutes earlier was no more and once again, I could feel time speeding up.

Sophia was taken to the nursery and Julia and I slept; she in the bed and I in the chair next to her.

You would think that my sleep would have been filled with visions of bullets, blood, horrible photos, guns, and red and blue flashing lights, but it wasn't. It was a void. A sleep so deep, even dreams couldn't find me.

When I woke, Julia was breastfeeding Sophia. She looked at me as I woke up. Her expression wasn't angry but it wasn't forgiving, either. It was worried. Expectant.

'So,' she said with a slight nod to the door. Through the small rectangular window, we could see a cop leaning against the opposite wall, talking to a nurse. 'Do you have something you want to tell me?'

And I did.

I told her everything. I told her about getting fired. I told her about the insurance. I explained to her why I lied. I didn't ask for forgiveness and I wasn't expecting any. I only wanted to give her the total picture.

'Lucas,' she began to protest. 'You should have told m—'

I held up my hand. 'I know. I should have told you but you were going into the home stretch and I didn't want to upset you.'

'But how are we—?'

'We'll figure that out, but for now, please let me finish, because losing my job is the most boring part of this story.'

I went on to tell her what happened the night before: about picking up Damon, having a gun held to the back of my head, Damon's threat of coming for her, being zip-tied and trapped in the trunk of the car, Damon shooting the police officer, Henford, our escape from Walsh's office, Northrup's trap, the police chase through the Hollywood Hills and Mulholland Drive, and finally, Damon's confession and bloody end.

Julia listened in shock, her mouth opening more and more with each passing detail. By the end, her frozen expression had me worried.

'Please don't lose your grip on Sophie,' I said with a nod toward our daughter, who at that point was sleeping in her arms.

Julia blinked, looked down, adjusted her arms and her gown to cover her breast. She began gently rocking Sophia as she gathered her thoughts.

'What are we going to do?' she finally asked.

'Believe me, if these last twenty-four hours taught me anything, it's that the most important thing is that you and Sophia are safe. We'll figure out the rest. Is it going to suck until then? Yes, but we'll figure it out.'

'Lucas, I wasn't talking about the money stuff. I know we'll figure that out. I'm talking about last night. I mean, are people going to find out about it? Because if they do, what happens to us?'

I shook my head. 'I'm going to tell them everything. I have to, but after that, I'm going to do everything I can to make sure that it's over. I don't want any part of it and I promise, it won't get anywhere near you and Sophia.'

'You can't promise that.'

I take her free hand and kiss it.

'I know but we'll be okay.'

*

And for the most part, we are.

Two days later, I was summoned downtown. I thought it was going to be the first of many lengthy interviews about what happened that night. Instead, I was questioned by two detectives for about an hour and a half. Afterwards, they thanked me for my time, suggested that I not speak to anyone about it, and then they sent me on my way.

Los Angeles was buzzing for a few days. People wondered what the big police presence in the Hollywood Hills had been. There were rumors of celebrity binges or a gas leak at one of the palatial mansions, but the real story stayed under wraps.

Sophia, Julia, and I returned to the apartment and began that 'honeymoon' phase of having a newborn child. It actually worked out fairly well to have both of us there for that first month. Julia and I traded off on the feedings, diaper changes, and walking/rocking shifts when Sophia was fussy in the dead of night.

However, when it was my turn to take one of those shifts of

walking around the studio with Sophia in my arms at 3 a.m. until she fell asleep, I would find myself flipping through the news channels on the TV or scrolling on my phone, waiting for the story to break, for the announcement of an investigation into Fletcher, Northrup, Walsh, Henford, Graham, Castillo, and whoever else was involved. They're all still alive, although no one has seen Northrup since that night. The official story from his publicist is that he has checked into rehab and has requested that everyone respect his privacy during this difficult time. My guess is that he won't show himself until the devastation Damon wrought on his face heals.

But that investigation I was expecting never materialized.

At first, I told myself that it must be coming, that a district attorney was building a case and getting their ducks in a row before going public, but nothing happened.

Finally, I was forced to accept that the whole thing had been buried.

How could it be otherwise?

The police kept the story from the reporters and who was left to bring a case? And then there's the obvious: Randall Fletcher is one of the most powerful people in Hollywood. Of course he has the clout to make it all go away, especially if it never leaked. The intrigue about what happened that night in the Hollywood Hills was talked about for a week or so, but with no updates, other news stories came to the front, and everyone eventually moved on.

Damon's plan failed.

I'm not really sure how I feel about it. I tried to stop the police from killing him, but it wasn't like Damon was my friend. I don't care that he shot out the tire to keep me from killing us both. There were multiple times throughout that night that he could have gotten me killed. Yes, those guys should pay for what they did to his daughter, but that doesn't mean Damon was right to do what he did. I guess I don't have very strong feelings about his death.

I've moved on, too. Both Julia and I have. A newborn baby takes up a lot of your time and we haven't been able to dwell on the past.

Our parents are in town.

Julia's parents put their differences aside to come out and meet their granddaughter.

I called my dad to let him know that Sophia had been born. When I told him her name, it shook something loose in him. Maybe he realized that it was time to start living again. He flew out a few days ago. The first time he saw Sophia, he just melted. He and I had a long talk. He apologized for how he behaved and I apologized for not being more understanding after Mom died. It's not like everything is okay between us now, but I would never have thought we could have gotten this far in only a few days. He wants to help us out financially, too. Just for a little while. Julia and I are taking him up on it on the understanding that we're going to pay him back.

I'm starting a new job in two weeks. It'll be a steady income so we can start digging out of our financial hole. We'll get there and the job offers great insurance, but getting back to work means I need a car, hence this visit to the scrapyard with the insurance adjuster. Julia and I have been sharing her car, but once the job starts, neither of us wants Julia at home alone with Sofia and no car.

The police released my wasted car from the impound this afternoon after weeks of me calling, begging them to do so. It's not as if it's a crime scene. They're not dusting for prints or combing the car for hairs or fibers. They got their man. There has to be plenty of bodycam footage to document what happened. Damon aimed a gun at me, and the cops shot him, a lot, which is what he wanted. During my interview with the detectives, I told them that Damon wasn't going to shoot me, but they didn't seem to care.

Damon is gone.

I'm reminded of that fact by the dried blood on the back of

the car from when Damon fell against it after the bullets slammed into him.

'If you don't mind me asking,' the insurance woman says, pulling me from my thoughts. 'What happened?'

She might not know for sure that's blood, but the bullet holes are unmistakable.

I shrug. 'What happened wasn't my fault.'

The insurance company must have the police report. They know what happened, but they haven't told her. Maybe that's standard practice. Maybe in addition to the cops, Fletcher got the insurance company to settle quickly and keep it quiet. Either way, it has nothing to do with me, anymore. All I want is the check.

'Well,' she says, realizing that I've got nothing more to say, 'I think that about covers it. Simply sign here and the check should arrive next week.'

She offers me the clipboard and a pen. I scribble my name on the line.

'That should do it,' she says, taking the clipboard back. 'Is there anything else we can do for you?'

'No. You've been very helpful. Thank you.'

She smiles. 'Glad to hear it. Have a great day.'

'You, too.'

She turns and walks away through the columns of junked cars.

I step forward and place my hand on the roof, which has been warmed by the sun, and peer inside the car. There are still bits of glass scattered across the floor. The deflated airbags hang from the interior and protrude from the steering wheel. They were once white but are now yellow from the blowing dust and exposure to the sun.

I remember saying 'good-bye' to my first car. It was the one I traded in so that we could have a little extra cash for the move. There were fond memories of awkward make-out sessions in high school and road trips with friends. I drove this car from Pennsylvania to Los Angeles. It was the start of a new chapter in my life but there is no nostalgia in saying goodbye. Even if it had somehow survived that horrible night, there's no way I could have kept it. Every time I looked in the rearview mirror, I would have seen Damon leering back at me. Anytime I opened the trunk, I would have felt the zip ties cutting into my wrists.

I run my hand over some of the bullet holes and open the back door, which groans and squeaks.

There are more rusty brown spots across the upholstery. It's all that's left of Damon.

I don't even know what they did with his body. I didn't ask.

So, this is it. The check is on its way. I have a new job and my family is waiting for me so we can all go out to dinner. I'm done with the whole affair. I close the door, turn around, and begin walking away . . .

. . . Except I can't shake what Damon said, just before he aimed the gun at me so the cops would shoot him. I'm not talking about his belief that I would be a great father, but the part where he said that one day, I might have to make a choice.

What *choice*? What was he talking about? It has bugged me every day since.

It's over. It didn't go the way he wanted. Those men should have been punished but his plan didn't work. His two years of planning was all for nothing and it almost got me killed. And I'm sorry it didn't work. I wish it had. I wish the photos had been enough to put them all in prison, but they weren't and there's nothing to be done about it now. Julia and I have moved on. We don't talk about that night. We've never told anyone. What good would it do?

Thinking about it causes the memory of the photos to flash through my mind. I see Chloe's eyes staring back at me and try to block it out. I wish I had never seen those images. I wish I had never pulled that envelope from the backpack. I often wonder what the police did with the photos. I'm assuming they destroyed them all as part of the coverup. I wonder if Fletcher personally oversaw their destruction. Did he burn them? I wonder what he thought as he burned that last envelope that was meant for him. I guess I'll never know.

Wait.

What happened to that envelope? The one meant for Fletcher?

When Damon tossed the backpack onto Mulholland Drive, the envelope wasn't in there. The backpack only held the last of the zip ties. I know there was one last envelope in there. I saw it and it wasn't in there at the end of the night. Damon had to have taken it out, but why? And where would he have put it . . .?

'One day, you may have to make a choice . . .'

I slowly turn back to the car.

There's no way . . .

I race back to the car and throw open the back door. I stand there, looking at the bloodstains on the back seat from where he was bleeding out after the crash.

I climb inside and glance around. Where would he have hidden it? I search the obvious spot of the pocket in the back of the front passenger seat. Jamming my hand inside, my fingers hit the bits of broken glass hidden at the bottom. I quickly pull my hand back. There's a little bead of blood already forming on my fingertip. I shake it off and wipe my hand on my shirt. The seat pocket is empty. Of course, it is. If Damon hid it there, the police would have found it. That means there's really only one place left. Pulling up the flashlight app on my phone, I crawl out of the car, and kneel down in the dirt. I lean back into the car, and crane my head to look under the seat.

My heart stops.

There, crammed in between the metal lattice frame and the cushion of the seat, is a manila envelope. I reach in and begin working it back and forth until the envelope comes free in my hand.

I stand, return the phone to my pocket, and stare at the envelope. It's crinkled and spotted with Damon's bloody fingerprints. He only had a few seconds after I left the car. While the police were focused on me, he must have hastily stuffed it under the seat. It's been sitting here for three months, and it shows.

I'm suddenly worried that someone is going to see me holding the envelope and ask, 'Hey! Is that what I think it is?' I look around but, of course, I'm alone. The only sound is the whisper of cars on the freeway.

Instinctively, my hand goes to open the flap but I stop.

I know what's in here. If I open this flap and pull out the photos, I know what I'm going to see and I never want to see them again. Even though I try to fight it, the photos flash through my mind, but this time, for a split second, it's not Chloe in those photos, but a grown Sophie. Suddenly, I'm physically ill. That imagined image makes my blood race and every muscle in my body tense. I'm filled with the urge to scream. Just picturing it, only for a second, makes me want to find every one of those men, take their throats in my hands, and squeeze until their eyes burst from their skull and their struggles cease.

But it wasn't Sophie, I have to tell myself. Sophie's at home, safe and sound.

I stand there, clenching my eyes shut and waiting for it to pass, waiting for my pulse to get back on the rails, for the urge to burn the world down to subside.

I slowly open my eyes and stare in shocked awe at the car. It wasn't my little girl, but even thinking about it filled me with a sensation I've never come close to feeling and that sensation was only a small fraction of what Damon must have felt. I know what he said about keeping the men alive so that they could be exposed, but if it had been me, I'm not sure I would have left them alive.

No. I'm not going to look at the photos in this envelope. I know what they are. That's enough.

*

The envelope is sitting on the passenger seat as the red eye of the stoplight stares down at me.

If I go straight, I can be home in ten minutes. We can get in the car and go out to eat with our parents. Julia and I can talk about the type of car we'd like to get when the check from the insurance company arrives next week. I'm sure Dad will have some thoughts. We can talk about the new job. We can fawn over Little Sophie as she does the most basic of baby activities. We can try to get her to laugh. We can play peekaboo. Then, after dinner when the parents go back to their hotels, maybe we can get Sophie to sleep early and Julia and I can watch a movie or just quietly relax on the couch. We can get on with our lives.

Or, I can go right, get onto the I-5, and head downtown.

This is it. This is the choice Damon gave me in the seconds before he died. He knew it was coming or at least hoped it would.

'Whatever you decide is up to you . . .'

I glance at the on-ramp and clench my jaw. I shouldn't get involved. These men got the cops to cover for them. They're that powerful and how can I do anything without exposing my family? I should let go. I should just go straight, throw the envelope in the dumpster in the alley outside the apartment, and go inside to my wife and daughter.

But how can I do that? How can I do nothing?

And then I remember the question I asked Damon, about another route he could have taken to expose these guys, and I have my answer.

The orange hand of the crosswalk signal begins flashing. The light is about to change. I switch on my turn signal and hit the button on the steering wheel. I pull up Julia's number and call just as the light turns green.

'Hey,' she says as I pull onto the on-ramp. I can hear Sophie burbling in the background.

'Hey,' I answer back. 'How are the two ladies doing?'

'Well, one of the ladies was fussy, so she just had a feeding,' Julia says. 'Didn't you, you little missy?' she asks Sophie in baby talk.

Sophie coos.

'Are you on your way home' Julia asks.

'Yeah, but I have to drop something off. Going to be a little bit longer.'

'Okay,' Julia says. 'We'll be waiting, but you've got diaper duty when you get back,' she jokes. 'Isn't that right, Sophie? It's Daddy's turn to deal with your stinkies, isn't it?'

Sophie makes an amused sound while I laugh.

Julia and I have gotten over that initial shock of how something so small and precious can create so much of something so foul. Now, it's all part of the routine.

'I can't wait. Hey, can you do me a favor and let the folks we're going to be a little late for dinner?'

'Sure.'

'Thank you. I shouldn't be too long.'

'Pinky swear?'

I smile. 'Pinky swear.'

'Okay. Drive safe. I love you.'

'Love you, too.'

I hang up the phone and begin to merge. Once I've established myself in the flow of traffic, I commit the sin of looking something up on my phone while driving.

Chapter 39

I park in the structure and cross the street to the large art deco building sitting smack dab in the middle of downtown Los Angeles. The building houses the sixth largest newspaper in the country. In my hand, I hold the creased and crumpled envelope with Damon's bloody fingerprints on it.

I'm not going to get involved, but I'm not going to do nothing.

The entrance opens to the expansive lobby. There's a moderate amount of people moving about. Print media may be dying but this newspaper will be one of its last casualties.

I cross the lobby to the reception desk, where a man in an ill-fitting suit is sitting behind a computer.

'Can I help you?' he asks.

'You wouldn't happen to have a Sharpie I could borrow, do you?'

'Sure.' The man searches a drawer, finds a black marker, and hands it to me.

I thank him, set the envelope on the desk, and write *Edward Thorwald. Editor. 6th Floor*. Under that, I write the date of that infamous night and six names: Scott Graham, R.J. Castillo, Patrick Henford, Julian Walsh, Alex Northrup, and Randall Fletcher. For a second, I consider using the marker to blot out Damon's fingerprint, but decide against it. That was the price Damon paid.

I return the Sharpie to the man and then carry the envelope over to a panel with two slots built into the wall. One slot is marked 'Outgoing.' The other is marked 'Internal.'

I've wrestled with what Damon did or at least tried to do. He was right. I didn't fully understand until I had a daughter, but I'm not doing this for him.

I'm doing this for Chloe.

I will do this for a daughter I've never met and for every other daughter these men have harmed.

I hope this finds its way to Edward Thorwald, the editor of the paper. I hope he sees the photos and the date and the names and starts putting everything together, but this is as far as I go. I'm doing this anonymously so that I can keep my new family safe. Damon said it would be my choice and this is the choice I'm making. He tried to go to the cops and it didn't work. I'll let the press have it. Either the photographs will be enough to implicate them or they won't. Hopefully, Randall Fletcher won't be able to silence the paper like he did the police. I hope I'm lighting the fuse to the bomb that Damon wanted to set off. I hope this leads to those men never being able to hurt anyone else ever again.

I hope that for Chloe.

I drop the envelope into the slot marked 'Internal,' turn, and walk to the exit.

Now, that night is finally over.

I hope all of that happens, but if it doesn't, I've done all I can.

I've got a life to live.

I have a daughter to raise.

And it's all going by so damn fast.

Los Angeles Inquirer
January 10th

SEXUAL ASSAULT AND BLACKMAIL AT ONYX PICTURES

Some of the biggest names in Hollywood have been implicated in crimes of sexual assault and blackmail.

A seven-month investigation has found that the head of Onyx Pictures, Randall Fletcher, Academy Award-winning director, Alex Northrup, and others routinely lured young women to various locations with promises of job opportunities in the film industry. There, they would sexually assault the women, take photos of the encounters, and threaten to release the photos to keep the women from going public with their stories.

Throughout the course of the investigation, more than a dozen victims have come forward, confirming the allegations.

When asked for comment, a representative from Onyx Pictures stated that Randall Fletcher had stepped down as the head of the studio and that filming had stopped on Alex Northrup's latest movie.

Los Angeles police chief, Dominic Voller, held a press conference this afternoon, where he announced the opening of a criminal investigation into the allegations, as well as an internal review amid victims' statements that police knew of the allegations and covered them up at the behest of Randall Fletcher.

The investigation began after an anonymous tip was delivered to Edward Thorwald, the lead editor of the Inquirer. The identity of the individual who delivered the tip remains unknown . . .

The Good Husband

How far would you go to protect your family?
Mark Burcham and his wife Amy live the perfect life: they
have a happy marriage, a comfortable home in Los Angeles
and a beautiful daughter, Tatum. But one night Amy fails to
come home from a business trip to Boston, and her office has
no record of a client on the east coast.

Then Mark gets the worst news of all; Amy has been found
dead. But nothing makes sense. Why was Amy still in town,
when he'd waved her off at the airport a few days before? Who
was the mysterious client she'd been meeting with for months?
There's only one thing Mark knows for certain: his wife was
keeping secrets.

As he digs deeper into the life Amy tried to keep hidden,
Mark realizes that someone is trying to stop him, someone
who is watching his every move. And when they threaten
Tatum to keep him from discovering the truth, Mark will stop
at nothing to keep his family safe . . .

**Don't miss this utterly gripping thriller from Steve Frech,
perfect for fans of Chad Zunker, Joe Hart and
Robert Dugoni.**

Secrets to the Grave

The girl was lying face-down, the soles of her socks covered in fresh grass stains. Her wavy, chestnut hair fanned out across the pavement, as if across a pillow. She almost looked as if she was asleep . . .

When a teenage girl is found dead on a quiet suburban street, Detective Meredith Somerset is called to the scene. The victim is shoeless, the only clue to her identity a silver heart-shaped charm hidden in her grass-stained sock. Did she run from her killer across the smooth lawns of Willow Lane? And if so, how did no one in the surrounding houses see or hear a thing?

As Meredith investigates, she's haunted by flashbacks. Years ago her little sister disappeared in broad daylight, and no one saw a thing then either. It's the reason Meredith became a detective—to get the justice her sister never did—and she won't stop until she gets the truth.

Meredith needs answers. But Willow Lane has more than one mystery behind its doors—and to find the killer, she must venture into a community that's determined to take its secrets to the grave . . .

A nail-biting crime thriller with a shocking twist, perfect for fans of Kendra Elliot, Robert Dugoni and Lisa Regan.

Want You Dead

The backyard is full of balloons and streamers, and a piñata hangs from a tree branch, circling lazily in the breeze. But beneath the table of party food, a body lies half-covered by a brightly coloured tablecloth, blood seeping onto the floor . . .

A child's birthday party ends in chaos when one of the parents is found brutally beaten to death. With no way for anyone to leave unnoticed, it's clear the killer must be another guest, but with twenty high-spirited children as a distraction, anyone might have had the opportunity to slip away from the rest of the party.

Detective Meredith Somerset soon discovers the victim had no shortage of enemies, and everyone has a potential motive. Fractured marriages, jealousy and betrayals all come to light but Meredith can't seem to cut through the lies and find the truth.

When another party-goer disappears Meredith knows the clock is ticking before the killer strikes again. But when everyone has a motive, how can she be sure who was the one who struck the fatal blow? Who is innocent—and who is out for blood?

A gripping thriller you won't be able to put down, this is perfect for fans of Robert Dugoni, Rachel Caine and Melinda Leigh.

Acknowledgements

The process of writing every book is different, and this book was no different . . . wait . . . What?

I was more than halfway through writing my next novel when The Good Husband took off and I realized that the story I was working on was not the one to follow it up. So, I did something I've never done before; I scrapped the book. I decided to start over, and I needed to deliver a first draft in five months.

To do that, I leaned on a lot of people.

First and foremost, thank you Sandy Comstock, for letting me bounce ideas off you while you kicked my ass at marbles.

Thank you, Mom & Dad, for all the stories of what it was like to be expecting a child in your very early twenties.

Thank you, Abigail Fenton, not just for this book, but for taking a chance on Dark Hollows and for being a part of every one of my books since.

Thank you, Jon Appleton, for coming in clutch to get No Turning Back over the finish line.

And thank you, Georgina Green and the whole HQ family, from the marketing team, graphic designers, and every department in between. These books don't get off the ground without you.

Dear Reader,

We hope you enjoyed reading this book. If you did, we'd be so appreciative if you left a review. It really helps us and the author to bring more books like this to you.

Here at HQ Digital we are dedicated to publishing fiction that will keep you turning the pages into the early hours. Don't want to miss a thing? To find out more about our books, promotions, discover exclusive content and enter competitions you can keep in touch in the following ways:

JOIN OUR COMMUNITY:
Sign up to our new email newsletter: http://smarturl.it/SignUpHQ
Read our new blog www.hqstories.co.uk

𝕏 https://twitter.com/HQStories
𝐟 www.facebook.com/HQStories

BUDDING WRITER?
We're also looking for authors to join the HQ Digital family!
Find out more here:
https://www.hqstories.co.uk/want-to-write-for-us/

Thanks for reading, from the HQ Digital team